# THE TUTOR'S SECRET

LIA GOODACRE

The Tutor's Secret

Lia Goodacre

This is a work of fiction. All of the characters, organisations, and events portrayed in this novel are either products of the author's imagination or are used fictitiously.

The Tutor's Secret. Copyright ©2023 Lia Goodacre.
All rights reserved.



Ebook ISBN: 978-1-915717-06-1
Paperback ISBN: 978-1-915717-08-5

# 1

B ath, England 1840

ADELLA TOOK a confident step through the doorway, and her eyes swept around the elegant drawing room. This grand house in South Parade was as good as any other in the finer end of Bath.

She looked down at the richly patterned Axminster carpet, and dared not guess how much it cost. Then around at the furniture; it was of the best quality. The piano with the lid closed; such a waste of a fine instrument, the tall vase of lilies on an exquisite mahogany table, and then the elegant lady reclined on a chaise longue.

She had come to the house because she was running an errand for her half brother; Dr Leonard Preston. Being at his disposal for such things, she often went to the Apothecary on his behalf and such trips were becoming more frequent as his practice grew. Now she had arrived with a package for his newest and, possibly richest patient.

She took a few more light steps into the room, unafraid to disturb the quiet.

"Ah, Adella!" her brother said motioning her to come further in.

She took the opportunity to observe her brother's patient more closely. Very much a Lady, and dressed in a fashionable green silk dress that Adella could only dream of owning. She was beautiful; blond hair tied up flawlessly, with an oval face. A pale face. She was obviously unwell.

"May I present my sister, Miss Maxwell. She has brought those tonics I told you about. Adella, this is Mrs Polwarth," Leonard indicated.

"Polwarth?" her mind whispered. Her brow furrowed. Polwarth? She only knew one person by that name. Surely this lady was not related to *him*?

Adella went forward and presented herself. The lady looked at her with an expression of neutrality, then, after a few moments she stared and her eyes widened.

"You. . ." Mrs Polwarth muttered, and she seemed unable to speak further.

A quiet cough came from the other side of the room, and Adella looked up. She caught a movement out of the corner of her eye and saw a gentleman. She hadn't noticed him when she entered.

She gasped as she took in those features she knew so well from five years ago.

Her reaction to him did not go unnoticed by the other occupants of the room. He cleared his throat, then, not even glancing at Adella said to her brother, "Excuse me, I think I should leave you two alone with my wife."

"Please do not go Joel, you know how I depend on you,"

Mrs Polwarth said as she feebly held out her arm. He hesitated for a moment, unsure what to do. Then he conceded to his wife's pleading, and resumed his former position by the window. Mrs Polwarth threw a suspicious glance at Adella, then at her husband.

Adella felt herself flush deep red, and tried to not stare at Mr Polwarth.

*After all these years, she was finally in the same room as him.* She never thought it would happen again.

Of course, she was not introduced to him. A doctor's errand-girl would not be deemed worthy of such an honour. Just as well. Their eyes met and they held each other's gaze for a few moments until her brother's voice roused her.

"Adella, is there something wrong?"

"Oh. . .no," she said turning back to the patient. "Sorry, here are the tonics you asked for."

"Thank you. If you wait a moment, I will accompany you back. It should not take much longer to see to Mrs Polwarth."

Adella nodded and stepped backwards against the nearest wall while her brother tended to his patient for a few more minutes. She tried to remain as invisible as possible, though that was difficult given who she was in the room with. Try as she may, she could not get over the complete and utter feeling that she wished the ground would swallow her up. All the while he stood across from her; not six paces away. Most of the time he looked out of the window, but occasionally she noticed his eyes would flicker to her.

After the first few glances, her pride took over and she met his brief looks with proud defiance. After all, she had nothing to be disgraced about. He was the one who should be ashamed.

She noticed he was dressed in expensive tailoring, but

then, that was not surprising, he was very rich. He wore a dark green jacket and a fine dark green waistcoat, no doubt from the best tailor. His hands clasped behind his back, she could see the rise and fall of his chest as he breathed. Five years had taken little toll on his handsome features. She calculated he must be at least 26. Yes 26, his birthday was the 24th February she recalled frustratingly quickly, and it was April now. His hair was longer than before, and still the darkest raven black. She stopped herself from remembering how she used to run her fingers through it.

Adella tore her gaze away from him, and turned to Mrs Polwarth. So, this was his wife. She was beautiful, but there was a shrewish look about her she hadn't noticed straight away. Her hair was insipid and lack-lustre, but she supposed that was no surprise under the circumstances. She checked herself from further criticism. It was not right of her to do such a thing. This woman was his wife and she deserved pity and not only because she was ill.

When her brother finished tending to his patient and took his leave she made for the door, eager to escape.

"Actually, Adella," she heard her brother say, "Would you mind waiting for me downstairs? I would like to speak to Mr Polwarth about a few matters."

"Of course," she murmured and showed herself out, wishing he had realised ten minutes previously that he needed to speak to Mr Polwarth alone.

Mr Polwarth nodded to her in a polite manner as she left. Protocol required it, but she did not acknowledge or return the gesture. No, she would not. Nothing could bring her to acknowledge him.

She closed the oak drawing room door behind her, shut her eyes and let out a long deep breath. Today was supposed to have been an ordinary day. One thing was sure, she had to get outside. Her legs almost gave way with each step and she ran down the flight of stairs, then out into the street.

She took a deep breath as if she had been suffocated before.

Her life would never be the same again, at least not while he was in Bath. If she ever thought she would see him again, then she wouldn't have reckoned on it being now, five years since their paths first met, and in Bath, a place far from where they knew each other before.

Her heart thumped hard as she blushed and re-lived every second of the last fifteen minutes when she was forced into his presence. He recognised her straight away, she knew that. She remembered every expression on his face, learnt from those six short months they shared.

How did his wife recognise her? They had never met before – she was sure of it.

She walked a few doors down, just out of sight from the house, and the window on the second floor. A few moments later she walked back. What had she to hide? What if he did see her from the window? It was a public place. He could look on her all he pleased. The world seemed oblivious to her torment and mercilessly carried on as if nothing was wrong. But how she wished to cry out. Why now? Why here? How she wished she had been more prepared to be in his presence again. One thing was certain, she must master her feelings. If Leonard suspected something, it would only make matters worse. She would only end up telling him everything.

Eventually Leonard emerged from the house and they walked towards their home in Horse Shoe Walk. "I must stop at Mr Alther's very quickly before we go home," he said.

"Of course."

But as her brother turned left down a side street that led to the Alther's Apothecary Shop, Adella continued on, a thousand thoughts swimming in her head. Her brother grabbed her arm, and she looked up, seeing where they should be going.

"I'm sorry," she shrugged in apology.

Leonard smiled at her, "You can tell me all about it later. Until then, I have business."

They made their way a few yards down the side street. It was by no means the only Apothecary in Bath, but it was the nearest to their home, and Mr Alther was lenient about the time it took Dr Preston to pay his bills. The familiar shop front greeted them, dressed with a myriad of coloured bottles, boxes and jars of the current medicines all claiming to cure illnesses and ailments. When they entered, the pungent smell of chemicals, herbs and other brewing concoctions that were cooked up every day was a warm welcome. They waited a few minutes while an elderly gentleman was served. He left with a number of bottles and packages until Mr Alther turned his attention to them.

"Dr Preston, Adella! You here again! You can't stay away can you?" he grinned, "Always nice to see you both, even if it was just a short time ago."

Adella smiled back. Her previous stresses forgotten, because it was impossible to dislike Mr Alther. He had such a happy manner about him, and always lifted her spirits. He was a tall pole of a man, with large eyes, and the thick glasses he wore made his eyes look enormous.

"Miss Maxwell is here again Mary!" he shouted over his shoulder to the doorway behind.

A short moment later, Mrs Alther appeared. As was her custom, she wore a large amount of jewellery and an extremely frilly dress which, Adella always thought was to draw emphasis away from her face. She was not the most beautiful in Bath, but certainly not plain. She never seemed far from the counter, always hiding in the office, and appearing at a moments notice. Today she was carried a pestle and mortar with a small quantity of yellow powder in it.

"Oh Miss Maxwell! Dr Preston. How lovely. I was about to make some tea!" she said.

"I'm sorry Mrs Alther, we cannot stay. I have another patient to see soon," Leonard replied.

"Very well," crestfallen, her smile disappeared and her shoulders dropped. She took to studying the contents of the bottles on the counter.

"But maybe we could come in the next few days. Things are a little quiet tomorrow and Wednesday," Leonard added as an afterthought.

"Oh good! I will look forward to it. You can tell me all about Mrs Westmorland's conjunctivitis."

Leonard shook his finger at her, "Now Mrs Alther, you know I can't tell you anything of the sort. I can't break my patient confidentiality."

"You know I love to tease you!" she said. "One day you will slip up and then how I shall laugh!"

Mrs Alther returned to her office, and Leonard finally got down to the real reason he was there: a prescription.

"Sleeping draughts for Mr Polwarth," Mr Alther read on the paper. Adella tried not to flinch at the mention of his name again.

She had nearly forgotten him.

Nearly.

"Hmm an unusual one, I shall have to make it up especially. But it is a good choice Dr Preston, one of the less addictive types."

"I shall send Adella to collect it later and she can drop it off to Mr Polwarth."

Adella felt the blood drain from her face. "B-But surely, someone else could take it?"

Leonard turned and studied his sister.

"All you need do is hand it in at the servants' entrance Adella." He said in a low voice.

She nodded as Mr Alther said, "Now Adella, surely you would rather use the servants' entrance eh? None of that "la de da" that we all hate, and that's just the footmen that answer the door! They look down on people like us, when we all know they are the same as us. Except we don't have to be nice to people all day in case we get thrown out on our ear."

"Yes, I suppose." Adella managed a smile.

"Good, that's settled then," said Leonard.

Adella did go back to the Polwarth's, and at Mr Alther's suggestion, she used the servants' entrance. She was gone within a minute of the door being answered, but all the way there and back, she kept a watchful eye about her in case she saw him. Thankfully he was nowhere to be seen.

All through the day she was conscious of herself, wondering every time she walked out if she would see him. One thing was certain, she would not speak to him, and a part of her wished to see him in the street, just so she could snub him.

Seeing Joseph again, no, it was Joel; that was his real name, shocked Adella beyond anything she had felt for many years. Five years in fact. It all flooded back, every painful moment of his betrayal, his deceit and his wanton abandonment.

What was he doing here in Bath? Why had he asked her brother to be his wife's doctor? He was mocking her, she was sure of it. He had come to seek her out, and to torment her even more than before.

ADELLA NEED NOT HAVE FEARED ACCIDENTALLY MEETING Joel Polwarth. He never ventured out that day, so she could have gone about unheeded and without worry. That night, Joel sat on the side of his bed, his head cradled in his hands.

Hopefully the next day would not prove so troublesome. The next time he saw Adella, he vowed not to be so stilted, so awkward. He did not expect to see her so soon. He smiled to himself. She was as beautiful as he remembered. Her plain blue dress and her brown hair tied up in a simple knot made no difference to her attractiveness. Her blue eyes still with the long dark lashes framing them. She had simply grown more bewitching in five years. Cynthia recognised Adella, he was sure of it. Cynthia's face always showed every emotion she was feeling. But how she knew about Adella, he could not comprehend. Unless of course she had secretly looked through his sketches.

Cynthia, now sleeping in her own chamber, was more than difficult this evening. The chair was too hard, the chaise longue uncomfortable, her tea too cold, the chimney smoked. He attended her until his patience was at an end. He called for her maid and went to sit in his study for the rest of the evening.

They had only been in Bath for two days and already Joel was exasperated. This time away was supposed to be helping her, but instead she seemed more agitated and fretful than normal. Still, his closest friend Frederick Garner was due to arrive in about a week and he looked forward to a time when he had an excuse to be away from home a little. Perhaps she would settle down in a few days.

He was sure it was not the house or their location that troubled her. He chose this house in particular on a glowing recommendation and it was one of the smartest and fashionable area's. Cynthia seemed pleased with the idea of spending time in Bath, goodness knows she needed a change of scene. Bed-ridden for many months and although her illness was real, she seemed to play on it, mentioning symptoms that their doctor said was not a result of the underlying problem.

The whole trip to Bath was difficult from start to finish. They travelled by coach, but Joel knew that rail would have been quicker and more comfortable. Cynthia insisted that the fast speeds the trains travelled would make her more ill than she already was. Consequently the journey took three arduous days and they were both exhausted.

He sat up and poured one of the sleeping draughts into a glass of water. He needed as much rest as possible. As far as he could see, things would only get worse. He drank the contents in one gulp and lay back in bed waiting for it to take effect.

Adella's face filled his mind, and he drifted off to an induced sleep a few minutes later.

IT HAD BEEN a long and stressful day for Adella, and she was glad when after dinner, they retired to the sitting room, but not until everything was cleared away and tidied. She kept an ordered house for her brother, even if it was modest in size. She was proud of his medical career, and was happy to be of use to him.

"I saw George Fadden on the way back this afternoon," Adella said after a few minutes.

"Oh really? How is he?" A small playful smile spread across Leonard's mouth.

"He is well, thank you, and you need not smile like that."

"Like what?"

"You know."

"Well, I can't help it. The poor man can hardly speak when he is around you." Leonard said.

"I have noticed. He stutters and stammers and eventually gets a compliment or two out." She smiled at the thought of Mr Fadden's blushes whenever she looked at him. If she was of a flirtatious and cruel nature she could have played with his feelings.

"He likes you very much," Leonard said.

"I know."

"Yet you give him no encouragement. Why is that? He is a son of a successful grocer, he is a good man, handsome, a little quiet, but a girl like you could help him rid himself of his shyness."

Adella looked away, "I have sworn off men. As I have told you countless times."

"Hmm, you have never told me the reason *why* you have sworn off men," Leonard raised his brows.

Adella placed her sewing down for a moment, "No, I have not told you have I?"

"Then, do you think now is the time?"

Adella faltered for a moment, one man alone was the reason, and it was time she told Leonard about him. She drew a deep breath and said in a low voice, "It is because of Joel Polwarth."

"Mr Polwarth? My new patient?"

"Yes," she glanced at her brothers face; it wore a confused frown.

"Adella, you reacted in a very odd manner to Mr Polwarth this morning. Was there a reason you disliked the idea of going back to their lodgings? You know him?"

Tears formed in the corner of her eyes and threatened her composure as she whispered, "Yes, I know him."

Leonard sat back in his chair and gestured that she continue.

"I know him, or at least knew him very well. But his name was not Joel Polwarth. He called himself Joseph West then."

She stood up and walked behind her chair, feeling claustrophobic under her brother's gaze.

"I knew him five years ago when I was governess in Sidmouth." She dropped her head to hide a tear that had fallen onto her cheek.

"Why are you crying?"

She pushed back her tears, and wiped her cheek, "I'm not crying."

"Did he do something to hurt you?"

"Yes, no. He did not hurt me physically. He -"

"You have history with this man?"

"Yes."

"Did he court you?"

"Yes."

"You loved him?"

She looked up, "Yes," she said, "Yes I loved him more than any other man. I was completely and utterly in love with him."

"Tell me, you did not do anything you now regret?" He raised his right eyebrow slightly and it was full of deeper meaning.

She took his meaning immediately. "No, no! He was honourable in that respect. I was prudent. I would never do such a thing, however much I loved a man. You must believe me." She shook her head.

Leonard's expression went from anguish to comprehension, "So he is the reason for your disappointment five years ago. Mother alluded to that time, as have you, but I never knew all the details. I have often wondered why you have not spoken of it though I have been curious."

"I wanted to forget. Talking about it brings it all back. Besides, mother and father thought it best that it was not widely known. You see, the whole situation is incredibly awkward and when I tell you everything, you will realise why I have kept it to myself. Yet now, here he is in Bath, and you are his wife's doctor."

"Then please, do tell me. I am more than intrigued to know."

"Very well. I will tell you everything. I think it is best you know it all. I have been wondering about telling you. Today, it was such a shock to see him. I cannot describe it. The last time I saw him was five years ago. Then suddenly he was there in front of me, and his wife in the same room. I did not know what to do with myself."

She started to chew the end of her finger and then deciding that there was no time like the present, drew courage and sat back down, ready to begin her story.

Leonard waited silently as she composed herself. She had hidden a secret love all this time from him. Leonard had always professed to love her. Despite their different fathers and the six year age gap, he had taught her a fair amount of boyish pranks. Teased her, fought with her and many times made her life a misery. But if anyone bullied or was cruel to her, he was the first to defend her.

She felt his gaze as she fought back emotions.

"Adella, if you would rather not speak of it tonight, I understand."

"No, it is alright, I need a few moments to think where to start. It is all so difficult to know where to start."

"From the beginning?"

"Yes, I suppose that is the best place. How much do you know of what happened at that time?" she asked.

"Nothing really, except that you were a Governess weren't you?"

"Yes."

"Mother and Father said little more. I can remember they wrote and told me you found a position and they thought it might be good for you; you often professed a desire to see more of the world."

"Yes, I did get to see more of the world. A small part of Devon at least."

She smiled grimly, took a sip of tea and began.

**2**

———

ylesbury, Buckinghamshire. Five years before.

"ADELLA, ADELLA," her mother shouted from the bottom of the stairs.

"Yes Mother?" Adella appeared at the top, still in her cotton night gown and robe, her hair hanging loose.

"The morning post is here, this letter is for you and it's postmark is Sidmouth."

Adella didn't need any more explanation. She ran full pelt down the worn wooden stairs, grabbed the letter, and ripped it open. Her eyes scanned the contents, then she let out a scream.

"They have given me the job! I'm going to be a Governess!"

Her mother hugged her, "I am so pleased for you. Though I will miss you dreadfully," she dabbed her eyes with a handkerchief. "When do they want you to start?"

Adella re-read words quickly, "As soon as possible. It says they gave me the job because they were impressed with my reference from Mrs Peters and the open minded content of my curricula for their daughter. They will pay me a salary of thirty pounds per annum, that should be more than enough to help until father is completely well again."

Her mother nodded, "Yes, more than enough."

"I am so happy. I can't wait to go. I have so much to do!"

"Yes, yes," her mother said, "But first come; you must tell your father..."

She followed her mother through to the dining room, where her father was eating his breakfast. He looked up from his newspaper. Adella was struck anew with how pale he was, there were dark patches under his eyes and as he held his cup, his hand shook a little. His illness had been long and hard all through the winter. It was just as well that she had this opportunity to earn some money.

"Father, I am going to be a Governess!"

"Really? Where?"

"It's the position in Sidmouth I applied for weeks ago."

"Sidmouth? Well, well. The sea air will do you good."

Adella noticed the unconcerned tone in his voice, "Are you not pleased?"

His expression softened, "Of course I am pleased my dear, but it hard for me. I should be the one earning money, not you."

"But it will be a great adventure. You know how I long to see more of the world. Why not start with Devon?"

"Why not indeed. But I want you to promise me that if are home sick, or your employers treat you badly, that you will come home immediately?"

Adella took hold of her fathers hand, "I promise."

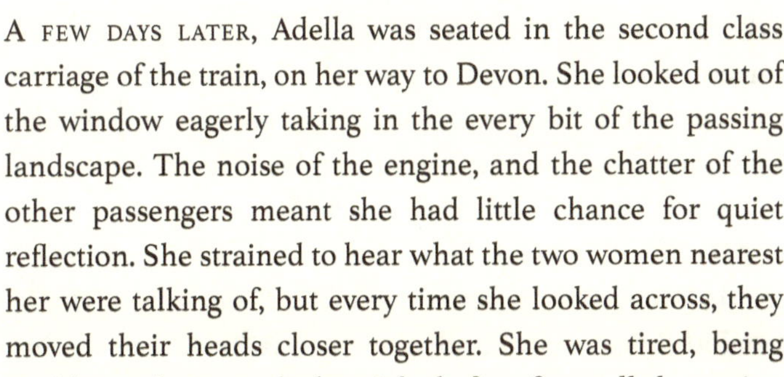

A FEW DAYS LATER, Adella was seated in the second class carriage of the train, on her way to Devon. She looked out of the window eagerly taking in the every bit of the passing landscape. The noise of the engine, and the chatter of the other passengers meant she had little chance for quiet reflection. She strained to hear what the two women nearest her were talking of, but every time she looked across, they moved their heads closer together. She was tired, being unable to sleep much the night before from all the excitement, but she didn't notice her exhaustion too much. There would be plenty of time to sleep once she arrived.

The first part of the journey was long and arduous, and several times she checked her pocket watch, to see if the train was running to time. It was. Her mother and father had waved her off, and though sorry to be leaving them, she was touched by her father making the effort to come to the station.

She arrived in London to change trains, and hurried to the correct platform in good time. She briefly thought about leaving the station to have a look at the outside; it was a few years since she had been to London, but she didn't want to miss the connection, or the opportunity of getting a window seat again. Eventually, the connection arrived, and she was on her way to Devon.

When she arrived at Axminster, a carriage was waiting for her. It took her the few miles to her new home: and her new employers, Mr and Mrs Waters.

The house was moderately sized, and not as grand looking as Adella imagined. Still, it was prettily situated a mile from the sea in it's own well kept grounds. She looked forward to exploring them.

"How was your journey my dear?" Mrs Waters said shaking her hand. Adella stood inside the hall and tried not to be too overwhelmed by the size of the staircase and the fine brocade wallpaper.

"Very good thank you. The trains ran smoothly and to time, and I met a few interesting people on board."

"You must have had to leave early?"

"Yes, the train left Aylesbury at six o'clock this morning."

Mr Waters gave a polite nod of his head, "Well, what a wonderful age we live in that you can be in Aylesbury this morning, and Devon this evening. Look, it's just past seven." He pointed to a gold clock sat on the mantle piece.

"Well," Mrs Waters said, "I expect you are tired and hungry, and would like time to unpack?"

"Yes." Adella lied. She wasn't hungry, having been given enough food for a week by her mother. But she didn't like to refuse Mrs Waters offer. Especially this early on in her employment.

"Then I shall take you to your room, and have cook send up supper for you." Mrs Waters said. "Come to breakfast tomorrow morning with us, and we can discuss the finer details of your tasks, and you can also meet Mary. I'm sure you two will get on well."

"You also have a son I understand?" Adella asked.

"Yes, Harry is twelve and away at school; at Harrow. Mr Waters was a Harrow boy, and was determined Harry should go there too, weren't you?" she looked over at her husband, who nodded. "He is doing remarkably well, his reports are glowing and all the teachers love him."

Adella nodded her approval, bid farewell to Mr Waters, and was shown to her room by Mrs Waters. It was comfortable, adjoining the school room on the third floor. The wallpaper was plain, and there was no other decoration. There was a washstand, a bed, wardrobe and chest of draws all made of plain matching oak. Everything was functional, clean and in need of a few feminine touches.

"Thank you, this is very comfortable," Adella walked to the open window, and though it was dark outside, she looked out and asked, "How far are we from the sea?"

"It's half an hours walk. Not far at all."

"I can smell the salt in air, even from here."

"Can you? I have lived here all my life so I don't notice things like that."

"I would have loved to have grown up by the sea."

Mrs Waters walked to the door, "Well, I am sure the sea air will make you sleep well tonight. I will have your supper sent up. Goodnight."

When she was alone in her room, Adella sat on the bed, her mind full of the task ahead. She had a nervous anticipation, but was certain she was up to the task. She wondered what little Mary would be like, and whether they would get on. If she was anything near as pleasant as her mother, they would do well.

Adella set about unpacking her clothes, and when she finished, she sat back and admired her room. This was her new home. She wasn't home sick, not yet. But first things first, she wrote a letter to her parents to let them know she arrived safely.

The next morning, Adella went to breakfast with Mr and Mrs Waters. She slept well, but woke early and was still a little fatigued, her lack of sleep the night before catching up on her. She entered the dining room and tried not be intimidated by its size and elegance. The table was made of mahogany and the chairs looked so finely carved she feared she might break them. There was a young girl sat at the table.

Nine years old, with most adorable blond curly hair. Mary.

"Do come in Miss Maxwell," Mrs Waters said. The girl stood up, and Adella went straight over to her.

"You must be Mary," she said holding out her hand, and smiling.

"Yes," said the girl shaking it, and smiled back.

"I am Adella Maxwell, and I'm very pleased to meet you."

"Can you play croquet?" Mary asked looking up at her, an inquisitive look on her face.

"Yes, yes I can."

She jumped up and down and clapped her hands, "Oh good, can we play later? I love Croquet."

Adella looked over to Mrs Waters, who nodded.

"Yes, we can play later. But first, breakfast?"

Mary sat down, and continued eating her toast.

"A lady always eats breakfast," Adella commented, "It helps her concentrate and not fatigue before lunch."

"I love toast, with lots of butter and marmalade."

Adella smiled, "So do I. But I like Kedgeree too."

"Errrghhh, fish. I hate fish."

"Oh dear."

"She used to eat it when she was younger," Mrs Waters said, "but lately she has taken a dislike to it. Such a shame seeing how close to the sea we are."

Over breakfast, Mary proved herself to be what Adella thought; a delightful girl. She was outspoken and bold, but was not pretentious or spoiled by her parents. She showed Adella around the house, and grounds, they held hands as they went, Mary dragging her from one room to the next. They spent the day talking and getting to know each other and of course, they played Croquet. Adella let Mary win.

Alone in her room that night, Adella mused that Mary was the ideal child to be governess to. In fact, they were inseparable after two days. Mary had never received her mothers full attention, she was too busy running the house and with social engagements to give herself full time to her daughter, so having a governess suited them perfectly.

A FEW MONTHS LATER, and Mary was responding well to Adella's tutoring, though it hadn't always been smooth going. She wanted to play sport all the time and longed to be outside most of the day. She didn't like sewing, and Adella despaired several times when she produced such bad stitches because she had done the work too quickly. So Adella wrote to her mother for advice, and was told to withhold Mary's favourite activities until the sewing improved. It worked, and though Mary always sewed under protest, she did improve enough for Mrs Waters to be grateful to Adella.

One fine morning, the two were together in the schoolroom at the top of the house, the sun shone brightly through the windows and Mary practiced her French verbs. Adella was seated next to her, patiently listening and correcting where she needed. They were interrupted by Mrs Waters bursting into the room in a fluster. She was holding a white lace covered handkerchief and waved it about as she spoke.

"Adella, Mary my dear, Mr Waters and I have received some terrible news." Her face was pale.

"What is it?" Adella asked, a hundred terrible thoughts going through her head.

"It is dearest Harry. We have heard from his school; he has whooping cough!"

"That is terrible. How long is he into the illness? Is he going to be alright?"

Mrs Waters started to cry, and Adella ran over to her and put her arms around her. They stood there for a few minutes as she tried to tell her what had happened, how Harry was, but her speech was incomprehensible.

Eventually she calmed down and they noticed that Mary had her arms around her mother too.

"Don't cry Mama," she said, "Is Harry going to die?"

"No, no he's not going to die. He is strong and will get through this," she sobbed.

Adella led them all to one of the sofas as Mrs Waters explained.

"An express arrived about half an hour ago from Harry's headmaster. He is in the school infirmary. The letter said that he is at a critical stage and if he makes it past today they think he will pull through. Mr Waters wants to go and see him but I am afraid that he will catch it too and die. I don't know what I would do if they both died."

"But you said Harry wasn't going to die and now Papa is going to die too!" Mary started to cry, and covered her face with her hands.

Adella was a long time trying to comfort both mother and daughter. She wasn't sure her efforts to console them was helped at all. Some time later, Mr Waters entered the school room looking for his wife, and Mary flung herself at him,

"Papa! Mama said you were going to see Harry and that you are going to die!"

He picked up his daughter and looked at her, "Of course I am not going to die my little one."

"You are! You are!" she rubbed her eyes, "Please don't go."

But he did travel to Harrow the next day, to be near his son and heir. He reported a few days later that Harry had pulled through and was to be removed home for proper recovery at home. Mrs Waters was as relieved as any mother would have been and prepared the house for her son's arrival. She double checked everything, was fractious on more than one occasion to Mary, and took to lecturing the servants much more frequently than she normally did. Luckily, Adella was not often on the receiving end of her remonstrations.

Harry returned home and he made a slow recovery. He suffered badly with his illness and needed much care. His mother was the main provider of this, and fussed over him, insisting the doctor visited everyday for the first month, regardless of cost. He seemed to enjoy the attention.

After two months, he was well enough to take part in lessons with Mary and Adella.

"And what do you think of the story, Harry?" Adella asked one day after reading to them both in the schoolroom.

"I think it's stupid. It's for babies, like Mary. Can't we read something interesting." He slumped back in his chair and folded his arms.

"Like what?"

"We had just started Homer at school."

Adella looked over at Mary. She was far too young to be reading the classics. Besides, Adella had barely read them herself.

"We could try something not so advanced for Mary. She is a lot younger than you remember."

"Boring. I don't see why I should have to put with this." And with that, he stood up, and with one sweep of his hand, sent all the books on the table flying across the room.

This wasn't the only time Harry misbehaved. Each day,

he became more and more difficult, until a few days later, Adella couldn't take any more disruption, she decided to speak to his mother and father about the issue. She was nervous of the reaction she would get, although Mr and Mrs Waters were pleasant people, she had limited contact with them. They clearly loved their children, but still, this was the first time she had gone to them with a problem, and she did wonder if they would just tell her to get on with it. That was her worst fear. Her second was that they would think she couldn't do her job.

She sought out Mr and Mrs Waters and found them in the drawing room. They were sat next to each other on a sofa drinking tea, enjoying a quiet morning.

"I am sorry to disturb you both," Adella said, spacing her words carefully, "but I would like to speak to you about a matter that concerns Mary and Harry."

"Come in, Miss Maxwell. Do sit down. What is the problem?" Mr Waters asked, indicating the chair opposite.

Adella perched on the edge of the seat, her hands clasped tightly together and explained the problem. They both listened intently and with serious expressions.

"Can you not manage somehow?" Mrs Waters asked after Adella finished speaking, "There must be something you can do to occupy his time?"

Adella shook her head, "I have done everything I can think of, but Harry has been used to fast paced intensive teaching and I simply am not trained for that level of tutorship. Even if I were, I believe Mary's education would suffer, and she is my primary charge."

Mr Waters stood up and paced around a little, his wife watched as he thought over Adella's words.

"What do you propose we do?" he asked, "Send him back to school? He is not well enough yet."

"I do not think you should send him back either. He still has many months until his recovery is complete. You are right, he is not strong enough for school at the moment." She paused, knowing that she already had the answer for them. All she must do was persuade them. She took a deep breath, "You could hire a tutor until he returns to school. That way, he will not be too behind in his work when he goes back."

"Yes!" Mrs Waters sat up straight, "Oh Mr Waters, that is an excellent idea. We can keep Harry here, and he can continue to learn. Why did I not think of it!"

Mr Waters stopped pacing, "I am not against the idea, although, do you think it will be possible to hire a tutor for a few months?"

"I am not sure, but I would have thought there would be a gentleman who would be able to take the work knowing it was a few months. Perhaps someone who is looking for their first position and needs a reference."

Mr Waters started pacing again, weighing up the idea. Then he stopped and said, "Very well, I will start proceedings to hire a tutor immediately. Thank you for your concern Miss Maxwell. In the meantime, I will try and give Harry some school work so that you and Mary are not interrupted so much."

Adella let out a deep sigh after she left the room and ran up the stairs to see Mary. Everything was going to be alright.

Mr Waters was true to his word and tutored Harry a little each morning, and gave him enough home work for him to have more than enough to do each day. He wanted to please his father more than anything, so he was a complying student.

She heard nothing of the quest to hire the tutor until three weeks later. Mr Waters came into the schoolroom after

Mary was in bed and said, "I thought you should know that tomorrow Harry's new tutor arrives. Would you mind showing him the ropes, so to speak?"

"Of course. I would be glad. What time he is to arrive?"

"He should be here by late afternoon."

She nodded, glad that finally she would be able to concentrate solely on Mary once more. A tutor would be able to control Harry completely.

The next day, she tidied the school room after tea. Mary was outside in the gardens playing with Harry and her dog after finishing her lessons. Mr Waters walked in.

"Miss Maxwell, this is Mr Joseph West. Harry's new tutor," he stood aside.

Mr West came forward, somewhat tentatively. Adella saw his nervous smile and stepped forward with a smile and offered her hand.

"Mr West. I am very pleased to meet you. Please call me Adella -oh Mr Waters, you do not mind such informality?"

"Not at all, you know we are very relaxed here are we not?"

Mr West's eyebrows raised in surprise, but then softened.

She took the opportunity to look at him properly. He was a tall man, dark raven hair, clear blue eyes, a handsome face. Not the sort of man you would expect to be a tutor really. His clothes were old, but smart. Adella noticed an air about him; it was awkwardness as well as confidence. A bizarre mixture. How could someone be both at once?

"I shall leave you in Adella's capable hands. She will tell you everything you need to know and show you around the house and so on."

Mr West's awkwardness remained when Mr Waters left

the room, he stood looking as though he didn't know what to do with himself.

He looked at Adella and she smiled back at him again. There was silence for a few moments as they both allowed themselves to become accustomed to each other. Adella couldn't take the awkwardness any more and began tidying the room again, "I expect you are hungry?"

"Yes," he said, still looking at her.

"I will get cook to send some food up. While we wait for it I will tell you everything you need to know."

"Thank you."

She rang the bell and the children's maid, arrived a short time later promising food and drink as soon as Cook could get it ready.

"I believe you are to have the room next to Harry. Has anyone shown you where that is?" Adella asked.

"No."

"Well, I will get Harry to show you."

He smiled. At last he smiled. She vowed she would get more of those out of him yet.

Before either of them could say anything else, Mary and Harry burst through the door in a flurry of noise and excitement. When they saw Mr West they stood frozen looking up to him with their wide eyes.

Adella walked over to them, "Mr West, this is Harry Waters, your charge." Harry stuck his hand out, and Mr West shook it, a serious expression on his face.

"Pleased to meet you sir," Harry said.

"And I am very pleased to meet you too."

"And this is Mary my charge." Adella said. Mr West turned to her and Mary gave the most perfect curtsey Adella had ever seen,. She held her hand out to him as though she were Queen Victoria herself.

"How do you do?" She said. Adella's lips twitched into a smile. Her charge was doing her proud.

Once the introductions were over, Adella sent the children outside, despite their protestations. She told Mr West about the children's current daily routine, what Mr Waters had been teaching Harry and anything else he needed to know until his food arrived. Then she left him in peace. She took the children for a walk, and when they returned an hour later, he was gone from the school room and was nowhere to be seen.

"Do you think we will see him again today?" Harry asked.

"Probably not. He is most likely unpacking," Adella said.

"You said I was to show him where his room is, he might be lost!"

"I am sure one of the servants has shown him," she replied.

"Do you like Mr West?" Mary asked Adella after she had finished reading her a story and was tucking her into bed.

"Yes. He seems pleasant."

"He didn't say much and didn't smile either," she said in a sad tone.

"No, but you must remember that he needs time to adjust to being here. It must be very daunting. We all know each other and he doesn't know us at all. We must make friends with him and then I am sure he will smile more."

"Shall we start tomorrow?"

"Yes, first thing at breakfast. I'll tell you what, the first one of us to make him smile tomorrow wins a bag of sweets."

"I hope I win," Mary said turning over.

Adella went into the school room. She sat and read by the fire, as was her custom in the evening. She sometimes went to the kitchens and spent the evening with the cook, and a few of the other servants, but that night for an unknown reason she wished to be on her own. She thought over how to bring Mr West out of himself for the primary reason that she wanted to win the bag of sweets.

"I will soon rid him of his withdrawn ways," she said to herself.

She sat reading a book, and sipping her tea until she heard a noise behind her. Someone had come in. She looked around, "Mary, are you awake? Did you have a nightmare?"

She stood up.

"Oh, I'm sorry Mr West. I thought you were Mary," she said.

"I am sorry to interrupt your solitude. I – er, wanted to see the school books to see whether I needed to purchase any." There was a distinct uneasiness in his voice.

"They are on the shelf over there."

"Thank you," he said walking over and inspecting them.

Adella opened her mouth to speak to him, but then decided it was not the best idea to disturb him from his task, so she sat back down and opened her book. It soon became evident that she could not concentrate on reading with him in the room. He made no sound to disturb her, but she felt his presence keenly. She turned the page and still did not know what the words said. She heard him walk a few steps towards the door and looked up, "Did you find everything you needed?"

"Yes thank you, I mean, no. I shall have to order a few books after all."

"Would you like some tea? The pot is still warm."

He hesitated, but Adella smiled at him and he gave a small incline of his head, "Thank you, I would like that."

"There is always plenty of tea at Brayfern," she said pouring him a cup. "Mrs Waters is the local tea merchants' best customer. I think the grocer's in Sidmouth make all their annual profit from her. She prefers tea from China, but I prefer Indian."

She handed him the cup, he was still stood near the door, candle in his hand.

"Will you not come and sit down? Unless you are tired. I do not mean to trespass on your time. Perhaps you would rather be alone and take your tea back to your room?"

He shifted about a little, unsure what to do, "Thank you, I will sit with you for a short while," and he seated himself in the chair opposite.

He said nothing. Offered no conversation. They both sat watching the small fire burn, until she asked, "Is your room comfortable?"

"Yes."

Adella was bursting with questions to ask him about himself, but thought it imprudent to ask soon in their acquaintance.

After a minute or so, he asked, "How long have you worked here as Governess?"

"Nearly five months."

"Do you like it here?"

"Yes, very much. I am extremely lucky to have such an excellent appointment. I know of several women who have to put up with a great deal from the family who employ them. Not so here."

The corner of his mouth curled into a smile and for the first time Adella believed that given time he would come out of himself. She liked him, despite his reserve. She knew they would be friends. She was determined they would be friends. There was something about his face that was handsome, yet it was indefinable.

"'f you do not mind me saying, you look very tired," she said, then realised that she probably should not have said such a thing, he must think her very blunt. She searched his face for a flicker of annoyance, but there was none. He must have taken it well however, and said,

"I am not surprised I look tired. I have not slept much for several days."

"I hope you sleep well tonight then."

"Thank you. I am sure I shall."

"I found the sea air helped me sleep well for many days when I first arrived. I am sure you will be the same unless of course, you have already been living near the coast."

Adella hoped her sly enquiry might be answered.

"No, I have not," he replied and looked down, unwilling to divulge any further information.

He sipped his tea, and left to retire for the evening about half an hour from the moment he first sat down. Adella watched as he left the room, her eyes never leaving him until he was out of sight. She couldn't help from wondering what secrets Joseph West was keeping about his past.

## 3

B<sup>ath 1840</sup>

ADELLA LOOKED over at her brother who, although listening intently, was looking fatigued. She had noticed his eye lids droop several times in the last fifteen minutes.

"I think I should continue with my story tomorrow night. There is still so much to tell you."

Leonard yawned, "Very well. I am sure it will keep. I have an early morning appointment, so I think it best."

"Yes, it will. It has kept this long."

It took Adella many hours to fall asleep. Her heart was in turmoil. The darkness of the room was oppressive, she knew candlelight would prove to be no respite. She was re-living her time at Brayfern, and wished her memory did not serve her so well. Even through the darkness, her mind could not put aside that man's face. It burned her vision, even with her eyes shut.

Now that she started to speak of that time, she knew that she would have to continue her story until its end. She was terrified by the possible repercussions of this. What if, after knowing the full truth, her brother refused to be the Polwarth's physician any longer? In the circles in which rich people as them moved, such a decision could have irreparable consequences for Leonard's livelihood and her own. She must persuade him no matter what, that he must not allow his personal feelings get in the way. Despite the fact that the very thought of that man turned her heart to stone. It went against everything she was, every single inclination, but she had to think of the long term effects on Leonard's reputation. He had come so far already, she could not allow his career to be ruined. Not now.

THE FOLLOWING MORNING, Leonard only had two appointments and for a Tuesday it was quiet. Maybe Mrs Alther would have the pleasure of his company for tea after all. He would rather she would forget, but he knew that was unlikely. It was not that he disliked her, far from it, but it was so difficult to get away. One cup of tea would invariably turn into three or four and before he knew it, half the day gone. He was not entirely sure he liked her fascination with diseases. She always loved to talk about them and their cures, and often asked his opinion on the use of herbs and drugs. Whatever happened, he decided he had to try and steer the conversation to other matters when he made his visit.

But he supposed, at least if she spoke of diseases there were no awkward silences, no lapses in conversation. Not that he didn't mind silence, but at the Alther's house, it seemed a little out of place. Leonard was more than happy to sit quietly with Adella, or one of his friends but Mr and Mrs Alther were different. He supposed it was because they met with so many people in their shop all day, speaking to people was the most natural thing. Doctors, like him, needed to be quiet and thoughtful.

He made his way to Mr Harris, who was suffering with severe gout, and pondered over the first instalment of Adella's story from the night before.

If he was more inquisitive by nature, he would have made her tell everything last night. But by inclination he was not a gossip. Well, perhaps he was a little like that with his own family. But as a doctor he was privy to much sensitive information and he was careful not to pass anything on to the point where he was sometimes secretive.

He would know everything in the fullness of time. But he was a little concerned for Adella. She was quiet at breakfast, not her usual self. She silently cooked Kedgeree, and served it with equal reservation. He had become so used to her steadiness and at times he knew he took her for granted. The presence of Mr Polwarth in Bath deeply unsettled her and he had never seen her like this. She was faithful, the one constant thing in his life. She never complained and he did not know what he would do without her should she ever decide to marry. He must remember to thank her more and let her know how much he appreciated her. But that would have to wait until later today. He had business to attend to.

The one thing that worried him more than anything was that Mr Polwarth used a false name. It was most abnormal and he wondered what a gentleman like him was hiding. Had Adella had a lucky escape? Who knows what evils she could have been drawn into under that man's influence?

And all this happened when he was in his final year at

medical school, he knew nothing of it. She had gone out to work to help the family, when really it should have been his job to do it. True, they had different fathers, but although he was never very close to his step-father, he admired and respected him.

He was not due to visit Mrs Polwarth until Thursday, by which time he would know all the details. But no, it was important to remain professionally detached. Was not the Hippocratic Oath written for such moments as these? He had sworn to live by it, and he would follow it to the letter. He would not allow his personal prejudices to affect his work. He would act the professional to the last, but that did not mean he would betray his sister. There was no choice. Adella won every time.

BREAKFAST AT SOUTH Parade was most often taken before ten o'clock, but it was eleven before Mr and Mrs Polwarth were seated to eat. Cynthia had waited for an hour in the elegantly furnished dining room. Breakfast was laid out on a table to the side of the room, and she looked longingly at it. She dressed for breakfast, something that she only did occasionally now. But being in Bath, she liked to try and make the effort.

"Oh Joel, I thought you would never come. I am famished. You are so thoughtless and uncaring. I hate waiting for anyone." Cynthia said, after Joel came into the room.

He said nothing.

"You might at least apologise."

"I took a sleeping draught, that is why I am later than usual, but I do not see why you do not take breakfast without me if you are hungry." He was already helping himself to food.

"You know how I hate to eat alone. You are not going to disappear all day are you?" she asked.

He poured the coffee, "No. Not all day."

"Good, I get so bored here on my own and I know no one. It is such a shame that we cannot be introduced to more people. Are you sure there are none of our friends here in Bath?" She nibbled a piece of toast and then screwed up her face as though she were eating poison.

"I am certain there are none. Once Frederick arrives, I am sure that will change. He always makes friends easily," he said.

Mrs Polwarth sighed, she was not fond of her husband's best friend, Frederick Garner. She knew that he had always despised her, something she found galling. She came from an honourable and respected family; the youngest of five children, her marriage to Joel was most agreeable and advantageous for both families in question, and her husband's fortune and position once his father was out of the way would elevate her to the height of the social sphere. If only her father-in-law would oblige her by dying.

So, she must put up with Frederick again. Always visiting Joel, always with a chill look of disdain in his eye whenever he looked at her. She never rose to the bait, never let it show that he annoyed her. Though she secretly hated him almost as much as she hated her husband. No, she enjoyed talking to Frederick as often as possible because she knew he disliked it. She was sure that he was glad she was ill. Well, once she was better, she would show him. How exactly, she was not sure. She would watch for an opportunity and devise a plan.

She was more than capable and willing to receive visitors. It irked her that Frederick was the one who would be making her friends. If she was well, she would have been out every day and made many new acquaintances.

"What about Dr Preston? We know him. He can be counted amongst our acquaintances now." Mr Polwarth said.

"A doctor! Why, he is not someone to socialise with." Then with a pause she looked at her husband, her eyes turning shrewish and said, "Why would you want to ask him? I think it very desperate. You are such a fool Joel. Why, you would be inviting that sister of his next. She would do well in the sitting room in her dirty worn clothes. We will have to put out a sheet for her to sit on! She is so ugly too. I believe I have never seen anyone so ugly in my life."

Cynthia studied her husbands face for a reaction. She noticed his jaw set hard.

"Well, I wish to invite the doctor to tea. Whether you like it or not is no consequence to me. Keep your condescending views to yourself," he replied in a sharp tone.

Cynthia screwed her face up again; she could guess why he wanted to invite him, and it was not for his medical expertise. She knew how far she could push her husband when they argued but all in all, and after a moment's thought she realised a social visit by the doctor would be something to fill a morning and entertain her. But what depths she had sunk to. . .

"Very well. Invite him if you must. But not the sister. I do not mind the doctor, he is pleasant enough. His hair is curly. I wonder why he does not straighten it. His face is a little round, but not unpleasant to look at. I suppose his conversation might be agreeable. At least when I speak of my complaints he listens without judgement."

"Cynthia," he said, "I will invite whoever I like to tea,

whether you approve or not. On this occasion, I wish to only invite Dr Preston and not his sister."

Mr Polwarth concentrated on eating his food and there was precious little conversation for the rest of breakfast, and afterwards he stood and said, "I will be in the study until lunch."

"Painting again I suppose?"

"Yes. I find Bath very inspiring."

And he left the room.

~

THE DAY so far for Adella had been full of domestic work; cleaning, cooking, tidying. She did these long overdue tasks simply in order to keep her in the house. Only once did she briefly venture out to buy a few groceries. She did not expect to see *him* in the part of Bath she lived, for it wasn't one of the fashionable area's, but she still kept her eyes alerted to the possibility. She looked about suspiciously, expecting something untoward.

Leonard came home several times that day, and on one occasion came into the kitchen and kissed her on the cheek.

"What is that for?" she asked.

He shrugged, "to show you how much I appreciate having you here."

Then, after dinner, as they sat once more relaxing, Leonard spoke.

"Do you miss Mother and Father very much?"

"Well, yes – I always miss them, I hope they can visit soon?"

"I will write to them in the next few days and ask them. Would you like that?"

"Why, yes, I would," she smiled and the joy in her eyes

returned a little. "I think they would like to come to Bath again. They often say they would like to in their letters."

They descended into silence for a time, until Adella spoke, "Shall I continue my story from yesterday?" she asked after a pause.

Leonard nodded.


SIDMOUTH, **five years before.**


THE NEXT MORNING, the children were called for breakfast with their parents and Mr West. Adella ate with the other servants, she preferred their lively banter to a solitary breakfast alone in the schoolroom.

She did not see Mr West again until lunch time. He was to teach Harry in the main study, away from Mary. But Mary reported to Adella what happened at breakfast when they were seated ready for their morning lesson.

"Mother and Father asked Mr West all sorts of boring questions about himself and his family, and what he was going to teach Harry that I lost interest after a minute or so. I saw him smile only once and that he looked nervous. He ate toast and some bacon and a big bowl of porridge. I couldn't understand why he was so scared, it is only Mama and Papa! But you would have been very pleased with me: I ate all my food and didn't drop my knife and fork at all. I ate in small bites and chewed properly. Not that Mama noticed, she was too busy talking to Mr West," she sighed.

At lunch, they all ate together in the schoolroom with Mr West. This was to be a daily occurrence from then on, and Harry seemed a lot more settled. Half a day of lessons seemed to have made him happier. He looked brighter and sat chatting to everyone instead of sulking around complaining about everything.

Mary took Adella's suggestion of trying to make friends with Mr West literally. Perhaps it was the prize of sweets she was thinking of. She kept asking him questions at lunch, much to Harry's amusement.

"Mary," Adella said, "a lady does not ask a gentleman so many questions so soon into their acquaintance. It is not becoming."

"But Mama asked Mr West lots of questions this morning."

"She is the Mistress of the house and Mr West is her employee. She had the right."

Mary frowned into her plate, and Mr West leaned over to her and whispered something into her ear. She giggled and with a broad smile continued her lunch, leaving Adella to wonder what he had said.

In the evening once the children were asleep, Adella sat once more in front of the fire with her needlework in the deserted schoolroom. Mr West came in about seven o'clock and had some tea again. This time however, he was not so shy or reserved as the night before.

"Harry seems to have enjoyed his lessons, he was a lot happier in himself today," she ventured.

"Yes, he was an eager student. I hope I did not disappoint him."

"I am sure you did not. Did he tire quickly?"

"Yes. By about two o'clock it was clear he was having problems concentrating and his cough was growing worse. I sent him off for a rest and he did not argue."

His tone was easier and relaxed. Much better.

They chatted for a while about the children until that

subject was exhausted. Adella ventured to ask him a little about himself.

"Where do you come from Mr West?"

"Er - I come from Kent, although recently I have been living in Scotland."

"Oh? I have never been there. Is it nice?"

"Yes, although I am afraid I only know Edinburgh. I studied at St Andrews University."

"What did you read?"

"Literature and History."

"Not the most practical subjects for today's growing industry. Is that why you are a tutor?"

"No, I chose this career, and there are plenty others I could have chosen."

"I am sorry, I did not mean to offend you," though she obviously had. His face wore a frown.

He did not speak for a while, and stared into his cup. Adella thought she should try and repair what was obviously broken.

"My brother is in London studying Medicine. He is in his final year."

It had the desired effect. He looked up, a softened expression on his face. "Will he specialise in any area?"

"I am not aware of any preference at the moment, we do not correspond much at this time, he is very busy with his exams, and I would not want to disrupt him."

"You are not close to him then?"

"I don't see him often, but whenever I do, we never argue and are the best of friends. I admire him greatly. He is turning into a fine gentleman. But then, I suppose I am prejudiced towards him. But if you cannot have the support and admiration of your family, I do not know what would happen. Do you have any brothers?"

"Yes, I have three."

"Three? Tell me, are you the eldest or youngest? Or somewhere in between?"

"I am the eldest, James is eighteen, Henry is seventeen and Michael is fourteen."

"Four boys! Your mother must have been very busy. You do not have any sisters then?"

"No, but I think my mother would have liked at least one of us to be a girl. My father on the other hand. . ." His voice drifted off and there was a distant look in his eye.

He seemed to shake himself mentally and then stood up and stretched.

Adella tried not to look at him, but her eyes seemed to always fall upon him whenever he was in the room, making her sewing both slow and painful; she kept pricking her fingers with the needle. They were silent for a long time. Adella continued sewing badly, Mr West paced the room.

Finally, he sat down and had more tea. She glanced at him occasionally, and saw that he had a furrowed brow. She was not sure what to say to lift his gloom and was saved by him asking,

"Do you ever go to Sidmouth? I would very much like to see it. To see the sea I mean."

Adella looked up, "Yes, I take the children at least twice a month. Before Harry was ill Mary and I would go every day. I would prefer to walk, but Harry is not strong enough, so we take the carriage. You are most welcome to come with us. We will next go on Monday."

He smiled, and the dark clouds lifted.

He stayed that night nearly two hours in the end. Considering Adella thought she offended him at least once, he obviously did not bear grudges, because he left with a smile.

They did all go to Sidmouth on Monday. They set off mid-morning with a picnic lunch. The carriage dropped them off at the sea front and they made their way straight to the promenade. When they caught their first glimpse of the sea, Mr West stopped and stared out.

It was as though nothing else existed.

After watching him and not wanting to interrupt his reverie she couldn't stop herself from speaking; "Is this the first time you have seen the sea Mr West?"

He kept his gaze fixed on the sea and said, "No. But it has been many years since I last saw it, and I always loved it. It makes me feel like a child again." He looked at her, "And please call me Joseph."

"I always think it is the smell of the seaweed and the salt that I like as well as seeing the water itself," she said.

"For me it is the expanse and the sound of the waves on the pebbles."

The children ran on ahead and left Joseph and Adella to walk behind. He stopped several times to look out again as they walked on, each time he appeared deep in thought.

It was a clear day and the English Channel looked like a still pond rather than a dangerous sea that could thrash the cliffs and sink ships. They walked along the front then stopped to eat their lunch in the gardens overlooking the sea.

"It is so beautiful here," Joseph said.

"Yes it is. And it gets more beautiful further along the coast. On one of my days off I walked as far along as Otterton. I do not think there are finer views or such varied landscape."

"I would very much like to see it. I enjoy walking. Would you show me the way sometime if it would not be too much trouble?"

"Of course. I had no plans to take that route again so soon, but I would be glad to show you. You enjoy being outside I think," she commented.

"Yes, I do, very much."

"Have you walked the grounds at Brayfern?" she asked.

"Yes, every evening I go out after supper. I don't like to be inside for too long."

Adella smiled at herself. She was starting to bring him out of himself, and the more she saw of him, the more she liked. His eyes were the clearest blue she had ever seen.

Later on, Harry and Mary played near the water, Mary looking for crabs and Harry trying to scare them away. But by late afternoon, Harry began to tire, and Adella knew they must make their way home.

Before they left, Adella had an errand to run for Cook at the fishmongers. It took a lot longer than anticipated, so that by the time she was finished, everyone was in the carriage awaiting her return.

"Sorry I took so long," she said climbing in. "Cook had extremely specific instructions, and I had to follow them to the letter. Besides, she said she would show me how to cook Devilled Oysters in my next lesson, and I don't want her to change her mind!"

"You have lessons with the Cook?" Joseph asked, with a small smile.

"Yes. What of it?"

A grin appeared on his face and he was obviously trying not to laugh.

"Why do you find it amusing?" Adella crossed her arms.

"I am sorry, I do not see you as someone who would cook. I cannot picture it."

"Well I have cooked a great many times for my mother and father, every day in fact from the age of twelve. We are not rich enough to have staff. Who cooks in your family for four boys and your mother and father?"

He stuttered a little, paused and said, "My mother."

"Well then, now I can see why she wanted a daughter; to help her with the cooking!"

He said nothing and looked out of the window, his smile gone.

On the way home they were a cheerful party, except for Joseph who remained quiet, although not altogether out of spirits. They laughed and made jokes about the characters they had seen; The old gentleman who nearly tripped over himself when Harry stuck out his tongue at him, the old lady who thought Mary adorable but believed her to be a boy. Surely she had seen that Mary was wearing a dress?

Mary was ecstatic when they nearly reached home, when Adella pulled out a crab purchased from Mr Davis' shop. It was bought with the express reason for her to claim that she had caught it. It was one of the largest any of them had seen and they wondered how long they could convince everyone.

THAT EVENING JOSEPH and Adella sat together again in the schoolroom after his walk. He apologised for his comments about her cooking lessons, and she quickly forgave him. It was fast becoming a habit for them, sitting together, although Joseph would stay for different amounts of time. One night he took his tea straight to his room and Adella did not see him again. But that night, he seemed in high spirits and there was a sparkle in his eyes. He stayed the longest time yet, and it was only when Adella yawned several times and professed a wish for sleep that they parted.

She walked to her room, and closed the door. Her head was full of him. Over the last few weeks he had become a welcome companion. She had not realised how lonely she was before he arrived. Mary was adorable, but sometimes she craved adult companionship. And his was captivating, almost compulsive. She was sorry he would only be working there for six months. But at least those months would be brighter. She wondered whether he felt the same about being with her.

**4**

———

B<sup></sup>ath 1840

"Did you love him by that time?" Leonard asked.

His question took Adella by surprise, "I had not thought about when I started to love him before, it all happened so naturally. You know, I think I did. I fell in love with him very quickly." Adella paused, "I cherished every evening that we spent together, it was like a reward for a hard day's work. I wish I could say the same for him. He certainly gave the impression that he enjoyed my company. I thought he felt the same. But knowing what I know now, it was all a lie."

Her voice drifted off and she pushed back tears. She would not cry. She was determined. Leonard moved himself next to her, and put his arm around her shoulder.

"I am sorry. I cannot believe what a fool I was," she said.

'Shh, Adella. You are no fool. You are not. I should not have let you continue your story tonight. This has affected you more than I realised. He seems like a complete scoundrel; changing his name like that and pretending to be a tutor. You will tell me everything won't you, Adella?" He looked into her tear-glistened eyes.

She was about to continue, when there was a loud knock at the front door.

Leonard went to answer it. Adella heard the conversation at the door; a patient of Leonard's was asking for him.

When he came back into the room, she held his hat, coat and bag ready.

"I am sorry I must go; old Mr Richards this time. I'm afraid we must continue tomorrow."

Adella nodded. "I think it is best anyway, I'm tired. Besides, your patients must come first."

Poor Leonard, he was forever being called upon by his patients. If he got two nights free from interruptions a week he was lucky. It would be an understanding woman who would be a doctors wife. She did wonder whether Leonard would ever meet someone he could marry. What would become of her then? She would be in the way if he did marry.

The following day, Adella opened the door to Mr Alther's Apothecary shop and walked inside. The musty smell of chemicals filled her nose instantly and she started feel at home to the once alien smell. There were several items to collect and deliver on behalf of her brother; an ointment for Mrs Havers, and cough medicine for Mr Harris.

She resolved that morning not to hide away any more. She was happy to get out and she went out with her head held high and a spring in her step. The streets of Bath were busy, and she made sure she didn't hide her face from beneath her bonnet.

"Adella my dear, come in, come in. I thought it was about

time we saw you. Mrs Alther was ready to come and see you this evening if you had not turned up!" Mr Alther said.

"I'm sorry, but I'm here now, and very glad to see you. Is Mrs Alther in?"

"She's out buying a few items for the stock. She's got it into her head that we are going to run out of castor oil, though we have two barrels out the back. I think she wanted to get out for a short while, which is fine for me. Gives me a chance to get on with the things I want to do."

Adella smiled, "Then I will not delay you from your 'things' very long."

Mr Alther was behind the counter as usual. For once, the shop was tidy from the normal array and clutter of bottles and equipment lying around.

"I do not mind dear. You are always a welcome interruption. What can I do for you?"

"I've come for those items my brother ordered earlier."

"Ah yes, I fear Mrs Havers will need her ointment as soon as possible if it's for what I think it's for! I'll get the items for you. You know where to deliver them?"

"Yes, Leonard gave me the addresses."

"Very well," and he disappeared behind a shelf for a moment, and returned with the medicines, "We'll see you again tomorrow no doubt."

"No doubt." Adella turned and walked to the door.

"Oh, by the way," Mr Alther added, "Before you go; you and Dr Preston must call in a few days time for tea. My niece arrives tomorrow and is to stay with us for a year or two. She lives out in the country at the moment and I think my brother wants her to meet a rich man to marry here in Bath. I'm not sure his plan will work though, if I remember her rightly she was an ugly baby."

Adella tried to hide her shock, "I'm sure that is not true.

But isn't it the case that ugly babies turn out to be the prettiest women?"

"If that is the case, then you must've been a very ugly baby!"

Adella gave a small laugh, "You will have to ask Leonard. He will tell you."

"No doubt. See you tomorrow then. I would be grateful if you would befriend her, pretty or not," his face was suddenly serious.

"It would be an honour. I'll call the day after tomorrow to give her time to settle in. What is her name?"

"Helen."

"A very pretty name."

Mr Alther nodded and she stepped backwards out of the door, closing it.

She turned quickly around, and as she did, she bumped into a gentleman.

"Oh, I am so sorry. Please, I beg your pardon!" she said.

The gentleman turned to face her.

They stared at each other for a few seconds. Both speechless. This was the moment Adella had dreaded for the last few days.

Against her will she felt her face drain of colour. Her mind was blank. All she could hear was the thud of her heart.

It was Joel Polwarth.

She turned around and began to walk briskly in the opposite direction.

"Adella!" he called .

She walked faster.

"Adella!"

Joel's voice got closer.

"Please, Adella."

He was faster, he ran past and blocked her path. She tried to get away from him, but he blocked her again.

"Let me pass." She stopped but would not look at him.

"Adella, please. Will you not speak to me?" he demanded.

She looked up at him.

"You dare call me by my Christian name after what you did!"

He stepped back, as though stunned by the bitterness in her voice.

"I'm sorry."

"What for? For your lack of propriety a moment ago, or for all you did five years ago? Or for both?" She knew all along that if she ever started, she would find it hard to stop her abuse at him. Her face burned hot with anger. She was desperately trying to contain it. She wanted to lash out at him; to hit him, to make him feel the pain that she had suffered these five years. Now that he was confronting her, she wasn't going to run away. This was the moment she had waited for all these years. All those nights she laid awake thinking about what she would say to him if she ever saw him again.

His voice softened, "I am sorry, yes for both. Truly I am. I understand your bitterness towards me."

"You cannot even begin to know how I feel. You say you are sorry. But why should I believe a liar like you?"

He shrugged, "You have no reason to believe me."

"What are you doing here in Bath?" She lifted her chin and stared at him.

"My wife is ill."

*His wife.*

The words stung her, and she had to look away.

She was supposed to have been his wife.

She looked back at him, "You think I care about your wife? You think I care about you? I hate you. I don't care that you are here in Bath. I have a better life without you. You are a liar -"

But she couldn't continue because he interrupted her, "I am a liar, but – I wish I could tell you why. I can't. Not while Cynthia. . ." His voice drifted off and he suddenly looked vulnerable. His face was so familiar to her. Every contour, every part. She had tried to blot it from her memory over the years, but she knew the colour of his eyes and the shape of his mouth. Oh yes, the shape of his mouth she knew intimately. She had tried to forget it, tried to forget what it was like to feel his loving kisses.

He suddenly drew himself up and took a deep breath in. "I cannot tell you today. But I will. I swear I will."

He took hold her hand. But she quickly pulled it out of his grasp.

"You promise? Just like you promised to marry me?"

He looked down at his feet. It annoyed her. He couldn't even look her in the eye now.

She continued, "You promised to marry me. You denied me; you cast me off. I don't believe any promise you make."

"You have no reason to I know. But I have not come to Bath to hound you or to spite you – whatever you may think. I've come because my wife is ill."

"If you did not come here to hound me, then why are you using my brother as your doctor? Why are you talking to me now?"

"I had to see you."

There was honesty in his face for a moment. But no, she had to remember what he did before.

"If you think you can fool me again, then you are mistaken. I am not that easily lead girl you once knew. I'm older and wiser and I warn you now: stay away from me. Leave me alone Joel Polwarth. Do not speak to me. Do not look at me. I hate you, you evil depraved, vile, cold-blooded man!"

She walked around him, and swiftly stepped into the road to get past.

This time he let her go.

JOEL MADE his way back to South Parade, his steps slow. His mind was in turmoil. He had gone out in order to get away from his wife and was only walking for fifteen minutes before his encounter with Adella. He made his way around the narrow side streets for a while, unfamiliar with his surroundings, the streets all looked the same; such a nuisance. It was a complete chance that they met. Part of him knew that it was likely to happen at some point in time, and part of him dreaded it. He had no business talking to her, he should not have done it. Then, following her, demanding she speak to him. It was not right. Yet he could not control himself. Her outburst had left him speechless, but not altogether surprised.

He arrived back home, pleased to find out that Cynthia was resting in her room. She was in a vile mood today; disconsolate and irritable. He hated it when she was like that. She always mocked him and bated him too.

He pondered what he should do with himself to fill his morning, and heard the front door bell ring. A short time later, he heard footsteps coming up the stairs, and the door opened. A familiar dark haired gentleman stood in the doorway.

"Joel?"

Joel stepped forward, eager to greet his best friend since boyhood. "Frederick! I thought you would not be here for at least a few more days."

"I had the feeling you may need me here sooner; for your sanity if nothing else."

Joel nodded, "You are right. Cynthia grows worse in every way."

"Is the prognosis the same?" Frederick asked.

"Yes. That hasn't changed."

"But if I know you and the fact you are here in Bath, I sense that she is not entirely the source of your chagrin? Or the exasperated tone of your voice?"

Joel sighed, "You mean Adella?"

"Of course. Who else."

"I've seen her twice already. Both times were. . ." he paused trying to find the right words, "they were tense."

"Understandable. You are still determined in your decision regarding her?" Frederick asked.

Joel nodded, "Yes. But let us talk of other things. I'm so very pleased you are here. How was the journey?"

Frederick rubbed his eyes. "Very easy, the trains ran perfectly to time and there were only a few people travelling. I was quite comfortable. Can't understand how anyone could put up with second or third class though."

"You never were one to skimp on comfort."

"Just as well I was born into a wealthy family," Frederick said with a grin.

~

ADELLA RAN straight home after her encounter with Joel, and it was only after a good ten minutes she managed to get control of her feelings that she saw the package in her hands. The errands for Leonard must be done.

She washed her face, looked in the mirror, and paced about for a bit to allow her red eyes to settle down. Only after half an hour did she have the courage to go out again. She duly left the house, and could think of nothing else as she walked, occasionally dabbing her eyes as she fought back the tears. It was a vain effort to try and forget her encounter with Joel.

If she had only spent another minute talking to Mr Alther it would not have happened. In a strange way she was glad that the event was over with, but she was angry at herself for handling it so badly. Her words stuttered out. Regretfully, now, she could think of a thousand clever things to say to him. Things that would have made her feel much better; that were suppressed for five years.

What did he mean that he would tell her, but not now? He was twisting the knife, she was sure. The whole conversation ran through her mind again and again. Each time more painful than the last. She tried to clear her head by thinking of Miss Alther; what she may look like, whether she bore any resemblance to her Uncle, how old she was. She had forgotten to ask, but after a moment's thought, realised that she was probably nineteen or twenty.

As the evening came and they were seated once more. She told her brother of the day's events, not leaving out her meeting with Joel and his insistence on speaking to her. Leonard was sympathetic, but she felt he did not fully appreciated her restraint, or the turmoil it caused her. But then, he did not know all the facts yet. He had to know, it was time he knew the truth.

All of the truth.

"Leonard, when I continue with my story tonight, I wish

to conclude. To tell you it all," she said over dinner, "Regardless of how long it will take."

"Of course. It will take longer than the other times?"

"Yes. You must know why speaking to that man was not pleasant for me."

"I think that's for the best. I don't believe I can wait any longer either."


**SIDMOUTH, five years before**


"ARE YOU READY TO LEAVE?" Joseph asked. He stood in the doorway of the schoolroom.

"Yes, I think so. Let me check I have everything." Adella opened her small bag, and searched inside. Water bottle. Food. Handkerchief.

She looked up and saw Joseph surveying her, one side of his mouth curved into a smile.

"Yes. I'm ready now," she said. "The walk will take most of the day, so I have lunch."

"And I have my sketch pad," he said and held up a leather folder.

"And what are you intending to draw?"

"Something beautiful I'm sure," he said looking directly at her.

Adella looked down embarrassed. Did he mean her?

The day was clear and bright; perfect for walking. It took half an hour for them to get to Sidmouth sea front, and as they were to take the coastal route, they made their way along the promenade. The path turned into a rough ground, and Adella was glad that she wore sensible walking boots.

The incline was steep for much of the way, and they stopped frequently, not only to admire the view, but to draw breath.

They had already been to Sidmouth a few times since that first trip. Joseph still seemed to adore looking at the sea as much as ever and each trip he would drift into a silent reverence on more than one occasion. Adella longed to ask him what was going through his mind. But something always held her back, it was as though she would be intruding some way. There was a secret part of his mind that she knew he would not allow her access to.

They were by no means silent on their walk today and spoke of many things; the freedom and the space seemed to liberate them both from the stilted awkwardness of their positions as governess and tutor. That day, they were Adella and Joseph.

Eventually they arrived at Branscombe beach and they found a quiet grassy spot just a few yards from the pebbles. They seated themselves on the grass and ate lunch.

"Branscombe is supposed to be a peaceful village, it's similar to the one I grew up in," Joseph said.

"Really? I grew up in a town; Aylesbury. Sidmouth is quite small enough for me already. I'm not sure I could endure being in such a rural area all the time."

"Oh, it has it's advantages, believe me."

"Such as?"

"Country sports for one. My best friend Frederick and I used to spend hours fishing and hunting when we were boys."

"Not poaching I hope."

"No, not poaching."

After they had finished eating, Joseph got out his sketch pad and started to draw Adella.

After ten minutes or so of quiet sketching, Adella couldn't stay silent any longer.

"Let me see what you have drawn," she tried to peer at the pad.

"No," he pulled it away so that she could not view it, a smile on his lips. "Not yet."

"I only want to see if you are any good at drawing. You could be drawing that cow over there."

His grin widened, "You can judge that later when I have finished."

"So, you will let me see it then?"

"Yes, but how can I finish it, if you will not sit still?"

A few minutes later, he sighed. "It is no good. There is something not right."

"Let me see and I will tell you."

"Are you such a great art critic?"

"Only when I'm the subject."

"Let me take a closer look to see what I have got wrong." He held her chin in his hands and silently studied her face as he held it, looking in turn at her eyes, her nose, then her mouth.

She didn't know where to look at first. But her eyes betrayed her soul and she looked back at his face. It was a novelty to be studied so closely, and to have him touch her. He was so close that she could not help from studying his face in return.

Then, his eyes fell on hers again and he held her gaze long enough for a silent mutual affirmation. Before she knew what was happening he leaned forward and placed his soft lips onto hers. She forgot to breathe, and when she remembered, it was because he pulled away a few moments later.

"I'm sorry," he said and looked down at the blanket they were sat on.

She felt herself blush then put her hand on his arm to reassure him, "No. Don't be sorry. Please. I – I liked it. Very much."

It was obviously the opening he needed.

"You did?" he said looking up.

"Yes."

"I have wanted to do that for such a long time," he said and gave a long sigh of relief.

"And I have wanted you to."

"Really?"

She nodded.

"I was hoping you would say that, but I was not sure. I don't know how to read a woman's thoughts."

"I have tried to make my feelings plain, but it has been difficult, given where we both work. Of course, it is highly irregular for a woman to just profess her feelings for a man."

"That's true," he said.

"I think you should kiss me again," she looked up at him, her eyes pleading.

He obeyed her without question; reaching out, he placed his hand behind her neck, and drew her in. This time, he kissed her for longer, and more confidently. Adella was in heaven. His nearness was exhilarating and she eagerly put her hands around him, daring to touch his head and feel his soft hair.

She tried to forget that it was the first time she had been kissed. Well she wasn't counting the time Simon Taylor kissed her when she was fourteen; it was a dare and he kissed her on the cheek, not the lips.

They were both oblivious to the fact they were in the

open and anyone could see them. Just as well there was nobody else about.

When they pulled apart, she bent her head and breathed a kiss on his neck. "Sweetest Adella." He whispered into her hair. "I - I think I love you," he said.

She looked up to gauge the truthfulness of his words by trying to read his expression.

"I've never met any woman like you. You're so beautiful, so perfect. I don't think you realise how perfect you are."

She met his gaze, and had never been so happy before. His words were what she longed to hear.

"Perfect. You used that word twice, but I assure you, I am far from perfect. Just ask my mother." She took hold of his hand and he closed his fingers rounds hers. "It is you who are perfect."

He shook his head in disagreement, but was smiling all the same. Then his face became serious, "If you ask my father, he will tell you that I am the worst of men."

"Well, I will have to set him straight on that matter then. I have admired you since the moment I first saw you. Couldn't you tell? These last few weeks I have been unable to stop my feelings from growing into something much stronger. To know you feel the same warms my heart and I do not think anything could quash it. Except you yourself of course."

He lifted her hand and kissed the palm. "That will not happen. I know it. You have entered my heart and there is no escape for you now."

They walked back hand in hand, and at each kissing gate Joseph would make Adella pay a toll; a kiss.

As they approached Sidmouth, Adella became more serious.

"Joseph. I think we ought to keep our feelings a secret

for the time being. Mr and Mrs Waters frown upon any fraternising between the staff and I have to keep earning money for my mother and father."

He stopped, and pulled at her hand. It made her turn around to face him. "How am I going to be able to restrain myself from kissing you when we are back at Brayfern?" He was smiling, but there was a serious tone to his voice.

"You will have to bear it, as will I! However hard it may be."

"Then I will take my share now," and he drew her to him and kissed her again.

That evening as usual they spent in the schoolroom. But this time they sat next to each other, and Adella found she could not sew; Joseph would not let go of her hands.

"It has been agony with you night after night, wishing I could kiss you, and touch you," Joseph said.

"It has?"

"Yes. Could you not tell how much I looked at you. Whenever you are in the room, I find it hard to look at anything or anyone else."

His smile made her pulse race. "Joseph," she sighed, "Such sweet words you speak to me."

"I mean everyone of them."

When Adella retired to her chamber, she was so happy, so content. But she knew they must to be discreet. Her Father was almost well enough to return to work, but it would still be weeks until that happened. She could not risk being dismissed. She could not but feel that they had been thrown together somewhat, but what good luck that he was hired as Harry's tutor and not some other worthless man. Adella could think of nothing except how warm and tender he was in every way. He never behaved too inappropriately.

Indeed, she was glad of it, and it was what she expected of him.

She loved above all else being able to touch his face, his hands and sit close to him. It was a kind of intimacy that she only dreamt about, but thought could never happen to her. It opened a floodgate. She felt elated, alive and cherished.

From then on, they were normal attentive employees during the day, but every evening they would continue to sit together, to speak, read and talk and at the end of the night before they parted Joseph would kiss Adella goodnight.

Occasionally, they would have half a day or a whole day to spend together, and would make up some excuse to leave the house separately, and then meet in secret. Sometimes it was in Sidmouth, but mostly it was in the surrounding countryside. When she looked back, Adella knew that it was a very indiscreet way to behave. But her feelings were so strong that though she knew she was behaving like a love sick girl, she was acting from the heart. It was like a tide, pulling her in regardless.

Barely a month later, there was a dance in Sidmouth for all servants and employees in the area. Joseph and Adella were to attend and Mr and Mrs Waters kindly lent their carriages to carry their servants.

The dance was held in a large marquee in the cliff top gardens and Joseph and Adella danced all but one dance together. Adella loved every second of it and Joseph was a changed man from the nervous quiet one who came to work at Brayfern four months previously. He was talkative, attentive and vibrant. She had never seen a man look so alive as he was that night.

When the dance finished, they both made their way back to Brayfern in one of the carriages. Adella helped the grooms with the horses before she returned to the house. As she was leaving the stable block and heading back towards the house, she heard her name being called.

"Adella."

She looked around in time to see Joseph's smiling face peeping around the corner of the stables.

She walked back, turned the corner and found him waiting. He was leaning against the wall, but his whole demeanour was agitated. He came towards her, and grabbed her arm, pushed her against the stable wall and kissed her with such force and passion that her breath was taken away.

"Joseph, are you drunk?" she managed to say when he finally released her.

"I have never been more sober in my life," he said looking into her eyes.

He kissed her again, then broke away and said, "Adella, I love you. Say you'll marry me. Say you'll be mine, I could not bear life without you now."

She looked into his eyes, inquisitive, yearning. Willing her to say yes. His smile now gone; he waited for her to answer.

## 5

———

"Yes," she said. "Yes, I'll marry you," she replied immediately. It was an easy question to answer. She had known what her answer would be if he asked. For a moment she thought she was dreaming.

She flung her arms around his neck and he pulled her into a tight embrace. Then he spun her round and laughed aloud.

"You said yes!"

"Shhh. Someone will hear us!" she giggled.

"Soon there will be no secrets. Soon we can tell the whole world," he whispered and kissed her again.

The next day, Adella was walking on air. She couldn't believe that she was going to be a married woman soon. She looked at her hand and imagined a ring on it, and how it would sound being called Mrs West. At breakfast in the schoolroom with the children, Joseph and Adella exchanged smiles and knowing glances. Earlier she worried that he may have regretted asking her, but one look at him allayed all her fears. His face wore a soft smile. One she knew well, and his eyes seemed to pierce through to her heart. It was as though he could read her every thought.

That night, Joseph was a little quiet. As usual, they sat together in the schoolroom, and Adella glanced often at him and wondered whether she should ask him what she feared the most; that he regretted his proposal. He had been silent like this before, but it never lasted this long.

"I wish I could buy you an engagement ring, but I can't afford one at the moment," he said at last.

"I do not need one," she spoke quickly, secretly relieved that that was the reason for his quietness. "I really do not care about a ring."

"You deserve the finest jewels. Are you sure you do not mind?"

She laid aside her sewing, "Do you really think such a thing matters to me? I am happy beyond words that you wish to marry me. I - I would prefer to have a wedding ring. I am not sure how much they cost, but we could buy one together? I have some money saved– "

He took hold of her hand. "I promise you, you shall have a wedding ring. A gold one and I will buy it myself, if I can't I know my best friend Frederick would lend me the money."

She smiled, "Very well. But gold wedding rings are not cheap. Any will be sufficient. Please, do not fret about a gold one."

"Hmm we will see. Will you not mind living on a tutor's salary?"

"So that is what troubles you, is that why you are so quiet?"

"You could tell?"

"I knew something wasn't right. I know you well enough already," she said her eyes full of love for him.

"You have not answered my question."

She stood up, "Well, I need at least 20 dresses a year, fifty pairs of shoes to replace the two I own myself, and if I do not have a house that has at least fifteen bedrooms then I will be very disappointed!"

He laughed at her as she sat down next to him, and took his hand.

"Joseph, all I need is you. I have never wanted to be rich, only happy, and you make me so very very happy that I can't find the words to express it. It's like I have always known you and when I look to the years ahead; the years we will share, my heart is full of gladness."

"Mine is too. I have never been happier than these last few months. Who would have thought that a woman such as you existed in the world." He let go of her hand only to gently stroked her cheek, "You have no pretence, no false-ness, you just want to share my life."

His hand slid down and he cupped her chin. He drew her in and kissed her, sealing their promises.

FOR THE NEXT MONTH, they planned their future together. They were both eager to marry quickly, Joseph more so than Adella. This surprised her, she thought there would be at least a period of a year for their engagement. She knew they could not afford an extravagant wedding, but after a bit of thought, she realised that the notion of waiting that long was something she saw happen to her friends. There was no reason to wait if they didn't want to.

She couldn't help but think on occasion that Joseph's eagerness to marry lay in his passion. He was at times fervent, and Adella was forced to put a stop to his ardent kisses on more than one occasion. In fact, how quickly they could marry was all he spoke of some evenings. They agreed that once his time at Brayfern was over, they would have to spend time apart while he sought full time employment. But he was confident that he would find a position quickly. She was anxious about them being parted. She could not bear the thought of him leaving, and although she offered to come with him when he left, he declined. It was for practical reasons than anything else. They could not afford the rent of two separate rooms, so, as soon as he found employment, she would quit Brayfern and go to him. Then they would be married immediately. He was to make sure that the Banns were read before she arrived, or he would obtain a special licence. Everything was settled and planned for.

One afternoon, Adella had been out for a long walk with Mary. When they arrived back and were settling down for tea in the schoolroom, Daisy, one of the maids, rushed in.

"There is such a turmoil downstairs," she was out of breath from having run up the stairs and gasped a few times.

"What is it?" Adella said standing up.

"Oh Miss Maxwell, the whole house is in disarray! A gentleman arrived in ever such a grand carriage about two hours ago. He walked in on Mr and Mrs Waters taking their lunch and demanded to see Mr Polwarth. Well obviously nobody knew who he was talking about, there is no one here by that name. The man then said that he worked here as a tutor. 'Mr West you mean' was what Mr Waters said. Anyway, they got Mr West from the study and it turns out the Gentleman is Mr West's father, and his name isn't Mr West – it's Mr Polwarth – Joel Polwarth and they were both locked up in the study for half an hour and when they came out Mr West said he was leaving immediately and didn't have time to pack but would have his things forwarded to his home address in Bedfordshire, which is a really big house and he's really rich and the eldest son too!" She spoke so quickly and without pausing for breath that she panted for a few moments.

Adella stood for a moment silent, her brain took in everything Daisy just said.

"Joseph is leaving?" Adella repeated.

"Yes miss."

"His father is here?"

"Yes."

Adella couldn't move.

"Go quickly, before it is too late." Daisy said and she pushed her towards the door. "They are fetching his father's carriage. They leave in the next few minutes."

Adella rushed to the door, her mind was all confusion. "Yes, yes, I'll go. Look after Mary for me?"

She didn't wait for and answer, and rushed downstairs and out of the house. Her legs couldn't carry her fast enough. Sure enough, outside there was Joseph stood beside a carriage, waiting to get in. Daisy was right; one quick glance at the carriage showed it was of the best quality.

"Joseph?" she ran up to him.

He turned his head slowly. He was the same man, but not her own Joseph. His face was different; his eyes were cold. Distant.

Finally he spoke.

"Miss Maxwell. I am leaving immediately. It has been a pleasure working with you."

"Where? Why? Joseph, why are you leaving so quickly? You were not due to go for another four weeks. Daisy said you were going to Bedfordshire. Is that where you live?"

At this, a man; an older version of Joseph, approached. He was taller than Joseph. His hair was grey and his face wore deep frown lines in his forehead. Mr and Mrs Waters followed behind as his father spoke.

"Miss Maxwell, is it?" the man said eyeing her up and down.

"Yes. I am the Governess here."

"My son is leaving with me immediately. I would thank you not to delay us any further with taking your leave." His tone was one of unaffected boredom.

Joseph stood still, but was looking away from her, at the carriage.

"Joseph? Please, where will you be going? Home? I do not know where that is. Please, will someone explain what is going on?"

His father spoke again in an angry voice, but this time it was to Joseph, he ignored her.

"Hurry up. I want to leave now."

Joseph turned to Adella again. "Goodbye Miss Maxwell."

He started to get into the carriage and she grabbed his arm to stop him.

"But Joseph, is this any way to treat me? Please, just explain. Is this anyway to treat your fiancée?"

At that, he stopped. Father and son exchanged glances.

"Fiancée?" his father repeated, "are you telling me you are betrothed to my son?"

"Yes."

At that he laughed. "Surely there must be a mistake. Joel, are you betrothed to this governess?" He looked her up and down again with disdain.

Joseph slowly turned to her, his glance clouded, "No. I am certainly not betrothed to her."

She gasped and managed to stammer out, "Joseph, do you – do you deny me?"

"Miss Maxwell. It has been a pleasure working with you,

but I do not understand why you are under the illusion that we are engaged. Perhaps it is because I was friendly towards you, which I see was a mistake, for now you know I am rich, you now think me your fiancé. I will have you know, that I am shortly to be married to a fine lady. Miss Anderson has, as my father has told me today finally accepted my hand in marriage."

He removed her hand from his arm.

Adella could not speak. Then made one last attempt to reason with him.

"But we are engaged, we have been engaged since the 18th August."

His father intervened then. "Miss Maxwell do you have a ring?"

"No. Joseph could not afford one."

At that he scoffed, "You delude yourself, girl! My son could afford the largest diamond any jeweller could provide. Besides which, you do not even know his real name."

He got in the coach, closely followed by Joseph. They shut the door and his father said, "Mr Waters, I bid you good day and advise you to reconsider who you employ as your governess. Drive on Jones."

The coach pulled away and Adella and Mr Waters stood watching it, the sound of hoof beats echoing in her ears. When it was out of view, Mr Waters turned to Adella. "Miss Maxwell, you will come to the study immediately."

His face wore a deep frown. She knew he was about to attend to the elder Mr Polwarth's advice. She followed him with nervous steps through the front door, and beyond the hallway to the study. She stood as he seated himself behind his desk. He looked at her with clear scorn and spoke in a cold voice.

"Miss Maxwell, I never thought you of all people would

be so mercenary. Do you still claim that you are engaged to Mr West – er Polwarth?"

"Yes."

"Then I have no alternative than to dismiss you. I cannot have a woman such as yourself here in my house. Why, no wealthy man would be safe to visit here without you claiming something of him!"

She dropped her head, "I understand." She knew argument would be fruitless.

"Do you have nothing else to say by way of apology?"

"Sir, I cannot apologise for something I am wholly innocent of. If Mr West chooses to deny our engagement there is nothing I can say that will persuade you or anyone else."

"Then you will leave as soon as you have packed."

She nodded, and summoned enough presence of mind to beg, "May I leave first thing in the morning? If I leave now, it will be dark for most of my journey and I must travel alone."

"Very well, but make sure you are gone before breakfast."

"Yes sir."

Adella went directly to her room to pack. She knew she must gather her belongings together quickly, but something stopped her. She did not seem to believe what had happened. Surely there was a mistake? Surely, the man she loved, the man who loved her, or at least said he loved her could not act so cruelly. She suddenly felt completely alone, and deep in the pit of her stomach she knew the only thing that could alleviate her pain was Joseph. Yet as each minute passed, he travelled further and further away.

If only he had told someone of their engagement, then Mr Waters would believe her, and she would not have to leave. But there was no one. Oh, the injustice of it all. To accuse her of all people of being mercenary, nothing was further from the truth.

His father called him Joel. If that was the case, then why had he masqueraded under a different name, and if he was already engaged, why propose to her?

He had proposed to her hadn't he?

She flung herself on the bed and wept bitterly as the things she should have said and done whirled in her head. Some time later, as it was growing dark, there was a knock at the door. Adella gathered herself together, wiped the tears from her eyes and opened the door. It was Daisy.

"I thought you might like something to eat." She carried a tray with supper on it.

"Thank you Daisy, that was very thoughtful of you. But I am not hungry."

She placed the tray down on the bed anyway.

"Well I'll leave it in case you change your mind. Look at the state of you," she said, "You look positively dreadful."

"Thank you Daisy." She managed a small smile.

"Oh, don't mind me. I speak as I find, but you should have told Mr Waters that you weren't engaged."

"But that wouldn't have been the truth!"

"Aye, but you'd have kept your job."

"So you know I have been dismissed."

"Of course. The servants know everything, especially that you are to be out of the house before nine tomorrow."

Adella slumped down.

"I just can't understand why he would deny your engagement." Daisy said.

Adella looked up suddenly. "So you believe me?"

"Of course. Why wouldn't I? I know you enough by now. I know an honest person when I see one. But if you ask me, you're well rid of him."

"So it seems," she said quietly.

"Best eat your food, and get a good nights sleep. You'll have to walk to the Railway Station, Mr Waters says on no account are you to have the carriage."

"How charitable of him."

"You should know by now, that you're best to keep on his good side and not cause trouble."

"But I didn't cause trouble. Not willingly anyway."

"Well, what is done is done. You'd best make the most of it."

Adella left Brayfern House shortly after dawn the next day. She said goodbye to Daisy, then slipped out. She walked to the railway station at Sidmouth and arrived home late that night. Her mother and father were astonished to see her. Their pleads of why she was so suddenly returned home caused them much anxiety, especially when fuelled by their concern and the tiredness of the journey, she found it difficult to get the words of explanation out for some time. She was too stunned, too upset. Not only had she lost the dearest man she loved, but also her position, reputation and hope.

When she told her story, they believed her. How could they not? Her father wanted to go directly to the Polwarth estate and confront him, but she managed to persuade him otherwise. Besides, her father was just back at work and she did not want anything to jeopardise his health or his reputation. And anyway, she was not sure where Joel lived in Bedfordshire, she would need to find out.

In the end, she did find out where he lived from Daisy and wrote to him at the earliest opportunity.

*Joseph,*

*I do not know what to call you. Joel seems as though I am addressing a stranger, not my Joseph with whom I shared such precious moments.*

*You must know why I write? I am at a loss to know why you denied our engagement and I am more confused than ever about your name.*

*Please write and tell me why you behaved as you did, indeed, I think my heart will break if you do not.*

*But still, I remember your cold manner when you left Sidmouth, and if needs must, I release you from our engagement if you have changed your mind.*

*Please write soon, if only to say you are well.*

*Yours*

*Adella*

THE REPLY, nearly a week later was not from Joseph, but from his lawyer.

MISS MAXWELL,

WITH REFERENCE *to your letter to Mr Polwarth, I must warn you not to contact my client, or any member of his family in the future in any form. If you do so again, I will be forced to take legal action against you in the form of a restraining order.*

*Mr Polwarth is about to marry and is happy in his choice. I trust this will put to an end any delusions of grandeur you have towards him.*

*I have kept your letter as evidence, should it be needed in the future.*

*Yours etc,*

· · ·

*Mr Thatcher.*

   *Attorney to the Polwarth Estate*

HER RESPONSE upon reading such a reply was as any heart that loved would react. It was not a letter to be recovered from easily and Adella was at a loss to know what upset her the most; that the letter was not written by Joseph, or the threatening nature of the content.

She was devastated, and was inconsolable for many days. Her mother and father tried their best to help her recover but they knew only time would heal her wounds. Adella's sudden arrival home was covered up; they told their friends and acquaintances that her charge had been sent to a school. Her services were no longer needed. But Adella's absence from social gatherings sparked more than one persons notice, and her parents did everything they could to quell any gossip.

A month later, and Adella was slowly recovering from her disappointment. But she suffered a setback, when, as expected she found in The Times what she dreaded in the marriage announcement section.

6TH DECEMBER, Mr Joel Polwarth, the eldest son of Mr and Mrs Michael Polwarth of Biggleswade Bedfordshire, to Miss Cynthia Anderson only daughter of Mr and Mrs George Anderson of Woking, London. The wedding took place at 11am at St Mary's Church Woking. The couple will honeymoon in Italy for three months.

· · ·

**BATH 1840**

"HE REALLY DID ALL THIS?" Leonard asked.

"Yes. Now you see why I hate him? Not only did he deny our engagement, but I left my appointment in disgrace."

"I cannot believe it." He shifted about in his chair.

"Oh, please. Do not say that! I have had enough people say that they do not believe me. Mother and Father did, why can't you?"

He moved himself next to his sister and took hold of her hand. "I do believe you. I find it difficult to understand why he would do such a thing. Why would any man be so cruel, lie, cheat and leave you? It is beyond comprehension."

"I wish I knew the answer, I have tried to think of a reason these five years, and have yet to come to a satisfactory explanation. I think, it was because he was about to marry and wanted to seduce me. But it does not explain why a man as wealthy as he would become a tutor. What possible reason could he have, especially when he was so rich?"

"Yes. That is beyond all my understanding. I am speechless." Leonard managed to stutter, "To sully your name in such a way, to make it look like you made up an engagement and then to warn you off just because you wanted to know why!"

"I did not write what was in my heart, I wanted to say so much to him, truly I did, but I merely asked in the politest terms for an explanation of his recent behaviour to me and released him from our engagement. That was all. He told me so many lies: that he could not afford an engagement ring, yet he could."

Leonard stood up and paced the room for several minutes.

When he managed to calm himself, he noticed Adella was silently crying and so sat back down with her.

"He cut my heart open and it bled for a long time," she said.

"The scar remains still. I can tell," he said, his voice full of sympathy.

"Yes. I vowed never to trust a man again. If he changed his mind, which he obviously had, I would have released him from the engagement. Indeed, to find out that he was gentry, too far above me, I think it would have been impossible for us to marry anyway. If he only asked I would have released him, I would."

"You are not beneath him. He is the lowest of men! Indeed he is!" He clenched his fists and shook his arms. "If I knew all this before -" but before he could continue, Adella interjected.

"If you knew, you would have acted properly and professionally as a doctor should."

Leonard sighed deeply, "Yes, you are right. I would, but it will not stop me disliking him. I am due to see Mrs Polwarth tomorrow. I do not know what I shall say!"

"Leonard please. These people are extremely influential, and I am sure you are charging them a fee that will be very helpful to your income."

"Yes, but I would rather not see him again. I don't want his money. Knowing what I do now, I sent you back to take his sleeping draughts too. Oh Adella I am so sorry."

"I am well enough. You mustn't let it show that you know what happened. Besides, you are principally treating Mrs Polwarth aren't you? For all we know she was an innocent party in all of this."

"We cannot know."

"Please Len, please. Take their money. Be her physician and when she is better, they will be gone."

Leonard ran his fingers through his dark curly hair. "That is the problem Adella. Mrs Polwarth is not going to get better. She has a malignancy. It is only a matter of time before she dies. Four or five weeks at the most."

**6**

———

Leonard made his way to the Polwarth's house in South Parade at a fast pace. The rain that was so frequent in Bath caught him unprepared today. It only started a few minutes after he left, and he was angry at himself for not bringing an umbrella. Unfortunately it was the type of rain that was not only heavy, but penetrative.

He was taken straight up to his patient and as he entered the salon he saw Mrs Polwarth seated near the window. A quick scan of the room showed no other person present and he was glad that Mr Polwarth was not there; knowing what he did, he was the very last person he wished to see.

He stayed with his patient for half an hour, his treatment of her major illness taking up little of his time, for there was nothing else he could do for her in that respect. However, she was weakening considerably fast and had many other minor ailments all of which contributed to her being uncomfortable.

"Mrs Polwarth, I do hope that next time you are feeling as ill as this, you will call for me immediately," he said as he packed away his bag.

"Very well, though I do not like to trouble people with my little complaints."

"It is no trouble. I am your doctor, you must call for me if you need me. Take this pain relief every six hours and you will be more comfortable, but if it is not strong enough, then send for me. You will promise?"

"Very well," she said as she sank back in the chair.

The door opened and Joel walked in.

"Oh Joel, I do wish you were here sooner. Dr Preston has been here nearly half an hour and now he is leaving. I do so hate being alone," Mrs Polwarth said.

"I beg your pardon Cynthia, I was replying to my father's letter and he required an immediate response."

"You are your father's slave."

"Indeed, as I am yours also," he replied. He held out his hand to Leonard, who after a moment decided to shake it. He remembered Adella's words the night before, "act properly and professionally as a doctor should".

"We have finished and I am ready to leave," Leonard said avoiding eye contact and looking at the door longingly. If he could only get out of this house quickly he might be able to hide his aversion.

"I will see you out then," Joel said and he gestured to the door.

As they made their way down the stairs, Joel asked, "How is she?"

"She is weakening quickly and has worsened much more than I expected over the last few days. I do not believe she has very long left." His tone was lowered and he stopped half way down. "Is there somewhere we can speak more privately?"

"Yes of course," and he led Leonard to the study at the bottom of the stairs.

After they entered, Joel closed the door and indicated a chair. The study was dominated by an oak desk. To the left there was a fireplace with two dark leather armchairs.

"No thank you. I will stand," his expression was hard, and resentful, though he was desperately trying to hide it.

"Very well. What is it you wished to say to me?"

"Your wife still does not know that her illness is terminal?"

"No, I believe it would be better if she did not. She has a delicate temperament as you are aware, and I do not want her last days on this earth spent fretting or worrying that she is dying. She would become hysterical I am sure of it."

"It is not unusual to keep knowledge of terminal illnesses from the patient. But I would let you know in the strongest possible terms, that her family at least should know so that they can be prepared for the inevitable."

"They already know, and they agreed it was for the best to keep it from her."

Leonard raised his eyebrows. "Very well. In that case, if they wish to see her before she dies, then you must ask them to come immediately. I would recommend that I visit every day from now on. If she continues to deteriorate as she is doing, then it will only be a matter of weeks. I have given her more medicine for her pain and told her to fetch me if she needs me."

"Thank you," Joel said.

The two men having concluded their business, stood in silence for a moment, yet there was still something unspoken between them as they looked at each other, and neither made a move to leave the room.

"Adella has told you what happened between us, hasn't she?" Joel said in a quiet voice.

Leonard lifted his chin, "Yes. Yes she has."

"You are not good at hiding your disdain," Joel said, with a wry smile.

"I am sorry, I tried to hide my feelings, but my brotherly affection is strong."

"I understand those sentiments completely; I have three brothers, all are younger than me."

"Yes I know. It seems that is one thing you did not lie to Adella about."

Joel turned away and walked to the fireplace, deep in thought. After a few moments he turned back and said, "She told you recently, didn't she? You didn't know of our engagement a few days ago. Certainly not the first time you visited? I wonder why she did not tell you before."

"So you do not deny you were engaged?" Leonard stepped forward quickly.

"No," he shook his head, "I have no wish to deny my engagement to Adella now, and to you of all people; her brother. Whatever Adella has told you, I am sure it would have been the absolute truth. During the time we spent together, I became very well acquainted with her. She is no liar."

Leonard felt himself go red, and could no longer contain himself. "Mr Polwarth, I believe it would be for the best if I handed your wife's care over to another physician. Despite Adella's protestations that I should continue, I believe Dr Thanby, who is a good friend of mine and would very capable of -" but he was cut short by Joel.

"Dr Preston. Before you do that, would you allow me to tell you what happened five years ago? What I mean is, will you let me tell you why I did what I did?"

"I would very much like to know why you behaved so abominably to my sister."

"Do you have any other appointments this morning?"

"Yes, in half an hour."

Joel ran his fingers through his hair.

"Half an hour is not long enough, there is too much to say. Could you return one evening in the next few days?"

Leonard thought for a moment, "I can return in two days' time. Saturday. You will tell me why you abandoned Adella?"

"Yes, and after I have told you everything, if you decide to hand my wife's care over to this other doctor I will accept it. But in the meantime will you remain as her Doctor?"

Leonard nodded.

"Very well. I will expect you on Saturday evening, seven o'clock?"

Joel opened the study door, "One more thing. When I tell you everything, it must be kept confidential. You must not speak of it to anyone else – especially not Adella. Not yet anyway."

"But she deserves an explanation!" he spluttered.

"I know. But please, I will explain everything on Saturday, and especially why I do not wish Adella to know yet. But I can only tell you if you promise me that it will be kept to yourself, else I can tell you nothing."

"Nothing?"

"Nothing."

Leonard sighed. Joel's hard gaze was uncompromising. "Very well. I give you my word however much I dislike it."

"Thank you." Joel said.

Leonard turned to leave, he heard Joel say in a strained voice, "How is she? How is Adella?"

Leonard turned around and searched Joel's face, looking for a reason why this man would ask. What would he care? After a moment he said, "Physically she is well. But your appearance here in Bath has upset her greatly. You will not try and speak to her again as you did before? You will not demand that she speaks to you like you did outside the Apothecary's?"

"No. I will not." Then he added, "I promise you that. Tell her, tell her I am sorry for it. It was wrong of me."

After Dr Preston left, Joel checked on his wife, who was sat quietly content near the fire. Then, satisfied that she needed nothing, he went to find Frederick. He was in his bed chamber sat by the fire, reading the newspaper.

"It's very early for a visit. Who was it?"

"Dr Preston," he said as he sat himself opposite his friend. "And he is coming on Saturday night, when I will tell him everything about Adella and I."

"Everything?" he peered over his newspaper.

"Yes."

"Are you sure that is wise?"

"Yes. I need his help, and you need not look at me like that. He can help me, once and for all."

"I still think you should do as I say and follow my plan. It is an excellent plan after all."

"It isn't that I do not value your opinion Frederick, but I can't do as you suggest. It is out of the question."

"Well, after you have told Dr Preston, I think he will think my plan the best option. You'll see."

Joel stood up, "According to Dr Preston it seems it will be sooner than expected. He thinks it will be a matter of a few weeks."

"You seem upset about it?" he said and put aside his newspaper.

"Of course I am. How could I not be? She is my wife after all."

THAT NIGHT, Leonard mentioned nothing of his visit to the Polwarth's. Adella did not ask, although she thought of nothing else, especially the fact that soon Mrs Polwarth would be dead. She was sorry that anyone was ill, and especially terminally, but she wondered how much pain Joel was in because of his wife. If he loved his wife even a fraction of the way he had shown his love for her, then he would have suffered indeed. In a way it was a kind of justice. But, if there was proper justice, he would be the one who was ill. She hated her reaction to him, she hated what she was becoming, angry, resentful, unforgiving. She was mortified when she re-read the letter from his lawyer. Several times she thought about calling on him and demanding to see him and make him explain why he hurt her so. Her resolve to speak to him diminished, her hatred did not. She told herself that she must move on, and let her anger go again. She thought she had already done it once, and it was hard enough to try again. She wasn't sure she had the strength.

The next morning, Adella stood once more in Mr Alther's Apothecary Shop, for once not waiting for medicines, but for their niece, Miss Helen Alther to appear. The shop was empty, and Adella took a few moments to look at the bottles and boxes in the glass counter and cabinets.

"This is new," Adella said, pointing to a stack of cardboard boxes behind the counter. The label read "Mr Reed's Liver Salts".

"Oh yes," Mrs Alther said, "It just came in. It's been advertised in all of the newspapers, and we kept getting people asking for it. It's no different than any other liver salts, but the advertisement makes people want to buy it."

"It's more expensive than the others too," Adella said as she picked up one of the boxes and examined the label.

"Yes, Mr Reed must want the extra money to pay for the adverts!"

Adella put the box down, and looked at the clock high on the wall.

"They'll be out in a minute I'm sure," Mrs Alther said following Adella's gaze. "They arrived exactly on time." Mrs Alther seemed in a buoyant mood. There was a happy glow about her; her smile was wider, and she dressed in one of her prettier dresses.

"They?" Adella asked.

"Oh yes, Helen and Flora. Two of them! Well we only expected one," she laughed a little, "but two came in the end. Flora is the eldest . She's, well -" Mrs Alther drew herself closer to Adella and whispered, "she's thirty and quite the plainest girl I've ever seen. Anyway, she's come too and I suppose looking for a husband like her sister, although Helen thinks she's an old maid forever now. None of the men near her wouldn't have her apparently. It's a shame when a girl is so plain, don't you think? It is a good thing that neither of us have had to worry on that score."

"Here I am! You must be Adella. I'm Helen."

They both turned toward the loud voice that broke their silence. Helen was a small girl, with clear, bright skin and fashionably arranged light brown hair. She was light on her feet and glided forward.

"I am very pleased to meet you, Miss Helen," Adella said.

"I too! Uncle and Aunt have told me all about you!"

Behind her, like a silent shadow, another woman stepped through from the office. She remained under the door frame, shyly looking on. She was similar in proportion to Helen, though clearly older.

"And this is my other niece, Flora," Mrs Alther said. "Helen is a little wild, and needed Flora to look after her."

"I am not wild, Aunt!" Helen cried with a smile that showed her straight white teeth.

"Of course not, my dear. Your mother was always a little cautious that is all."

"Hmm. Well I did not want Flora to come, she'll spoil my fun. You'd better not spoil my fun, Flora."

Flora was silent, but Adella went around the counter and shook her hand. Flora smiled and quietly said, "I am pleased to meet you, Miss Maxwell."

"I know we will be best friends!" Helen said and she grabbed Adella's arm and dragged her out the door, "Come on, you must show me around Bath." She slammed the door shut behind them.

"My uncle said you live with your brother," Helen said as she linked her arm through Adella's and lead her down the street.

"Yes."

"And he's a doctor."

"Yes."

"Is he handsome?"

"You will have to judge yourself. I think him handsome, but you may think differently."

"Well, I suppose I should meet him, although a doctor is not rich enough for me to consider marrying. Still, he may be able to introduce me to lots of rich men. Rich men who are single and about to die."

Adella stopped walking. "Surely not."

"Oh, don't be like that Adella. I would make any man happy if he were rich. Very happy indeed. Do you know any rich men?"

"I am afraid I am not well connected at all. I know only tradesmen and servants."

"I'm sure I shall make friends quickly. Everyone likes me and I am excessively pretty don't you think?"

"Yes," she said somewhat reluctantly.

They continued on. Helen chattered and Adella was forced to agree with her whatever the subject. Adella looked across at her, her feelings were already swinging between hating and liking her. Helen was blunt and honest about her quest for a rich husband, but at least she did not her hide behind artfulness. Something Adella abhorred. Her brother was safe, but she could not imagine a worse sister-in-law. It was just as well. She turned around and saw Flora walking behind. She smiled shyly back at Adella, and wondered whether the elder sister would make a better friend.

Adella stopped again, "Flora, will you not join us?"

She ran up to them, and the three of them continued on.

"Shall we go and drink the water?" Helen asked.

"If you like, it does not taste very nice though."

"Oh I do not care. I can eat and drink anything. Besides, you can't come to Bath and not try the water," Helen said.

They continued on again. Through the centre of Bath Helen was enthused by every shop and tea room they passed and they were forced to retrieve her several times as she looked in the windows. When they finally arrived at the Pump Room, Helen handed Flora a glass. "You drink it first."

Flora took a tentative sip and grimaced "It's warm and very salty."

"Let me try," said Helen and she snatched the glass.

"Ergh. It's horrible." But she took another sip anyway.

"Here, you have some Adella." Helen handed her the glass.

"No thank you. I've already tried the water, and I think it

awful like you two. I don't need reminding of how it tastes thank you very much."

Helen giggled, then looked around the room. Adella watched as Helen's glances fell on each of the gentlemen. A couple of times, she caught a gentleman's eye, and she fluttered her eye lashes and smiled even more broadly than she was already. Adella was appalled, it was outrageous.

Flora saw Helen's flirtations too, and suggested they go to the Abbey. They managed to extract Helen from the Assembly rooms by each looping an arm around hers and moving towards the door. Outside, they looked up at the Abbey.

"It's certainly the finest Cathedral I've ever seen. Let's go inside," Flora said, dragging the others along.

"Do we have to?" Helen protested.

"Yes," Flora said, "You promised, remember?"

They toured inside the Abbey and returned home for lunch. Adella insisted they go to her and Leonard's house. As they sat in the small living room and sipped tea and ate bread and cheese, Flora opened up more.

"This seems a pleasant house," she said, looking around. "Well furnished."

"It is quite small, but it suits Leonard and I. He is becoming a more successful doctor every month. I have high hopes for him. He may come home soon for a short time, but it depends upon his patients. They come first."

"I do not know how anyone could be a doctor, all those sick people! Ergh." Helen said with a mouthful of cheese.

Flora gasped, "Helen! Do not say such things. It is so rude."

"How so?"

"Doctors are extremely skilled men who care for the sick and put themselves in danger to help others," Flora said.

Adella was right in her earlier assumption that Flora would make the better friend. She was sensible, controlled and extremely likeable. How Helen was from the same parents seemed so strange. To have two such different daughters! But one thing Adella thought was most odd was that Flora should be thought plain, because she did not think so at all. True, Helen was much younger, but Flora's large brown eyes complimented her oval face and red lips. No, Flora was pretty. Chances were, she had been treated badly by a gentleman too, and she did not wish to marry. Or no man had ever taken her fancy.

As they sat and talked, they heard the front door open and close. Leonard walked in, dripping rainwater everywhere.

"Adella, have you seen my umbrella? I am not very happy with myself; I forgot to take it. I should have learnt by now. Oh – " He stopped short, "We have guests! Of course, one of you must be Miss Alther?" he said as he walked in.

"Leonard, both these young ladies are called Miss Alther," Adella said.

"Two Miss Alther's!" he exclaimed. "Well, I am not sure Bath is ready for two of you!"

They both giggled.

Adella interrupted, "This is Miss Flora Alther, and this is Miss Helen."

"It is a pleasure," he said taking each of their hands in turn.

Leonard sat down, "Anyone with the name of 'Alther' is welcome in my house. Do you mind if I join you for lunch?"

"Of course we do not mind Dr Preston, this is *your* house after all!" Helen said with a slight blush and flutter of her eyelids.

"Indeed it is, but I would hate to disrupt you all. I know

how ladies sometimes prefer to be without a gentleman so they can talk more openly," he said with sly a smile.

"There's nothing I say to a lady that I wouldn't say in front of a gentleman," Helen said.

Adella and Flora's eyes met briefly in mutual understanding. Helen would do no such thing.

Leonard ate his lunch and chatted easily to both sisters. Although he found it disconcerting when, not only did Helen give him her undivided attention, but she kept interrupting Flora whenever he asked the elder sister a question. But Leonard bore it well, and was never rude to Helen.

"Well," said Leonard, "I must leave now, I have an appointment the other side of the city, and I mustn't be late."

"Oh must you leave so soon?" Helen said.

"I'm afraid so." Leonard stood up.

"But I was hoping you would stay at least another hour," Helen said.

"I'm very sorry to disappoint you, but I hope I will have the pleasure of your company again soon. You are most welcome here any time."

That seemed to placate Helen, and she allowed Leonard to leave without further protestations.

That evening, Adella took the earliest opportunity to ask her brother what he thought of the sisters.

"Well before I answer that question, I will tell you what *you* have decided about them!"

"Will you indeed!" the corners of her mouth turned up into a small smile.

"Yes," he said.

Adella placed her needlework down and listened attentively.

"Well, you think Helen an annoying twitterer, and you

would rather be left alone to get to know her sister, Flora, who you think sensible and likeable."

"You came to this conclusion just from today?"

"I can read you like a book." He crossed his arms.

"Hmm, very perceptive. Now all I need to do is think of a way to get Flora alone! It may be easier than I think though. Helen seems to want to be rid of her at the earliest opportunity."

"I wish you luck! But you would like to ask her to keep you company on Saturday evening, I have an engagement."

"I will see if I can get Flora alone that night. But, you have not told me what you think of them."

Leonard smiled, "One of them is very lovely."

## 7

The following morning, Adella was busy in the kitchen. She spent many hours there every day, and knew she could benefit from a few labour-saving utensils on display in shop windows. But they were expensive. She was a little unsure whether to ask Leonard for the money. It wasn't that she feared an adverse reaction from him, in fact, she knew that if she asked he would immediately give her the money. He wouldn't deny her anything he could afford to buy, it was only that it would be a large expense and she didn't want to bother him with it right now. She looked for the items in the second hand shops, but they were the same price as new. When it got closer to Christmas she would broach the subject of getting the meat mincer and a knife sharpener. Those two things would help the most.

Her mind wondered in this way as she cooked and baked, it was only after a long time that she remembered to think about Joel. Her face turned into an immediate frown at the thought of him, and she whisked the eggs a little too strongly and tenderised the meat a little too hard from then on. It was hard at times not to think about him, especially when she was alone like this. She needed company and as luck would have it, not long after the door bell rang. She wiped her hands on her apron and went to answer the door.

"Can we come in?" Helen said. Flora was stood next to her.

"Of course," and she ushered them in. "I'm so glad you are here, go through to the kitchen; I am baking."

They went through, "I am so excited, we are to go to the theatre tonight and you are to come with us!" Helen said.

"The theatre," Adella said. "I have not been for such a long time."

"I have never been, so I am very excited!" she grasped her hands together.

"What are we to see? And how did you get tickets?"

"Uncle got the tickets. They are the cheapest they had, and we will be so far up in the gods we won't be able to see or hear a thing! But the play is Richard III, it sounds a bit boring, but if it gets dull we could go to the buffet lounge and see who is about."

Adella didn't like the idea of that, but a quick glance to Flora allayed her fears. They exchanged a quick smile, and she knew Flora would not allow Helen to do any such thing.

"We have a ticket for Leonard too. Do you think he would like to come? Uncle says we need a man to accompany us, although I don't see why. At least he might know a few of the people at the theatre. Oh, please say Leonard will come too, for Uncle says he hates the theatre so he is our last hope."

"I am sure he will come, if there is no patient who needs him."

"Oh good!" Helen declared.

They stayed for a further half hour and chatted to Adella

as she baked. She sent them away with a cake and a promise to call on them at seven o'clock with her brother.

When he arrived home late that afternoon, Leonard already knew of the theatre plan.

"I called in at Mr Alther's this afternoon and spoke to Flora. She told me of tonight's engagement."

"You do not mind accompanying us?"

"No! Not all all. I would be glad to. What man could refuse to accompany three ladies out on an evening."

"I think we may have our hands full with Helen. Three of us to try and tame her may not be enough."

Leonard laughed then said, "I am sure we will have a delightful evening, despite the need to restrain Helen."

Adella and Leonard called at Mr Alther's at the appointed time. Helen and Flora were ready and the happy group set off immediately. Helen was dressed in a green gown, her hair was perfectly tied and Adella detected a small amount of rouge on her cheeks; they were unnaturally pink. Flora wore a plainer, yet not unbecoming dark blue dress with a matching shawl. The lack of frills suited her quiet demeanour.

Helen once more commandeered Leonard and made him walk with her all the way to the theatre. Adella took the opportunity to get to know Flora better. They talked a little earlier that day in the kitchen, but Helen continually interrupted, and wanted to be part of the conversation. Now at least, Adella had Flora on her own for a short time.

"Tell me Flora, whose idea was it for you and Helen to come to Bath?"

"It was my mother's actually. She does think Helen wild and I think she is glad to see her gone for a while. She caused a great deal of heartache amongst the men our family are acquainted with; young and old. You see, I am sure you can tell, Helen is a most determined flirt and loves to have the attention of any man. I am ashamed of her sometimes, she can be terribly embarrassing."

She gave Flora a sympathetic smile. "And what about you? Are there many broken hearts you left behind?"

"No, I am an old maid now, the only gentlemen who speak to me do so on the pretext of getting to know Helen."

Adella stopped and looked at her in disbelief. "How can you say such a thing?"

Flora shook her head, "Because it is the truth. I am too old to be considered by any man. There was a young man once, who I thought. . ." her voice trailed off.

"But it was not to be?" Adella filled in.

"No," she said and averted her eyes, "He turned his attentions to another young lady and they have been married these ten years."

Adella felt a new wave of camaraderie for Flora , "I too have had a similar experience. I will tell you about it one day, but I do not wish to spoil our evening by mentioning it."

"It seems we have much in common. My former love and his wife seem happy enough, and I simply have not met another gentleman who liked me as much as I liked him. Still, I am not unhappy to be an old maid. If Helen gets her rich husband as she keeps promising she will, I am sure she will need me as a governess or such."

There was a note of humour in her voice that made Adella smile.

"Besides," she said somewhat philosophically, "I have always believed that for everyone there is an ideal partner and that the man I spoke of a moment ago was not mine."

"Because he married someone else?"

"Precisely," she said with a firm nod of her head.

Flora's words struck a chord with Adella and she

admired her more with everything she said. True, she was six years older and the advantage of those extra years experience, but there was a deep earnestness and honesty about her that Adella liked.

There was a throng of people at the theatre when they arrived and they fought their way through one of the three arched doors. Gentlemen and Ladies milled about the foyer all dressed smartly and eyeing each other up. Helen and Flora looked about excitedly, they stood for a few minutes and watched and admired the other theatre-goers.

Their seats were as Helen described, the highest the theatre provided with only one other row behind them. Helen sat herself next to Leonard, with Flora on his other side and Adella on the end.

Over the din of the other people in the audience, Helen's voice could be heard as she chatted in an excited high-pitched voice. Adella let her eyes drift off around the theatre. She had been in it before of course, but it had been a long time ago. The stage and the décor inside were exquisite; the domed ceiling with ornate plaster covered in gold leaf dressed the room with majestic pride. She let her eyes drift from the stage to the boxes. Her seat was so high that she could barely see the stage. But she leaned forward and could see the boxes nearest to the stage.

She stopped breathing for a moment as her eyes rested on one of the boxes.

Joel.

She sat back quickly. He hadn't seen her. He was talking to a man next to him.

She leaned forward again. Tentatively at first. It was definitely him. She would know his face anywhere. So, he was here was he? Well, that wouldn't affect her. He was perfectly entitled to be there, as was she. She wouldn't let it affect her.

She gave him one last stare as though daring him to look up, then sat back.

It was as though fate had both slapped and caressed her at the same time. He was here, that was bad. But she knew he was here. At least she was prepared. She would slight him if he dared to look at her, or tried to speak to her.

Helen managed to stay in her seat for most of the performance. Although during both intervals she made her way to the nearest buffet and paraded about trying to catch the eye of any gentleman who would look at her.

Adella walked warily to the buffet each time, but didn't see Joel. Helen got her wish several times when a group of people spoke to her; one of the women admired Helen's gown spoke too loudly causing Helen to take the opportunity to join their party.

Flora looked mortified and several times apologised to Adella and Leonard. "I am so sorry for Helen's behaviour. I tried to stop her, but she is too strong for me to physically. It is all as I feared, she is a disgrace."

"I do not see how we can tempt her out of here." Adella said shaking her head. "There are too many gentlemen who could admire her. Perhaps it would be easier to get the men out!" She added with a laugh.

After the play was over, they made their way outside the theatre. Helen ran forwards suddenly when she saw someone in particular. Flora stood on her toes to try and view her sister, and saw her disappear down the road.

"There she is! Oh, but she is with another three ladies and four gentlemen. She is talking to one of them who was in the buffet lounge in the second interval."

Flora looked for Leonard's help, but among the many people, Leonard was nowhere to be seen. After a few moments, they spotted him, talking to a friend.

"What shall we do?" Flora frowned.

"Do not worry, I will tell Leonard we have gone to retrieve Helen and we will meet him back here in fifteen minutes."

She did as she said and Flora, who didn't lose sight of her sister, swiftly followed Helen.

Adella caught up with her just in time to see Helen disappear into a house with whoever she thrust herself upon. It was a terraced Georgian town house, like all the others in Bath.

"Oh dear!" Flora said, "She really has gone too far now. This really is most embarrassing. I am so sorry Adella, I really do not know what to do with her!"

"Do not fear. We will retrieve her and be on our way in no time. If there are two of us, we can drag her out!"

By this time, the door to the house was about to close. Adella ran up the stone steps and prevented the door from closing by pushing against it hard, shouting, "Excuse me!"

The door opened again, the servant looked bewildered, but a gentleman within bade them to enter.

"Are you here for Mrs Tate's soirée too?" The gentleman asked.

"No!", Adella exclaimed a little too loudly. "Er, I mean, I am sorry to intrude. My friend Miss Helen Alther is a little excited at being in Bath and I am afraid we could not stop her from coming in. I will go and retrieve her and we will both be gone."

The gentleman looked a little amused at Adella's words.

"Please, Miss -" he asked.

"Maxwell."

"Well Miss Maxwell. . ." and he stared at her for a moment. His face wore surprise, then he suppressed it quickly. Then as if remembering himself, he continued, "I

am sure we will all be very pleased if you and your friend -"
he said addressing Flora.

"Miss Alther," Flora said.

"Ah. Miss Helen is your sister then."

"Yes."

"Well, allow me to introduce myself. I am Frederick Garner, at your service, ready to guide you to your friend and sister." He gave a small bow to each of them.

Adella's heart almost stopped. Surely not. . .

She swallowed hard.

She knew that name. Suddenly she realised he knew *her* name at least. She had never met the man. He was described to her on many occasions five years ago by Joel. Frederick was his best friend.

He was also the man Joel had been sitting next to in the theatre. She had not recognised him at first.

He looked at Adella and, seeing the reaction he had expected on her face, he said, "Miss Maxwell, I fear now you know who I am, you may not wish to enter if you knew who else was in that room. I could retrieve your friend for you?"

She took his meaning immediately, but spoke with fresh determination. "You may try if you like, but I am not afraid of seeing whoever is behind that door, even if it were Lucifer himself."

"Very well," he said, one corner of his mouth curved into a smile. He led them through the threshold to where the other guests were. The two girls followed him through and held each other's arm for support.

Adella scanned the lavish room for Joel. She found him quickly and one glance told her that he was surprised to see her. He was in the corner of the room talking to a lady. He was in evening dress, and now, after five years of pain her heart skipped a beat as her head acknowledged how handsome he was. Mr Garner stayed with her and saw the instant recognition on both said in a hushed tone, "I do not think Lucifer will trouble you tonight Miss Maxwell. But if he does, I shall be here to help you."

"I thank you, but I don't need your help." She shot him an icy stare.

"Very well," He gave a short bow and went to join his friend.

Flora in the meantime travelled the short distance across the room to where her sister was.

"Helen, you must come immediately," she said.

Helen was busy chatting to at least five other guests and did not register their presence in the room. Everyone she was stood with, as well as her sister, all ignored her as she pleaded. "Helen, please come with me at once. We do not know these people and you have no business intruding on their private party." But it was no use, Helen simply carried on chatting and laughing.

Flora grabbed her arm, Helen turned around and with a wave of her hand said, "Oh you are here are you? And Adella too. You can stay if you like, but I am having far too much fun to go. I am sure one of these lovely Gentlemen will see me home," she smiled.

A few of them agreed, rather too loudly.

Adella went over to Flora and whispered to her, "You run and get Leonard. I will stay and make sure she does not make too much of a fool of herself."

Flora nodded and quickly left the room.

Adella suddenly felt very alone. She looked around. The others in the room were not paying her any attention except for a few contemptuous looks. She slipped to the side of the room and looked to the far end. Joel was gone.

*Where was he? She felt safer if she knew where he was.*

Then without warning, she saw him and Mr Garner approaching.

"I thought I told you not to speak to me," she said to Joel.

She turned away from them.

"Come come Miss Maxwell," she heard Mr Garner say behind her. 'You would not like to make a scene?" He paused then continued, "It seems you were at the theatre this evening too?"

She turned around a little, and cursing herself for doing it, said "Yes. Though we were in the cheap seats, so you wouldn't have seen us." She put strong emphasis on the word "cheap" and in defiance lifted her chin.

Frederick turned to Joel and they exchanged glances.

"Did you like the play?" Joel asked. "You are not a great admirer of Shakespeare I remember." She noticed he was grasping one hand with the other and his face wore a serious look.

She was momentarily stunned. Of all the things for him to say. She didn't expect that.

"You remember correctly. I didn't used to like Shakespeare. However, when I was younger I was much more naïve and I had different tastes. Not so now. I thought the play was excellent." She gave a curt smile, even though her cheeks were burning.

"Time has been kind on you Miss Maxwell," he replied. "I am also glad you have come to appreciate Shakespeare. If you recall, he was always a favourite of mine."

"I do not care to recall."

They descended into silence and Adella looked away again. She wanted nothing more than them both to leave. If only Leonard was here.

"I long for some music," Helen said loudly as though she wanted the whole attention of the room. She succeeded.

Adella saw Joel whisper something to Mr Garner, who in turn looked at her, then said loudly to everyone, "Miss Maxwell. I have heard you play and sing like an angel. Will you not honour us this evening?"

She blushed deeply again from pure annoyance. She knew that it was Joel's doing. "Have you?" she replied, "I fear you have been misinformed. For, I am sure whoever told you that must be the worst kind of liar." She gave Joel a defiant look in retaliation.

He said nothing, only for a fleeting moment met her gaze then looked away.

"Oh yes please do play," a well dressed lady said.

Adella looked around the room from one person to the other. They all stared at her. She was trapped; like a rabbit cowering in front of a pack of wolves.

"Come, come Miss Maxwell. I am sure you are being modest. You will not shame yourself or your family if you sing, for I play very badly," the lady assured her. A few other people nodded in agreement. But her words intended to sooth, only sounded officious and snobby to Adella.

Pride, fierce pride rose up in her. They all expected her to play badly, or at least barely tolerably well. If it was a performance they wanted, then that is what they would get. She had another motive: Joel wanted to hear her sing. She would, but he would not like what she chose to sing. It would be sweet revenge, all be it in a small way.

She cast a look to Helen, who was stood silently, and watched the proceedings like everyone else. At least, if she played, Helen could not get up to mischief.

So, Adella walked to the piano with all the dignity she could muster removed her hat and gloves and seated herself gracefully. She thought for a moment for something to play as she admired the piano. It was a fine instrument. It would be a shame not to use it. The rest of the room was quiet as they awaited her start. Joel, still stood in the corner with the others withdrew into the shadows to watch and listen.

It was many months since she had last played, but each time she sat in front of a piano it was as if she had never been away. She knew the perfect thing to sing, and so began:


'COME *all ye fair and tender ladies.*
   *Be careful how you court young men.*
   *They're like a star on a summer's morning.*
   *They'll first appear and then they're gone.*"


THE AUDIENCE WAS SPELLBOUND; she truly did have a rare talent.


'THEY'LL TELL *you some loving story*
   *They'll declare to you their love is true*
   *Then they will go and court some other*
   *And that's the love they have for you'*


ADELLA NOW HOPED that *he* was listening intently. The other day, he wanted her to speak to him, well now she would. But this time through song.


'DO *you remember our days of courting*
   *When your head lay upon my breast*
   *You could make me believe with falling of your arm*
   *That the sun rose in the West'*

. . .

AS SHE SANG THE WORD 'WEST' she sought his face and stared at him, half in the shadows she could still make him out. He looked away. She played on,

*'IF I HAD KNOWN before I courted*
   *that love was such a killing thing*
   *I'd a-locked my heart in a box of golden*
   *and fastened it up with a silver pin."*

WHEN SHE FINISHED there was hushed silence for a moment, and then applause. One of the gentlemen who had been paying court to Helen then approached. Adella looked him up and down, and hoped he wasn't drunk.

"Bravo, Miss. . ."

"Maxwell."

"Well Miss Maxwell, will you not play something else? I would dearly love to hear your sweet little voice sing again. Why, you play better than any woman I have ever heard and I have heard a great many."

"Thank you sir, but I fear I must allow the other ladies to play now."

"No, no, please, what can I do to get you play again?" he said gently and placed his hand on her arm. She looked down at his hand.

"Get Helen to leave now," Adella whispered to herself.

"What was that?" he asked.

"Er, nothing."

She looked about her once more, and realised that it was as she hoped; Helen was not misbehaving while she sang, sat back down again, "Very well, I will play once more, then I must go. With Helen." In fact she hoped that by the time she finished playing, Flora would have retrieved Leonard.

She thought for a moment and then with a smile began to play,

'EARLY ONE MORNING, *just as the sun was rising*
*I heard a maid sing in the valley below*
*"Oh don't deceive me, Oh never leave me,*
*How could you use, a poor maiden so?"*

REMEMBER *the vows that you made to me truly*
*Remember how tenderly you nestled close to me*
*Gay is the garland, fresh are the roses*
*I've culled from the garden to bind over thee.*

HOW COULD *you slight so a pretty girl who loves you*
*A pretty girl who loves you so dearly and warm?*
*Though love's folly is surely but a fancy,*
*Still it should prove to me sweeter than your scorn.*

SHE LOOKED up to see Joel walk slowly to the door with his back to her, and then leave. She made him go, and she was glad of it. She saw Mr Garner still watched her, apparently unaware that his friend had left. She continued,

SOON YOU WILL MEET *with another pretty maiden*
*Some pretty maiden, you'll court her for a while;*

*Thus ever ranging, turning and changing*
*Always seeking for a girl that is new.*


ONCE AGAIN, rapturous applause met her final notes, and she stood up as several other ladies and gentlemen came up to congratulate her and she struggled to master her confusion at such attention.

But despite this, she still felt they were looking down on her.

"I have never heard that sung so well in my life. Miss Maxwell, you are truly a rare talent," Mr Garner said when the majority of the guests went back to their previous groups.

"Thank you," she said and tried to sound as nonchalant as possible, "But next time you would like to hear music I would prefer it if you would pick someone else and not be Mr Polwarth's messenger."

"But to keep such talent to yourself is not right! The whole world should be able to hear you sing."

"The whole world can get on very well without hearing me singing. It has before," she said in a dry tone.

"Well, I heard from another that you sang well. You do not mind me mentioning it?" Frederick said.

"Why not? We both know who that 'other' is."

"Indeed," he said with a small bow.

"Therefore, I would prefer not to have to talk to you at all."

"Why ever not?"

"Have you never heard the phrase, 'My enemy's friend is my enemy'?" Adella asked.

"Enemy?" Mr Garner said raising his eyebrows. "Well I had no idea your feelings were that strong."

"Could you doubt they would be any less. Unless you, like the rest of the world believe me to be a liar."

He did not answer the question directly, only said, "My friend has made an enemy indeed. It only leaves me to say that I hope you will in time overcome your feelings and learn to live without bitterness. It will eat you up otherwise."

She didn't like being lectured and particularly not by this man. She despised him already for his obvious loyalty to his friend. He appeared to her to be somewhat smug and facetious and was making light of what Joel did to her.

"Your loyalty to your friend is admirable. If not somewhat misplaced."

"Miss Maxwell, I hope you do not think me a fool. However my friend has harmed you, he has never hurt me. In fact he has all the best qualities a gentleman needs in a friend."

"Then you have been treated better than me."

Their tête-a-tête was interrupted by the arrival of Leonard and Flora into the room. Leonard strode over to Helen, pulled her aside and spoke to her. She bowed her head and dropped her shoulders. A few moments later he led her to the door. He cast a swift look at Adella and she said to Mr Garner, "My brother has managed to persuade Helen to leave. I will bid you good night."

"Good night Miss Maxwell. I hope to have the pleasure of meeting you again soon."

Adella said nothing in return. If it was anyone else she would have returned the compliment. Instead she put on her hat and gloves, curtseyed, then left.

FREDERICK WENT STRAIGHT to retrieve his friend from whatever hiding place he found. It was a poky room, that matched the poky house. He really couldn't understand how anyone could manage to live in such a small place.

Joel stood by the window in an adjoining room and looked up as Frederick entered.

"You can come back in, she has gone," Frederick said.

Joel gave the hint of a smile. "I will be back in shortly."

"I am sorry if this was a bad idea. To come here I mean."

"No, it's alright. You were not to know that she would arrive," Joel said.

"Well, come back when you are ready."

Joel nodded and Frederick went towards the door.

"She is clearly still in love with you."

"What makes you say that?" he said immediately looking up.

"I had a conversation with her just now, and she hates you. Hatred like that does not come out of impartial feelings."

"If she hates me, then it is as it should be for now. But, I already knew of it. She told me so herself a few days ago," Joel replied.

"Then tell her the truth. You could go and get her now and tell her everything."

"I can't – not yet. You know I must wait. Please don't taunt me with it. It's bad enough as it is."

Frederick opened the door and said, "Very well. By the way, you were right. She does sing like an angel."

When Frederick had shut the door, Joel whispered to himself. "Yes, my own angel."

ADELLA CAUGHT up with the others outside. Flora was busy telling off her sister in the middle of the pavement, oblivious to passers by.

"I cannot tell you how embarrassing that was! You behave like a street walker! I am ashamed of you." She continued in this manner for some minutes as Leonard and Adella listened on.

"Whatever did you say to Helen to make her leave?" Adella whispered to Leonard.

"I said her Uncle told me to report any misdemeanour's to him and that if she did not leave now I would tell him to send her home tomorrow."

"Did Mr Alther ask you to do that?"

"No! But it can be our little secret," he winked.

Laughing, Adella then spoke at length to her brother about Richard III, though it was her least favourite of Shakespeare's work she needed to get her mind away from Joel.

By the time they both arrived home, she was glad to have the privacy of her room. It had been a long evening full of painful events. She shrank from the memory of what she said to Mr Garner. He was a strange man. He himself had not harmed her, so it was wrong of her to speak to him in such a way. Still, he was his best friend, and probably helped Joel masquerade as a tutor five years ago. Or perhaps Mr Garner was lied to as well. It was all very confusing. He seemed to know the truth; that Adella was the injured party. Yet he did not attempt to explain anything. How could he justify his friend in such a way to her? Oh he was a vexing man for sure. She did not like him at all, his main fault being his unrelenting friendship with Joel. He was handsome, but she was beyond being influenced by a man simply because he was admirable.

She was also angry at Joel for suggesting she sing. He spent many hours listening to her when they were at Brayfern House, why would he wish to hear her now if he cared nothing for her? Did his malice have no end? But she knew she affected him; he left the room didn't he? She hoped it was through guilt and shame. She couldn't believe the chances of seeing him again. Fate was certainly handing her a rough deal at the moment. She hated him. Hated everything he was and the sooner he left Bath the better.

8

The moment Flora and Helen arrived home, Flora summoned her Aunt and Uncle into the sitting room and told them everything that Helen did. Her Uncle looked shocked and serious, whereas she thought her Aunt was a little amused. At least she agreed with Flora that such behaviour was not to be tolerated, especially when it involved Dr Preston and Miss Maxwell. Flora stood nervously and shifted her weight as her uncle and aunt spoke to Helen. She still didn't know them all that well, and was worried that they would both be sent home. That would be awful.

"I promise I will behave better," Helen said. "But I really cannot see that I was that bad," she fluttered her eye lashes at them all. "I got talking to the same lady again outside of the theatre and she invited me into her house. She says she meets people like that all the time!"

"Helen, you always promise to behave, but still continue on afterwards." Flora said, then remonstrated herself; maybe she had given too much away about her knowledge of Helen's past behaviour.

Their mother and father had punished Helen many times. None of their previous discipline worked, and there was no reason to suppose that this time would be any different.

Flora continued on, "She could have been anyone, and it is dangerous to go into the house of someone you do not know. They could have done anything to you!"

"Well they didn't. There were several ladies who were very fine. Besides, the gentlemen were excessively handsome! Were they not Flora?"

Flora didn't answer, she folded her arms and stared at her sister.

"Surely you must have thought Mr Polwarth handsome. They say he is rich and is about to be a widower."

"Helen! How can you speak of a man in such a way, with his wife still alive. It is deplorable." Flora cried.

"Yes, yes," their Uncle said, sounding as though he was getting bored of the conversation. "Off to bed the pair of you and remember Helen, if you do not behave, you will be sent home and Flora will stay. How would you like that?"

Helen sloped off to her room and Flora followed a few minutes later. They shared a room. They both hated it. But there was no other spare bedchamber. Helen made sharp comments as they both prepared for bed, though Flora was wise enough not to reply. She knew her sister well enough by now, and answering her back only led to an argument.

After the previous night's trouble, Flora awoke determined to apologise to her new friends at the earliest opportunity. She wanted to set out early and call on Leonard and Adella, long before Helen would wake. But that wouldn't be difficult, her sister was lazy, and especially here in Bath. In fact, their Uncle and Aunt did not make Helen do any chores and had not asked Flora to do any either. But unlike

Helen, Flora was uncomfortable with that and she constantly asked for tasks to do. It was only right in her eyes.

She was about to leave, and went into the shop where her Uncle and Aunt were already busy with their daily tasks.

They were stood together talking and measuring a myriad of coloured liquids and powder. Containers were scattered across the counter and strange smells emanated from the liquids. Flora loved watching them at work. It was all still a strange world to her, yet she felt strangely akin to it.

"Morning Flora," her Uncle said without even looking up.

"Good Morning."

She stood watching them for a while longer as they poured and measured. What on earth was in the jars and bottles? What on earth were they were making? It was such a mystery, but one Flora wanted to find out. She wondered why she had not visited her Uncle and Aunt before. If she knew how pleasant they were, and how interesting it would be, she would have come a long time ago.

"I would very much like it if you would let me be useful here," she said when they looked as though they were not concentrating so hard.

Her Aunt gave a brief look and then said, "What do you mean? You are useful!"

"But I wish to help you more. The odd bit of housework is nothing. I could help you in the shop. Will you not teach me a little of what you do here?"

Her Aunt and Uncle looked at each other for a moment, until her Uncle said, "Of course Flora. But you do not think some of this may be too difficult for you?"

"I am sure with you to instruct me I will manage well enough. You could give me something simple at first and then see how I do. Though I had a good education and I am not unintelligent. To be frank, I am very interested in the shop."

"Then we would be delighted," her Uncle said. "Some days we have so much to do it is difficult to manage everything, and I have meant to start making house calls again. I've never had the time before. Besides, we can always do with an extra pair of hands. We can start right now if you like."

"Thank you," Flora said and went over and kissed her Uncle on the cheek. "I will make sure you will not regret it. But could we start later today? I must visit Adella and Dr Preston and apologise for Helen last night."

"Yes. I am sure they will be more than happy to see you," her Aunt said before Mr Alther could speak. "Although I think it will take a lot more to truly offend them. I've known them both a good few years now and they are everything that is amiable and friendly. But go and see them and give them our best regards, although I shall probably see them later today I'm sure!"

As she stepped out, Flora had great purpose. Helen pushed things too far last night, and she was mortified when she remembered the brazen unladylike things she did. But at least the events brought her closer to Adella, and she felt that she was becoming a true friend.

"I hope it is not too early to call," Flora said to Leonard when he opened the door.

"Of course not! Is Helen not with you?" he peered over past her shoulder and around the street.

"No."

He smiled then indicated she should enter, "Adella was about to make some tea and you are more than welcome to come in and share it with us."

Adella greeted Flora with a kiss on the cheek, and they

all sat quietly and chatted. They seemed to be avoiding any reference to the previous night until Flora finally got up the courage to broach the subject.

"I called today for a reason."

"Oh?" Leonard said.

"Yes, I came to apologise for Helen's behaviour last night. It was unforgivable, I am so ashamed of her and I hope you will be so kind as to overlook it." She looked down into her lap as she spoke, and dared not lift her head until one of her hosts spoke.

"Think nothing of it!" Leonard said, "I had a very pleasant evening. Very pleasant. Didn't you Adella?"

"Er, yes, very pleasant," she said a little tentatively.

"Well, there we are, we all had a pleasant evening, despite Helen's little misdemeanour's." Leonard said with a significant lift of his brows.

"I must say, that is a relief to hear," Flora said, "I thought you would never want to see or speak to us again. I was worried because I would very much like to become friends."

Adella placed her hand on Flora's and pressed it, "I would like that too."

Flora stayed and chatted for a while until Adella looked at the clock. "Len, look at the time! Do you not have an appointment soon?"

"Er, yes, I suppose I should go." But he did not attempt to move and continued to talk to Flora.

Adella got up and collected his bag and coat and handed them to him. He took them only when they were thrust on him. "I hope we can all meet together soon, perhaps if there is another play, or concert you wish to attend I can accompany you – er, both of you there."

"Thank you. That is a most gracious offer and I am sure Helen will have something planned very soon." Flora said.

LATER THAT EVENING, Leonard put his jacket on, and checked his reflection in the mirror; not bad. He combed his hair, pulled at his cuffs, and made his way downstairs.

"You off then," Adella said, when he reached downstairs.

"Indeed, and I shall be glad to have an evening off."

Adella smiled, "Enjoy yourself. Who is it you are seeing this evening?"

Leonard faltered for a moment, "Only a patient - a patient invited me over." He thought he answered a bit too quickly, and felt his face flush.

Adella didn't seem to notice and he left the house quickly.

He arrived at South Parade at seven o'clock as previously arranged with Joel. He was shown into the study where Joel was waiting for him and after preliminary conversation and politeness, he was given coffee and a cigar. They sat in the arm chairs in front of the fire.

"Cynthia is asleep already. She walked out into the garden earlier and it wore her out." Joel said.

"Yes, I should think it would. Although I dare say the fresh air would have done her good. Often patients keep themselves locked up inside for too long, when sitting outside for ten of fifteen minutes a day would help them immensely."

Joel contemplated the end of his now lit cigar. "She is very different now to when I first knew her. Oh, she was always sickly, but I always believed she put it on. She has always had weekly visits from our Physician in Bedfordshire throughout our marriage."

"Some Ladies do have delicate constitutions, and of course, physically, they are more complicated than men.

They can be prone to ailments which we cannot begin to contemplate."

At that, Joel smiled with one corner of his mouth and took a puff from his cigar.

"Yes, I suppose you are right. My mother has many complaints too, although she is better at hiding her discomforts than my wife. But you are not here to speak about Cynthia or my mother. . ." His voice drifted off.

Leonard nodded.

"I do not know where to begin," Joel sighed and ran his hand through his hair. He sat forward and gazed at Leonard for a moment.

"From the beginning?" Leonard said, remembering he used the same words to Adella earlier in the week.

"Very well," he replied and sat back.

"The beginning. . .the beginning must start at my home and my childhood."

"Naturally."

"As you know, I come from Bedfordshire and I am the eldest of four brothers. For the most part, my childhood was happy. I belong to a family that has a great heritage and reputation. In our area, the name of Polwarth is revered and honoured. We own a large estate and to be plain with you; we are exceedingly rich. Being the eldest, from an early age there was an onus on me to continue the traditions of the family and ensure that the Polwarth name was protected and continued. My father started to train me to run the estate when I was seven years old."

"Seven. Surely not that young?" Leonard said.

"It was nothing too bad; shooting, fishing, stable management and such, in fact most of it was very enjoyable. I took to Horse Husbandry and riding well."

Leonard felt himself relax.

"At the age of ten, I was sent away to school, to Eton. I believed I would be there until I went to University."

"Did you get bullied much? I was, although I did not go to such a prestigious school."

"Yes, there was a lot of bullying, most of which I managed to steer clear of by keeping the main perpetrator off my back with bribes. There was the odd incident," a wide smile spread across his face. "I was well trained by father. One time a boy dared to make fun of my name and he paid with a black eye and mud soaked hat. But otherwise, I was happy enough. I had friends, and achieved well in all the curricula. But suddenly one day when I was fourteen I was called out of class to the Head Master's office. He received a letter from my father that stated I was to return home immediately.

"Of course, I was a little surprised and naturally wondered what was wrong at home that demanded my return. However, when I actually arrived back, nothing was amiss. My mother and father were well, and told me to my astonishment that I was not to return to school. I was to remain at home and be tutored there. In a way, I was pleased to be home because Frederick, my best friend lived, still does live nearby. His family own the estate near to ours and we are a similar age.

"A few weeks later, my brothers were also pulled out of their school. My father watched our progress closely, but it was me he watched the most and would lecture me many times on my duty to the family." He paused for a moment. Deep in thought. His face frosted over and the glimmer that had been in his eye a moment ago was snuffed out.

"He told me I was to marry a respectable woman and continue the family line, I was to follow in his footsteps and to keep my brothers in tow so that the family name was not tarnished. There were other burdens I must take, but you understand what I mean when I say that he wanted me to be exactly like him and I was a complying pupil at first. I was such a fool, I adored my father, and looked up to him so much I truly thought he could do no wrong.

"Life continued on in a normal manner, until I was nineteen. Then, one day, my brothers and I were out hunting rabbits in the forest. We did not return until late and my father, who was normally firm but kept his temper, got very angry. More angry than I had ever seen him before. As my punishment he locked me in my room for a day. I accepted the discipline although he had never punished any of us in that way before.

"Things got progressively worse and quickly too. If I broke a rule then he would lock me in my room. If one of my brothers broke a rule then he would lock me in my room as punishment for not keeping them under control. If I argued then he responded that I must learn to control them so that when they were adults they would not disgrace the family name."

Joel shifted in his chair a little then continued, "My father believed that the family name was all and everything. More so than ever. I was not sure why he was so fervent about this issue, he was not like this before. At least not to this extent. When I questioned my mother about it, she simply shrugged and said that I should do as my father wished because he was the head of the family. My mother was and still is, compliant to my father and never disobeys him.

"Luckily, my brothers and I were close and they would rarely misbehave or disobey father. Though it was difficult for them at times, they would get carried away or fight as any children do. But my punishments were few and far between."

Leonard interrupted, "Your brothers were very good to you then?"

"Yes, but I have to confess, if they misbehaved while I got locked away, they got no dinner, so they had their own reasons to stay out of trouble."

Leonard gave small low chuckle, but checked it quickly. This was no laughing matter.

Joel continued, "When I was twenty years old, my father took me to London. I thought the purpose was to show me the city and extend my education, but this was not so. After we arrived at our lodgings he told me that the sole aim of the trip was to find a suitable lady whom I would marry. I did not know of it before, but he was eyeing London society for some years with this aim. He lectured me on my responsibility to continue the family line once more, something which I found strange,"

"Yes!" Leonard cried, "After all you have three brothers. Surely the odds of the family line continuing were excellent."

"Exactly. We spent many months in London and attended a myriad of social events. I was not very happy for most of the time. It was all awkward for me. One night after dinner father spoke to me and said that he had found my future wife. He had spoken to her father, she came from a long respected family and most importantly had a fortune of Thirty Thousand pounds. It was of course Cynthia.

"I objected immediately," he said rubbing his forehead with his fist. "I remembered Cynthia, she was insipid and sickly, always complaining about everything. Although I thought she was pretty, she was certainly not someone I wished to marry. Despite my objections, my father would not take no for an answer, and ignored my refusal."

"The next day, he took me to see Cynthia and her father, though I did not know their house was our destination until we arrived. I was shocked, words cannot – they cannot begin to describe. . ." His voice trailed off. Finally after a few moments he seemed to rally himself and continued. "There was the Rector, ready to set a date for the wedding and for the banns to be read. I was incredulous, and feigned illness and ran out of the house back to our lodgings."

"What happened next?" Leonard asked.

"My father came back half an hour behind me and he seemed more understanding. He said that we could return to Bedfordshire in order for me to think about the marriage. I readily agreed and we returned home."

"Did you not think it a little strange that he suddenly decided to let you think it over?" Leonard asked.

"No, stupidly I did not. And things were to get far worse for me. The morning after we arrived back, I awoke and dressed and was about to go downstairs for breakfast, when I tried my bedroom door. It was locked. I rang the bell for a servant, and after a short while my father came and stood outside. He told me that I was to be kept in my room until I agreed to marry Cynthia.

"Of course I refused and demanded to be let out."

"Of course! What a dastardly thing to do. Could you not escape some way, through the window?" Leonard asked.

"It appeared that my father anticipated my refusal. While we were away, he had metal bars placed over my bedroom window."

"Never!" Leonard sat forward suddenly.

Joel nodded. "I can hardly speak of the next two months, it pains me too much. You must allow me to skirt over it. But to put it plainly, he imprisoned me. To be confined for a long period of time was dreadful, but for two months he kept me there with only the basic food and water. Every day he would ask me if I would submit, but I would not give in."

Joel stood up, walked to the window and opened it a little. He stared out of it for a moment.

Leonard's eyes followed Joel. "Two months you say? That is awful. Did you not barge your way out when they gave you food and water?"

"The food was hoisted up to me through the window."

Leonard sat with his mouth wide open, then said, "But you got out somehow?"

"Yes. It was Frederick's doing that I got out in the end. I learnt afterwards that he tried many ways get me released, pleaded with my father, and my mother, what use that would have been, she was totally under his power. He went to the authorities to release me. But it was no use. They would not interfere. I was still not of age. I was still classed as a child, and my father could choose to punish me any way he chose. My release finally came on 24th February -my 21$^{st}$ birthday. I was officially an adult. Frederick arranged for the authorities to come and release me, but my father unlocked the door by the time they arrived."

"He did not put up any resistance to you leaving?" Leonard asked.

"No. In fact, he was very devious. He said that he kept me in my room because I had become mentally unstable and violent. He told them that they should not interfere, but he had no option other than to allow them to take me. They did not believe him for a minute."

"What happened next?" Leonard asked.

"Frederick took me away immediately. I was disorientated and weak by then, but he took me far away to Scotland. There I remained for a few months and recovered, until he informed me that my father had discovered where we were. I decided to take matters into my own hands. I left the house early in the morning, took with me money and clothes. I travelled to Glasgow and I found a cheap hotel. I left Frederick and my father a note stating that I would never marry Cynthia and I did not tell Frederick where I was going. I did not want him in any way to be persuaded to reveal where I was. It was not that I did not trust Frederick, but I believed my father would find an evil way of getting the information from him. When he wanted something he would stop at nothing.

"So, there I was in Glasgow, and I decided that I should to make a living for myself. My father would surely disinherit me, so I could see no other option. A few days before I remembered seeing an advertisement in the newspaper placed by an agency asking for tutors. I remember the advert exactly:

*"Male tutors required for teaching Gentlemen's sons. Locations throughout Great Britain. Only those with excellent character references need apply."*

I wrote to them, using a false name and references, followed by a short interview in Glasgow, and was given a position of tutor for six months with a family in Sidmouth, Devon. I travelled there the next day.

"So that is why you became a tutor," Leonard said. "I am glad was not for any underhanded reason, though I thought it was."

"It was purely out of necessity, I assure you." He paused for a moment, then continued. "When I arrived, I was greeted by Mr Waters. He seemed a kind man, if not somewhat austere. I was taken immediately to the schoolroom where I was introduced to. . ." he paused again, and swallowed hard, desperately trying to get the words out, "I was introduced to the governess."

Leonard noticed Joel's face had suddenly become anguished and serious.

"Adella." Leonard said in a whisper.

"Yes. Adella."

**9**

———

Joel stood up and walked about the room for a few minutes. The only sound was the fire gently crackling. His mind burned with the memory of her. Leonard did not break him from his reverie by speaking and suspected now why he was in his present state of mind. It was the first time either of them had mentioned her name, but it seemed to intensify the meaning of their evening together. Adella. One woman's name, a name that bound them both.

"I – I have not really allowed myself the luxury to think of her before now," Joel said, clutching the back of his chair. "I never would have thought that I would be here with her brother. She told me much about you during those months we spent together, she was so proud of you."

Leonard dropped his gaze and stared into the fire. "Yes, she was always the best sister a man could have. I have not realised until recently."

"You can sing her praises all you like. Tell me of her good qualities and I shall not grow weary of it." His voice was slow, full of passion. "Because I know her and for every good word you speak of her I can match it with a hundred more."

Leonard fixed his eyes on Joel's face, "You loved her then?"

"Can you doubt it?"

"Yes, after what Adella has told me. The manner in which you discarded her, of course I question it."

"Then, should I continue with my story?"

"Please do."

He nodded, and poured more brandy for them both, then seated himself once more opposite Leonard. This time as he began to speak, the words took more effort to get out.

"Mr Waters took me to the schoolroom and made the introduction. I will never forget how she immediately stepped forward and shook my hand with the most disarming smile I have ever seen. I was a little taken aback, I had not known such openness or warmth from a woman before, well apart from my mother."

"Did you love her from that first moment?"

"No. No, but I did think her extremely pretty," a wide smile spread on his face, "Her eyes, they are such a dark brown, I remember thinking that I could drown in them. I was too nervous to think much else. But she immediately put me at ease and after Mr Waters went, she guessed that I was hungry and ordered food. She chatted easily about the daily routine for the children and what was expected of me. I found it all a little amusing coming from a family and position like mine, but still I was nervous. Nervous because she truly believed that I was a tutor."

"You were tutored at home yourself, so you must have known what was expected of you as you took that place?" Leonard asked.

"I knew exactly what to do. My father employed only the

best and I witnessed my own tutors long enough to know how to behave. I was a little wary that I may give myself away through a thoughtless comment or such. Luckily, she did not ask probing questions, and when the food arrived left me to eat in peace." He sighed deeply. "And that was the first time I met Adella." He picked up a box of matches on the table next to him and began to examine it.

"It is all similar to what she told me," Leonard remarked.

Joel looked up and raised his eyebrows "I will not ask you to tell me what she said, but as I said before, I'm sure it was the truth."

"She is honest I do grant you that. Tell me what happened next that day."

"After I finished eating, I wondered about the house and found the servants' quarters. A maid showed me to my room and I unpacked. It was a good size, bigger than I expected a tutor to be given. But I found it oppressive. It reminded me of those months of confinement. In the end, after a few hours I could bear it no longer. I had to get out. There were only a few places for a tutor to go, most of the house being out of bounds. I thought about going to the servants' quarters again, the kitchens or such, but I wandered up to the school room. There, seated quietly by the fire was Adella. I did not want to disturb her so I turned back, but she heard me, thinking I was the girl.

"I think I made some excuse that I wished to check the books. Anyway I looked at them and then as I was about to leave, she invited me to sit with her. Her smile and voice were so warm and inviting, I defy any man to refuse her anything she asks."

"Like explaining why you denied her?" Leonard said sharply.

The question took Joel off guard because he reddened,

and attempted to speak. Leonard spoke before him. "I am sorry. The comment slipped out."

"No, you undoubtedly think me the worst hypocrite. And you are right."

"I will try and reserve my judgement of your behaviour until you have finished explaining fully. From what Adella told me, and from what you have already said, I think I can guess what happened when your father arrived. But please continue."

Joel closed his eyes briefly. Then as if drawing strength said, "She offered me tea and I thought it only polite that I accept. She did not seem to pay court to my anxiety and immediately put me at ease again. We sat talking for a short time until I thought I should be returning to my room. The calming effect she had on me did not make my return so frightening. It was as though her kindness wiped away any fear I felt about being alone in my room, like a tonic or something. Most of all, my heart was touched by her kindness. I vowed never to forget it. She didn't know me at all; didn't know who I really was, she thought me a lowly tutor. Yet she was genuinely interested in my welfare.

"The first week went very quickly and I sought Adella's company whenever I could. I must admit, I did not fall in love with her immediately. It happened quickly, oh yes, so quickly that it took me by surprise. But it was a good few weeks before I realised my heart beat faster whenever she was near."

He continued on, his eyes sparkled with enthusiasm, "Every night we would sit together in that schoolroom. I found her fascinating and I thought the whole situation interesting. Here was I, Joel Polwarth pretending to be a tutor, and sharing a small schoolroom with a woman!" He let out a small laugh. "The only women I knew were either servants (and father was strict in making sure that our behaviour to them was of the utmost of propriety), my mother and the so-called ladies who I met in London."

"There were none near your home in Bedfordshire? No Neighbours?"

"No, not really. Well I suppose a few, but I never got to know them at all because my father did not think it necessary. They were not suitable matches for his sons."

"Adella spoke of those evenings you spent together with fondness."

Joel smiled, "We would read to each other, discuss a wide range of subjects. Adella was particularly interested in learning about geography and history and luckily through my own education I was able to tell her a great many facts she had previously been unaware of. I am afraid I also lied to her several times when she asked me questions about my background. I mixed the truth with falsehood. I could not tell her the absolute truth of course, so I changed certain minor details. I was after all, masquerading as Joseph West. Adella was barely out of girlhood, but she was earnest, astute, intelligent. She had not been given a wide education, I could tell, but she was not lacking in other ways. She listened to everything I said with the utmost care, something that never really happened to me before. My father never listened to me because he was always too busy telling me what to do, and as for my brothers, well with three of them to compete against I rarely got heard."

He paused briefly and took a long draw from his cigar, "One of the qualities I liked the most about Adella was that she always thought carefully about what she said before she spoke. But in the same way, she did not lack spontaneity. As her brother, I am sure you know all this."

Leonard nodded, "Truthfully, I have not analysed my

sister's qualities, but what you have spoken appears to be an accurate picture of her."

"No, we do not tend to analyse those we are closest to. My comments come about after the event. But it does not make them any less correct."

Leonard smiled, "Adella said you spent much of your day together during those months as well as the evenings?"

"Yes, at breakfast, lunch, dinner and then in the evening after the children were in bed, we would sit by the fire in the school room as I said before."

Leonard remembered something Adella told him, "Can you tell me, why were you so eager to see the sea? You expressed a wish to go early on in your appointment. . ."

"Yes," he said, "Yes, she remembered that did she? I *was* eager to visit the sea. You see, when I was locked up by my father, I would get through the lonely hours and seek solace from the oppressive walls by remembering when I was a child playing on a beach. I do not know where it was. Somewhere on the south coast, but anyway, I longed to see it. To see the wide open expanse of the water, to feel the cool breeze on my face." He closed his eyes and for a brief moment, was once more on the sea front at Sidmouth.

Then, he opened them, swallowed hard and suddenly said, "This was a turning point, slowly I got over what my father did to me. My thoughts were often with my family. I did wonder how my father was treating my brothers. I tried to think and plan ahead, to try and work out what to do when my six month appointment finished. I was not sure whether I should try and return home, or not.

"I guessed that my father would probably have changed his Will and that I was now disinherited. But I did not seem to mind as much as I thought I would. I felt a strange release and freedom I never felt before. Not being shackled to duty, an estate, a family name and of course my father.

"But all my plans would go awry, because, before long, I realised that the one thing I least expected while I was away had happened. I fell in love."

"When did you realise you loved her?"

"I remember the exact moment I knew I loved her," he said, "It was the first time I heard her sing. I had been at Brayfern for about four weeks, and just finished teaching the boy for the day. I heard piano music and singing coming from the school room. I thought it would be the young girl practising at first, but as I walked through to the school room I saw it was Adella playing and the girl who seemed to be enjoying it as much as I did. I stood in the doorway and listened and watched." He smiled widely again, 'I knew her well by then, but there was something about the way she sang. She was singing a folk song; Sprig of Thyme, and now, whenever I hear that song, Adella is all I think of whether I wish to or not. Does she ever play that particular song at home?"

"No, we have no piano."

Joel sat forward."No piano! That is dreadful. I cannot believe it. No piano!" He slumped back in his chair and placed his cigar into his mouth.

Leonard stared at him.

"So, although you loved her, you had not told her?" Leonard said, quickly changing the subject.

"No, I was certain she felt something for me, but I was not entirely sure how deep it went. How do you tell whether a woman has such feelings?"

"Very true," Leonard said, his mind drifted off for a moment. "The female mind is a mystery to many men, including me."

"Each time I retired for the night I would argue with myself. On the one hand I believed myself to be disinherited. Adella and I were on an equal footing. Gentry I may be, but without money I may have the bloodline, but nothing else. On the other hand, a part of me knew that I would probably have to return to my family. If I could survive as a tutor, I promised myself to look after my brothers and I was neglecting them. I did not want to drag Adella into my sordid family, she deserved better. It felt like a pit of despair, whichever way I looked, whatever I decided, there would be consequences and someone would get hurt.

"In the end, my heart won out. Adella and I spent a day walking together and while we were out that day, I kissed her. I could not stop myself."

He paused, as though gauging the Leonard's reaction.

"I am not shocked," Leonard said. "Adella told me this herself. Besides, if one has such sentiments, it is only natural for such an. . .activity to be an outlet."

Joel shook his head, "One kiss of her lips and she stole my heart forever. To know that she felt the same – that she was certain of her feelings. It made my heart swell even more to know that she loved me for myself alone and not for my wealth. I knew from that moment on that there would never be another woman for me."

Despite his words of love, his face wore a grim expression.

"But there has been another woman You married Cynthia," Leonard said in quiet tone.

"No," his voice was low and serious, "I may have married Cynthia, but Adella was and still is the only woman I shall ever love. Indeed, the irony is, Adella as a governess in her plain dress, her lack of airs and self-importance, I would not have given her a second glance if we met under any other circumstances. Oh, I speak the truth, though it is shocking to speak of my dear Adella in such a way."

"It is the truth, a man of your position would naturally only look amongst ladies of his own class for a potential match. She told me that you kept your -" he paused trying to find the right word, 'love a secret, is her class the reason for it?"

"No. Relationships amongst staff were frowned upon and it was difficult to keep it a secret. I revelled in being with her and near her. Each day I would get up quickly and look forward to breakfast with her and the children. Then it would be a tortuous few hours until lunch and I saw her again. Then dinner and then once the children were in bed at least three hours alone with her as we sat together.

"Sometimes after we retired for the night, I went to my room and sketched or painted her from memory. I did not want her to know I was doing it. It felt a little obsessive sometimes. I still have all the drawings, though it is not often that I can bring myself to look at them."

"Has Cynthia seen the drawings?"

"Not that I am aware of, but she recognised Adella when they first met, I am sure of it. I have thought many times about destroying those drawings, but I could never bring myself to do it. It seemed as though burning them would be an insult to Adella. One final step to me finally removing her from my life. While I have them, there is still a part of her with me."

Leonard sighed. "If she knew all this then, oh I don't know. It is all confusing. I was so sure you cared nothing for her. When in truth, it is exactly the opposite."

Joel said nothing in return. He stared at the small flames in the fireplace.

Leonard stood up and walked to the window. He pushed the red velvet curtain aside a little and looked out.

"It has started to rain."

"We are in Bath," Joel said with a small laugh.

"I should have brought an umbrella," he said, as though he had not heard Joel's last remark. "Do you have one I can borrow?"

"Of course. If I had the carriage at my disposal I would have it brought for you. But it is being repaired at the moment; a buckled wheel."

"That's very kind of you to think of it. But an umbrella will be enough. Besides, it's not far."

Leonard sat back down. There was silence for a short time before he said, "So, you loved Adella enough to ask her to marry you?"

Joel nodded.

"That night I asked her," he said with a deep sigh, "it was the night of the midsummer dance. She told you that too? I believe that was the happiest night of my entire life -" he was about to continue but was interrupted by Leonard.

"Yes, it is no surprise you should say that! I remember Adella's exact words when she told me of you that night. She said, 'I have never seen a man look so alive as he was that night'".

Joel swallowed hard, clenched his fist and placed it up to his lips. It took a moment for him to continue. He managed to say, "She is right, I shall never forget when we arrived at the dance. It was held in a Marquee, a rickety old dirty thing. The floor was covered with straw, and it was packed full, the music consisted of three men who were drunk and played dreadfully. I smiled to myself when I wondered what my father would say if he could see his precious first born socialising with all those servants."

"What happened at the dance? Adella did not really speak much of it, only afterwards."

"I made sure I danced every dance with her except one. A footman from the estate next to ours asked her to dance when I went to get refreshments. I remember being very annoyed and whilst watching them dance desperately trying to contain my jealousy. When they finished, I quickly took her arm and made her promise not to dance with anyone else. She readily agreed."

"But surely, if you danced every dance with her, that would look suspicious?"

"Maybe it did. I did not care. I could not bear to see her with another man. I think that was the moment I decided I must ask her to marry me."

"Such strong feelings of jealousy are not to be sniffed at," Leonard said.

"I knew I could not let her go. I knew that I had to make her mine. When we arrived back, she helped with the horses, I waited for her and asked her. I knew we were young – and many people would scorn love so young because our characters were not fixed enough. But I knew in my heart that I could never love anyone else. When I thought about us together, I knew marriage did not have to be like my parents, where my mother was treated like a second class citizen and where my father was a tyrant only viewing her as bearer of his children. I knew with Adella marriage could be full of tender, passionate, wonderful moments where we loved and relied on each other. I vowed I would be the best husband to her, nothing like my father." He dropped his shoulders, as though speaking the words lifted a great burden.

"Yet though you wished to spend the rest of your life with her, you did not tell her the truth?"

"So many times I nearly told her who I really was and what had happened to me before I came to Sidmouth. But something always stopped me. I was much younger and I suppose I lacked courage. I was so much in love with her and she thought I could do no wrong. I could not face her disappointment. Disappointment that I lied to her. Of course, more than anything, I feared she might reject me. So in the end, I decided I would tell her just before we got married. After all, I couldn't marry under a false name it wouldn't have been a legal wedding."

"She told me that if she knew you were gentry, she would have called off the engagement." Leonard raised his eyebrows at Joel.

"I would have persuaded her not to, I am sure. I would not have let her go for *that* reason."

"I suppose, if you did tell her what you have told me, especially that your father disinherited you. I think she would have supported you through thick and thin."

"Whatever could have happened is irrelevant. I was living in a dream, a dream that was about to be shattered by the arrival of my father."

He threw what remained of his cigar into the fire, opened the mahogany box next to him and lit another. Then as an afterthought said, "Sorry, would you like another?"

Leonard shook his head. "There was about a month in between the engagement and your father arriving?"

"Yes. That month was -" he looked up, as if seeing far beyond the four walls, "it was a special time for me. That Adella would agree to marry me was a wonder in itself."

"So you really did wish to marry her!" Leonard whispered to himself, it finally sunk in.

Joel heard his words and nodded back at him. Leonard stood up again and he walked about the room.

"I wished to marry her more than anything. To think, she could be sat here now with us, well, not in a house as grand. But she could have been here and I could look at her face and have her near me. . ." his voice drifted off. "I will always regret not making her marry me immediately. If I had, my father could have done nothing."

"What happened the day your father arrived?"

"I was sat with the boy teaching him something. The door to the study burst open and my father walked in. His face was bright red with fury, and the look in his eyes, it was as though he was possessed by the devil himself. It was the most irate I have ever seen him. Mr and Mrs Waters were behind him. They quickly left taking the boy when my father started to call me every name under the sun. He proceeded to tell me that my stupid charade was now over and that I would be returning to marry Cynthia." He sighed deeply. "I was determined not to be cajoled by him. I told him in no uncertain terms that nothing could make me marry her, and I did not care if he disinherited me."

"Did you tell him about Adella?"

"No, I had to protect her at all costs. I thought it best for her own safety and future not to say anything. Besides, me being in love would not have stopped him. I did not think he would have physically hurt her but he has contacts and could have made it difficult for you all. He has always believed that anyone can be bought, and he has a number of lackey's as well as professionals who can call upon at any time to do his bidding."

"He must have said something to you to change your mind?"

"Yes. He told me that if I did not marry Cynthia, he would lock up all my brothers until they were 21."

"No! Surely someone would stop him?"

"I told him as much, but who stopped him locking me away? Nobody. Frederick tried to get me out but he failed. So, I had to choose: my brothers or Adella."

"And you chose your brothers?" Leonard said, his voice quietly resolute.

Joel rubbed his eyes and but could not look at Leonard, "Yes, I chose my brothers because of the promise I made to myself. If I was at home, then I could watch over them. I knew my father would be true to his word. If he made a threat he would always carry it out. I could not let them be punished for me. That one moment, I knew I must give Adella up, and I went with my father."

"But she arrived back at the house before you left?"

"Yes. I hoped to leave without a word. I wanted her to hate me. I hated myself. I could not face her and yet wanted so much to see her one last time. I barely remember what I said as we stood outside the house. I concealed my feelings, but it was so hard. The hardest thing I have ever done. I could not let my father think I cared anything for her; I needed to protect her from him. I have since tried my best to blank those minutes from my memory. Though her pleading voice often echo's in my mind. It still haunts me." He swallowed hard.

"It all makes sense now. Everything that she told me. Your coldness to her, your denial." Leonard shook his head. 'I thought you the worst of men when she told me what you did -"

Joel interrupted, "I am the worst of men. I am not excusing myself. Nothing can excuse what I did. I am simply trying to explain. I should have outwitted my father. But I was young and I was weak then. But not any more."

"I do not blame you for wishing to protect your brothers. Adella can look after herself."

"That is what made me decide. I knew that she would be upset, but I believed that in time she would get over me. It is better she hates me. I hate myself for doing what I did. How could I tell her that I chose my brothers over her?"

"I think she would understand, if you explained to her everything you have told me. She wants more than anything to know the reason for your betrayal. Did you know she was dismissed from her position at Brayfern? They thought her a liar because she claimed to be engaged to you?"

"Yes, I knew of it, but not until she wrote to me asking for an explanation."

"Ahhh, the elusive letter. You did receive it then?"

"Yes. To keep up the pretence with my father, I instructed our lawyer to reply. He read all my post you see. I knew that if he suspected for a moment I felt anything for Adella, he would use it against me. If I hated myself before, then I loathed myself after that. It was despicable."

Leonard sighed deeply, "I never thought that your explanation would be like this." He waved his cigar in a dismissive manner.

"What do you mean?"

"I don't know, Adella thinks it's most likely you were trying to seduce her before you married Cynthia. She couldn't be more wrong!"

"I never would have behaved improperly towards her. But if that is what she thinks of me, so be it."

Leonard sat for a moment thinking of the words Adella said to him - "I vowed never to trust a man again. If he only asked I would have released him from our engagement." Such words spoken from her heart! She was home that moment, hating this man sat in front of him, yet that same man did everything he could to protect her because he loved her.

"But surely, when Cynthia passes on, if you explained to Adella there may be a chance she would understand. . .you could marry her. . .once she has come to terms with the truth."

Leonard looked at Joel and awaited his reply.

**10**

———

Joel met Leonard's gaze and replied in a slow even tone, "Yes, when Cynthia is gone, I plan to win Adella back. I lost her once, and now I have this second chance my aim is to marry her."

"I think she will understand why you did it, but I am not sure she will be so easy to win over. She knows her own mind."

"I know that. I am not expecting her to fall into my arms. But I have come to Bath because of my wife's wish. It has quickened my wishes and desires regarding Adella sooner than I expected."

Leonard nodded. "You mean, if you had not come to Bath you would have waited until the mourning period was over to see Adella."

"No. I would not have waited that long. You see, I have another reason to wish for a speedy reconciliation with Adella."

"Oh?"

"My father. . .my father has already arranged who will be my next wife."

Leonard was unable to move or speak for a moment after yet another revelation from Joel. He rather wondered how many more there might be, and it was only half past eight.

"So, you see what kind of man my father is," Joel said, "He started looking for a new wife for me as soon as it was clear Cynthia had a mortal illness."

"It is an inhumane thing to do for sure. Forgive me, but your father seems to be the worst of men." Leonard said in a low tone. "Though I must admit, your being here in Bath and you speaking of your wishes to be reunited with Adella are very much the same as your father."

"It is true to a certain extent. But I have not acted on it. Unlike my father who has pretty much arranged everything with a wealthy widow."

He paused then continued, "I remember when I was very young he was not like that. He was never the most adoring father, but certainly, he did change the older I grew. I do not love Cynthia, and my marriage to her has never been happy. I only hope that she will not be in pain near the end." He gave Leonard an earnest look. "You will see to that? I owe her my daughter you see."

"You have a daughter?"

"Yes. Little Sarah. She is barely acknowledged by my father. She is the reason why he wishes me to marry again. I haven't provided a male heir. If she were a boy, then who knows? Perhaps he would not care who I married next, though I often think I am fooling myself. With the high death toll of children, he would most likely have wanted me to provide more than one heir. Just like he has."

"Your daughter, where is she now?"

"Sarah came to Bath a few days ago and is up in the nursery, I thought it important that she sees her mother before she dies. Not that Cynthia can stand to be in her company for too long."

"How old is she?"

"Three," he smiled, "She is everything to me, she is a little ray of light in our home. My mother dotes on her and was sorry to be parted from her while she is in Bath. I think she sometimes wished for a daughter herself."

"And Cynthia?"

His face darkened, "She only spends about half an hour a day with her, and she is not affectionate." His eyes were distant and then he added, "Adella would not have been like that."

"Indeed. She is very fond of children."

"Before my father arrived at Sidmouth, Adella and I would talk about what our children might be like. I told her, if they were half as beautiful and kind as she was, I would be a happy man."

"But Cynthia is a beautiful lady is she not? Sarah must be a pretty child?"

Joel was unable to suppress a grin, "Yes. She is adorable. If I can tempt my mother away from her, I too dote on her. I try not to spoil her, but it is so difficult." After a pause he added, "She has even won the heart of Frederick, who always claims he doesn't like children. He takes her out for walks and purchased a Shetland Pony for her last birthday and has promised to teach her to ride. That reminds me, Frederick will be arriving soon, he has been out visiting friends."

Leonard did not answer and they sat silently for some time, both deep in thought. Leonard's head was full of each and every revelation he had heard. He studied Joel's face. His anguish was clear, from the furrowed brow, to the distant gaze in his blue eyes. Everything about him, from the tone of his voice and the expressions over the last hour or so showed that he was haunted by everything that had happened. There was not a doubt in his mind that he loved Adella, but how much of his anguish was through guilt? Joel knew the Adella of five years ago, not the woman she was now.

The clock ticked and the room remained a quiet place of reflection until Leonard was roused from his thoughts by Joel, "So, Dr Preston, now that you know my story, you will stay as our Doctor?"

"Yes. Of course."

There was no other option was there?

"Thank you," he said, his tense shoulders relaxed.

"You could answer me one thing," Leonard said, "Why did you procure me as your wife's physician in the first place?"

"In hindsight, I know it was wrong, but it was because of Adella. I wanted, I needed to see her again."

"But surely you could have seen her without hiring me?"

"Yes, but I suppose, I wanted you to earn the money. In a way I suppose that was a reason. Or at least what I convinced myself."

Leonard nodded, not fully convinced that Joel wasn't at least a little bit strange.

"Now I must ask for your help," Joel said.

"Oh?"

Joel stood up and walked to his bureau, opened it and took out a small pile of papers. He sat back down and handed them to Leonard.

"What are these?"

"A few years ago I purchased an annuity for Adella. Those are the details. It is the sum of one hundred pounds a year until her death." He paused, before continuing, "Even after her marriage."

"After her marriage? But you intend to marry her yourself."

"Yes. That is true. I fully intend to win her back as I have said. However, in the case of my death or that she resolutely refuses me, that is for her."

Leonard glanced at the papers and was unable to hide his shock. "That is a generous amount, but why do you need my help?"

"She will not accept it if she knows it's from me."

"That's true."

"It is true at the moment. But if you do have to give it to her, I would like you to - that is, could you in some way convince her that a distant relative left it to her? Or something, anything so that she has the money and does not know it is from me."

Leonard breathed in deeply. "I do not wish to lie to her."

"You must," he said firmly. "The money is hers, it is small recompense for what I did, but I could never stand the thought that she could one day fall into poverty. Please, you must think of something. Though like I said. I fully intend to win her again and what we are discussing now will be a moot point."

"A hundred pounds a year is a good amount. Many people live on fractions of that," Leonard said.

"I simply wish her to avoid poverty and live a comfortable life – should circumstance contrive against us. Will you take the papers and by whatever means make sure she has the income if we are not married?"

"Of course. I will think through what the best action will be. But you must be assured that I would never let her suffer from want of anything."

"I know," Joel said. "But I want to help her. I have to. You see that don't you?"

Leonard nodded, "Yes, I see it plainly." He placed the papers in his inside jacket pocket. He started to wonder which was going to be more difficult; keeping Joel's secret from Adella or finding a convincing way to give her the money. Because he suddenly remembered now that he could speak of none of this to Adella. How would he sit down to eat with her every day without mentioning it? How could he see her anguish as she wondered why she had been treated so badly and not say anything? Yet he held it in his power now to tell her, to relieve her pain. But he was honour bound to say nothing.

Leonard was about to ask about Joel's father but they both heard the front door bell and a few moments later, Frederick came through.

"It's pouring with rain and I am soaked," he said as he entered, but he was smiling. "Forgot to take a damned umbrella again! Still, I think my overcoat took the brunt of the rain and I am only slightly damp underneath."

He patted his jacket and then turned to Joel and then Leonard. He stepped forward, offered his hand to the doctor. The two shook hands, "Well now. I hope I haven't missed all the interesting talk." He poured himself a glass of brandy and sat himself in front of the fire.

He paused briefly, looked at Leonard and surveyed him over his glass. Then finally placed the brandy on the table said, "So, you are the brother."

"Yes." Leonard threw him an appraising stare back.

"I have finished telling Doctor Preston everything," Joel interrupted giving Frederick a stern look, as if to warn him not to upset his guest.

Frederick seemed to take the hint, "And what do you think of Joel's story?"

"I think his father deserves to be transported to Australia for all he has done."

Frederick gave a small laugh, "Transportation is too good for him."

"I must admit, if there were a way to rid myself of him then I would have done it a hundred times over," Joel said.

"Now Joel, I know you, you would never carry through such a threat," Frederick said. "Though there are vast amounts of people who would be grateful to you if you did. Mr Saunders for a start. He hates your father more than you do. Then there's your mother, she will be more than happy to be rid of the tyrant that is the bane of her life. Mr Holden, Mrs Holden, your brothers, my mother. Goodness, how she runs to avoid speaking to him -"

Joel interrupted, "Thank you Frederick, I do not think Dr Preston would like a full list of those who have a griev-ance with my father. We will be here all night!"

Leonard chose his words carefully, "Your father has many enemies, but from the small amount you have told me, I think I can surmise what sort of man he is. Particularly when he is finding you a new wife before the other is dead."

Frederick stood up quickly, "Ah, but Dr Preston, when I heard that Joel was to tell you everything, I was a little surprised. But what do yo think of his plan?"

"What plan might that be?" Leonard asked tentatively.

"To hide his youngest brother Michael until he is twenty one." Frederick replied.

Joel covered his brow with his hand, "You should not have mentioned anything to Doctor Preston. I do not want to worry him."

"What do you mean?"

Frederick and Joel exchanged a glance.

"You should tell him everything," Frederick said. "He has a right to know."

"Very well."

"What is this?"

"After Cynthia is dead, I will confront my father. I have to. But I am not expecting him to give in at all."

"What do you mean?"

"I am not expecting my father to give in. So I must safe guard Sarah and Michael – the youngest of my brothers. He is nineteen. So I must hide him until he is 21. "

"Otherwise your father will use the same threat as before." Leonard finished for him."

"Exactly. But this time I will not give in. I am older and wiser and determined not to be at his mercy."

"What of your other brothers. Will they help you?"

"James is in India, in the army and glad to stay there while my father is alive. Henry is at University. He might help, but he too is happy to be away from home."

"Henry would definitely help, and Michael is a strong young man, he will stand up to him too," Frederick said.

"It seems to me," Leonard said, 'that this is pure surmising. Are you really sure that your father will really make you marry again?"

"He will try, yes. I told you before. I have not produced an heir, and he wants to make sure that I do. He has spoken plainly of it several times. I am sorry Dr Preston. I do not mean to overly concern you with my own problems. My aim in telling you all this tonight was to explain my behaviour to Adella, and give you the annuity papers. Nothing more. Anything else you must not trouble yourself with. Frederick, it was wrong of you to mention this to Dr Preston."

"I will help you in any way I can," Leonard said and turned his head to Frederick, ignoring Joel's protestations.

"It is a kind offer, but I can never accept your help. It would be insupportable," Joel said.

"You deny me the right to make my sister happy?"

"Look. Dr Preston, I appreciate the offer, really I do, but I cannot see what you could do. Even if I could allow myself to let you."

There was a knock at the door, and a maid entered.

"Yes, what is it?" Joel said.

"Pardon sir, but it's Mrs Polwarth, she is asking for you."

"Very well. I will be up in a moment." He placed his cigar in the ashtray. "Please excuse me."

"Of course!" Leonard said, "If there is anything I can do, send for me."

When Joel left the room Frederick waited for the door to close, then spoke immediately, "Dr Preston, if I think you can be of any help, I will let you know. Joel needs all the friends he can get with regards to this matter."

"He is determined to win back Adella. He has turned out better than his father I think."

Frederick nodded. "Yes. It is a wonder how having such a father can make a child the opposite." His face grew serious. 'Never doubt he loves Adella. I have never seen anyone so broken than when he returned from Sidmouth. He told me everything about her as soon as he could speak to me alone. The day he married Cynthia, I was grooms man and practically held him up through the ceremony. It was the only reason I did it; to help him through it, though I wholly disapproved of the marriage. Cynthia didn't notice of course, too caught up in the moment of marrying to such advantage. I probably should not tell you this, but I know he has been to Bath several times in the last few years with the sole purpose of catching a glimpse of your sister."

Leonard jaw dropped, "He did that?"

"Yes. He made sure that she didn't see him of course. But he told me about it one night when we both drunk too much. Couldn't hold him back once he'd mentioned her name. Talked about her for hours on end. I am an expert on her now."

"I wish I could tell her a little of what I have learnt tonight. She is deeply troubled by Joel's presence in Bath."

"Yes. She is very bitter isn't she? Something I told her myself the other night."

"You have met Adella?"

"Yes. Two nights ago when a young girl blundered into a little soirée we attended. Adella came in to retrieve her."

"Yes, you were there weren't you!" Leonard said, "I thought I had seen you before. I was there so briefly I hardly took note."

"Well, I too wanted to tell her everything then goodness knows how you will keep his secret. Anyway, Joel has made me swear never to tell her either. He has always been adamant that she should not know until Cynthia is dead. Too caught up in convention for his own good."

"This is all a little strange talk."

"What do you mean?"

"'All this talk of what will happen once Cynthia is dead. It's rather grotesque."

"I suppose it is." Frederick drained is glass and poured himself another drink. "The thing is, Cynthia has been a thorn in his side all through their marriage. She treats him with disdain, she talks down to him, sides with Joel's father with everything. She hates seeing her daughter, is ill all the time and blames Joel for it."

"She has little to recommend herself as a wife?"

"She is what Joel thought she would be before he married her; self-centred, selfish and uncaring. She cares for nothing except status and is the worst snob I've ever met."

"You have very strong feelings about her."

Frederick gave a small laugh when he saw Leonard's raised eyebrows.

"Yes. She has nothing but her beauty to recommend her, and that fast wares away once you get to know the beast within."

Frederick continued, "I think he should tell Adella now."

"Do you?"

"Yes."

"I told him earlier that I believe she would understand."

"I think if she is as discerning as I think she is, she will take time to come to terms with what happened in Sidmouth. I think he should tell her now so that he has plenty of time to win her round. They would probably have to marry before the mourning period is over, but that is a mere formality. He has a small quantity of money in his own right. There is some from his mother's side and what is left from Cynthia's dowry. He paid for the annuity from that. They could live very comfortable lives, and I will see that they will want for nothing."

"Pardon me, but did you say, he bought an annuity for Adella from his wife's money?"

"Yes, where else would he get the money from? He has to account for every penny his father gives him. I told you, do not doubt he loves her."

The door opened and the same maid from earlier came in.

"If you please sirs, Mr Polwarth must stay with Mrs

Polwarth for now and wished you to know that he would like you to stay as long as you liked."

"Thank you Claire," Frederick said dismissing her with a small wave of his hand.

When the door was shut, Leonard commented, "Cynthia seems to depend greatly on her husband."

"Yes. He is the only one who will put up with her. He has a strange notion that since he married her, he should look after her, even if he has no affection for her."

"A noble quality."

"Undoubtedly."

Joel returned a full hour later, by which time Leonard was ready to leave. He had exhausted all topics of conversation with Frederick. It wasn't that they didn't get on, but an hour talking with a new acquaintance was enough. He was given an umbrella as promised and made his way home through the downpour at a much slower pace than normal. All this time, Joel never stopped loving his sister. Circumstances and fate led him to make decisions no man should ever have the misfortune to do. But he knew his promise as a professional and gentleman meant he could not disclose anything until Cynthia died. Even then, it was up to Joel to tell her himself. Perhaps, in the fullness of time, things would work themselves out. It did give him a peace in his own mind to know that Adella was secure financially whatever happened. It was a generous gift, though somewhat unsavoury that Cynthia's fortune paid for the upkeep of a woman her husband loved.

It was such thoughts as these that filled his head when he finally arrived back home. The house was warm and there was a merry din coming from the sitting room. He entered to find his sister laughing along with Helen and Flora over a game of cards, coins were scattered over the table. The real warmth within was infectious joy, such a contrast from the house he left earlier.

"Leonard, you must come and help me. Helen and Flora are ganging up on me and fleecing me of all my pennies!" Despite her protestations, Adella was smiling broadly.

"I would not dare interfere in any dispute amongst ladies. I would make too many enemies!"

They all giggled as he sat down next to Flora.

"But Leonard, as my brother, you should support me."

"Ah," Helen said, as a customer and supporter of our Uncle's business, you should support Flora and I, for I am sure we will make sure Uncle always serves you first!"

"Once your game is over, I will play." Leonard said. 'Flora and I can be partners and -"

"No! You must partner me Dr Preston," Helen insisted.

But Leonard ignored her and when the time came to deal the cards he did as he chose.

An hour later, Helen and Flora left, their Uncle collected them.

"It was a happy evening," Adella said closing the front door. "Despite my losses. Remind me never to make my stakes higher than a few half pennies."

"I never knew you were such a gambler," Leonard said grinning.

"Neither did I! But I did enjoy it. Would you like more tea? I think the pot is still warm." Leonard nodded and after giving him the drink Adella sat down.

"Did you have a pleasant evening?" she asked.

"Yes," he said, trying not to colour, for since his arrival, he was desperately trying to think of something other than all he learned that evening.

"Who was it you visited again? I can't remember who you said it was."

"Oh, er – it was just a passing acquaintance. One of my patients who thought they might like to spend an evening with their physician."

"I hope they didn't ask you lots of medical questions."

"No, no. Not at all. We spoke of many things...." He gulped down the rest of his tea, stood up abruptly and said, 'I better get to bed. Busy day tomorrow!"

"But it is Sunday tomorrow, you have only one call to make," Adella said, "to Mrs Polwarth."

Leonard searched her face briefly for any emotion, but she betrayed none. Then she added, "I better air your jacket. It smells strongly of cigar smoke. You would not like your patients being offended by the smell? Particularly the delicate women!"

"Is the smell that obvious?"

For a moment Leonard wondered whether Joel smoked cigars during his time with Adella, and that she would know where he had been. But he pushed the thought away, there were plenty of men who smoked cigars.

In his room, Leonard dwelt long on the evening he spent in the company Joel and then Adella. Such contrast! Joel had been full of regret and longing love, Adella smiling and joyful. She was happy now. He suddenly regretted offering to help Joel. For he was struck by the severity and malice of Mr Polwarth's father and feared for Adella if she were made aware of the truth and her sentiments for him were renewed. She was happy these last few years helping him, running his house and assisting him. If she married someone other than Joel then she would be happier. Someone steady, trustworthy and with an ordinary family who would embrace her, cherish her and welcome her. There were several men he knew about in Bath who he noticed admired her. Surely she would be better off with one of them, one who would not ruin her happiness.

He fell asleep glad in the knowledge that he must keep Joel's secret, because now he felt it was better that Adella was not exposed to such a man as the elder Mr Polwarth. She would be an innocent girl at the hands of a ruthless tyrant.

## 11

"Did you say breakfast was ready?" Leonard said to Adella. He was stood in the kitchen doorway and Adella was busy in front of the stove.

"Yes. Best eat it now before it gets cold," she said over her shoulder. "You'd better be quick, your appointment is soon."

Leonard nodded, and was about to go to the dining room, "Here, take your jacket," Adella said. "I think the smell of cigar smoke has gone." She held it out and he took it. "Oh, and these papers fell out of the pocket."

The annuity.

Leonard snatched the papers. His heart skipped a beat, "You - you did not read them?"

Adella's mouth gaped open and she placed both hands on her hips, "Leonard! How could you ask such a thing! You know I would not do anything of the sort!"

He reddened. The danger passed, and his pulse beat slowed.

"Er, sorry. No of course not. It's just that they were given to me by a patient and are excessively private."

"Well, if they are highly sensitive then I'll take a look!"

she held out her hand still with the same indignant look on her face.

"Very amusing," Leonard muttered and walked into the dining room. But as he sat down to eat his breakfast, he scolded himself for being so careless. How could he have forgotten about the annuity papers in his jacket? It was too close a call. He only knew Joel's secret for twelve hours and had nearly faltered already.

He ran his hand through his hair and then suddenly stood up. He went upstairs and locked the papers in his writing desk. Adella may not look at them, even if they were hanging around, but he would prefer they were safely tucked away for the time being. Then he noticed he was angry. It was all aimed at Joel. He may have wanted to make sure that Adella never faced poverty, but it was an imposition to leave it to him, her brother to come up with an idea as to how to tell her about it.

A few minutes later, back in the dining room, Adella sat down with him. Their conversation was somewhat stifled.

"Will you go straight to church after seeing Mrs Polwarth?" she asked.

"Yes."

Adella nodded and took another bite of her toast as she regarded her brother.

"Leonard?"

"Yes."

"You do not mind seeing Mrs Polwarth. I mean, after everything I told you, I hope it is not too awkward for you when you visit her?"

"No, not at all. Mr Polwarth is rarely there when I call."

Adella's raised her brows, "perhaps he is out trying to seduce a governess."

"Perhaps."

Leonard placed his cup down, his face grew serious. "You know, George Fadden was asking after you again the other day when I visited his mother."

"Really?" her voice was nonchalant.

"Yes, and I think if you gave him a little encouragement, he would like it. He is a good man. I'm sure if you got to know him, you would like him too."

"I do like him, he is very nice, very pleasant. When he can stop blushing. . ."

"You should not let Mr Polwarth affect the rest of your life. Not all men are like him."

Adella stared at her plate and in a quiet voice said, "I know, and I have been thinking a similar thing recently. In fact, I think it would be a good thing to be open to the attentions of a man such as Mr Fadden. I like him, and his family. He is the sort of man who I can tell does not hold any secrets."

Leonard smiled, "Well then. Next time I see him, I will invite him for tea. What do you say to that?"

Adella nodded. "Very well."

LEONARD LEFT SHORTLY AFTERWARDS, and Adella's thoughts went to those papers that fell from Leonard's pocket. She wondered what might be in them that was so secretive. It was certainly true that people trusted their doctors with more than their health. She lost interest after a while and was soon thinking of other matters; the house work, the errands she was to run, and more importantly the fact that since her last meeting with Joel, she decided that she must move on. She wasn't quite sure how she would do it. But she knew she had to. The problem was, with him living so close by, the risk of running into him hung over her. She wondered whether she should be more open to receiving the compliments of other men. She would see what happened when Mr Fadden came to tea.

In the afternoon, Adella made her way into the centre of Bath. The streets were busy, and as she weaved her way around the people, and arrived at the Alther's shop, she found it closed. She rang the private bell, and waited. After a short while, a face appeared at the door, then the locks were thrown back.

"We were closed for lunch for a change! But the door is never locked for you," Mrs Alther said.

Adella smiled in return, "Thank you, but you should not make exception for me. You deserve a quiet break from all the customers for a short time at least."

"You are no trouble, besides, come and sit out the back and keep me company for a few minutes while Mr Alther does that prescription. I can tell you what Helen got up to yesterday when she visited Alexandra Park!"

Adella could well imagine what Helen got up to without any explanation, and wasn't entirely sure she wanted to know. But she said nothing and followed Mrs Alther into the back office. It was as cluttered as ever; Mrs Alther was brewing some herbs on the small stove, and there were a dozen empty jars sat waiting on the side ready to be filled. The rest of the room was filled with clutter; books and papers, jars and bottles. At least there was somewhere to sit down.

"She outdid herself this time!" Mrs Alther explained, "she was dressed up to the nines and paraded herself about whenever she saw any young gentleman. Flirting she was! No other word for it! Flirting! Fluttering her eyelids, dropping her handkerchief on purpose in the hope that a gentleman would pick it up. Poor Flora nearly had a turn! She tried to stop her, but Helen wouldn't listen. In the end, Flora hid behind the band stand for quarter of an hour, then ran home to get me."

Adella could not stop herself from giving a little laugh, "Poor Flora, she puts up with a great deal from Helen I think."

"Yes. It is my mission now that Flora finds a husband as well as Helen. She might think herself an old maid but stranger things have happened. I was nearly twenty nine when I married Mr Alther."

Adella was about to reply, when their conversation was interrupted by a loud banging on the door.

"Now who could that be?" Mrs Alther hoisted herself up from the table and walked out. Adella followed.

"Someone wants to come in," Mr Alther said, as he crushed tablets with the pestle and mortar.

"Hmm, not seen him before, but he looks desperate. Shall I open it?"

It was a boy stood outside the shop door peering through. He was small, about nine or ten years old with dark well combed hair. His clothes looked respectable. He must be a paid errand boy. As soon as he saw Mrs Alther he shouted, "Please Missus, please, will you let me in? It's an emergency!"

"Alright, alright," she said, as she took her large bundle of keys out of her apron pocket and unlocked the door.

The boy took off his cap and scrunched it in his hand, wringing it as he spoke. Still stood outside he said nervously, "Please Missus, there's a terrible emergency; is Dr Preston there?"

"Why no! But his sister is here." She indicated to Adella.

"Please Miss," the boy said, "It's Mrs Polwarth. She's hurt

real bad. She fell over and there's blood everywhere coming out of her arm. We need Dr Preston to stop it bleeding. I ran to his house, but he weren't there, the woman next door said you'd most likely be here."

"Dr Preston is in Perrymead and will not be back for at least another half hour." Adella said calmly and not betraying any emotion at the mention of Mrs Polwarth.

"You could go though couldn't you Adella? You've learnt a few things from your brother these last few years haven't you? You know how to bandage a wound?" Mrs Alther asked.

"Well, yes I suppose. But wouldn't it be better that you went?" Her voice trembled a little.

"Me dear! Oh no dear! I can't bear the sight of blood. Never could do, could I Mr Alther?" she gave a nervous chuckle.

Mr Alther still stood behind the counter said, "No. Never liked blood. Best keep her away from it if you don't want her fainting."

Mrs Alther gave a single firm nod of her head.

"Please Miss. Please," the boy pleaded. 'I'll get a thick ear if I go back alone."

She sighed deeply, "Very well. I will go and tend to Mrs Polwarth immediately, I know where it is. But you must run and get Dr Preston. He is at Mr Carmichael's, 19 Popes Walk. Run as quickly as you can."

The boy nodded, repeated, "19 Popes Walk," then ran off.

"I will need dressings," Adella said turning back to Mrs Alther.

"Coming right up." A moment later she was back, holding a large bundle. "Best take a bottle of iodine too," she placed a large brown bottle with a cork stopper on top of the dressings.

"Thank you," Adella said and took them. She had little time to think through the implications of where she was about to go. One thought flashed through her mind; would *he* be there? She quickly suppressed it. She was going to help her brother's patient. That was all. Everything else was of no consequence. Her legs almost gave way at the thought of entering his house again.

"Tell Flora and Helen I will call later to see them."

"Very well. Good luck."

She was pushed out the door found herself hurrying to South Parade. She calculated that it would take her about five minutes if she walked fast, and that Leonard could be there in about half an hour if he left Mr Carmichael's immediately. It would take great skill to dress the wound so that it stopped bleeding. And how bad would it be? She hoped it was not as the boy described; blood everywhere. She wasn't sure whether she could cope with a large amount of blood.

She found herself outside the house far sooner than she expected and ran up the few steps, rang the bell breathing heavily due to the exercise.

The door opened quickly and a pale-faced maid ushered her in after she explained who she was, not questioning her ability to perform the task.

"Follow me quickly, she is upstairs," the rustle of their clothes was the only sound heard as they quickly made their way up. But this time, instead of the drawing room, Adella was taken up to the next floor; one of the bedrooms. Her mind was a blur with each step. She tried not to notice the soft plush carpet beneath her feet, or the pristinely decorated stairway.

She walked into the room, and with a quick flick of her eyes, saw a crowd all stood around the grand four poster bed. The maid who opened the door made room for Adella and finally she saw Mrs Polwarth lying on the bed, a pathetic creature with one hand on her forehead and the other up in the air, being held by one of the female servants.

Adella did not look at the peoples faces to see if one of them was *him*. "Please, everyone leave, except you," she commanded and pointed to the maid who held Mrs Polwarth's arm. The servants obeyed, though she only noticed them gone after she heard a click from the door as it closed behind them.

Adella stood towering over Mrs Polwarth and took a good look at the task before her. She was under the covers, still in her night gown which was completely clean. There was a bloodstained towel next to her on the bed. Her hair was loosely tied in plaits either side of her pale face, that framed her sunken eyes.

"Please help me," Mrs Polwarth said in a pathetic tone, "I have lost so much blood already."

Adella walked around the bed and said to the frightened looking maid, "Get me some hot water."

"Yes Miss," and she left the room quickly, and paused only to hand over the arm.

Adella peeled away the blood soaked muslin that covered the wound. It instantly oozed a little, but bled no further. The wound was only a few inches along the upper arm, and not as deep as she expected. The errand boy's plea that there was 'blood everywhere' was somewhat of an exaggeration. She silently thanked Mrs Alther's foresight at giving her the iodine. But before she could do anything she needed to clean it.

"My brother will be here as quickly as possible," she said, and then after examining the wound said "It is not too bad, I will have it cleaned up presently."

"Very well," Cynthia said.

"How on earth did you do this?" Adella asked.

Cynthia turned her head away in defiance, so as not to answer, but then must have changed her mind, "It was an accident, with the letter opener. I fell over, and I was holding the letter opener the wrong way. It cut me as I fell."

"Well," Adella said, 'at least it didn't get you near your vital organs."

The water arrived quickly, the servants had obviously foreseen its need. She washed the wound with the water and then the iodine. If she was desperate to get out of the place she did not betray it in any other form than the speed at which she worked.

"I do not think it will need stitches, but it is best if I place a temporary bandage so that Dr Preston can decide for himself."

"Very well, I hope I will not need stitches, I would need a great amount of Laudanum if I do."

A few minutes of silent work and the bandage was fitted. "There. You must keep your arm elevated. It will help stop the bleeding."

"Very well. I was not going to get up today anyway," she sighed and lowered herself further down the bed. Then after a moment she stared at Adella, her eyes became shrewish, and her voice spiteful. "I know who you are."

Adella glanced at her, "Of course, we have met before. A little over a week ago when I came with your tonics. I am Dr Preston's sister."

"I know that. I know you are Dr Preston's sister and that we have met before. But I knew who you were the moment I heard your name that day. You are the girl who claimed to be engaged to my husband." She let out a small nervous laugh.

Adella felt herself instantly redden.

"It was not a false claim. Though it may well appear that way, since Mr Polwarth denied it."

Cynthia scoffed. "You still delude yourself now! Well, you must envy me very much."

Adella looked at her lying in bed, arm above her head. This dying woman. Pale and wane. Cynthia must have sensed at least a little of what she thought because she instantly said, "Oh, not my little illnesses. No, you envy me because you wanted Joel to be your husband. But he chose me. I am Mrs Polwarth and I am the happiest of wives. It certainly has been the happiest five years of my life. He is so thoughtful and considerate as well as being excessively rich. I want for nothing."

Adella picked up the towel on the bed and put it in a laundry bag.

"I will not deny that at one time in my life I wanted Mr Polwarth to be my husband much. But not any more. I cannot envy you."

"Not envy me?" she gave another irritating laugh. "How can you not envy me? I want for nothing."

Adella continued unperturbed, "You have a husband who lies and does not honour his vows. So, no Mrs Polwarth, I do not envy you."

"What impudence! He does not break his vows. You do envy me! You will envy me! Even though you say you do not. You. . .you little -" Cynthia stared at her in defiance.

Adella said nothing in return, though a thousand insults were at her lips, ready to be voiced. She kept her silence, if only for the sake of her brother and his reputation. But a quick look at the dying woman on the bed made her realise that insulting her would be a depraved thing to do. Besides, if she was to move on like she wanted to, she must let it pass.

"Would you like me to stay until my brother arrives? Or

should I ring the bell for your maid?" Adella said after she packed away everything.

"You can wait in the kitchen with the other servants until he arrives I suppose," Cynthia said. "I don't want you here."

"I would not wish to inconvenience your hard working servants. Good day Mrs Polwarth," she said mustering all the civility she could.

Cynthia said nothing, she looked up at Adella and gave a dismissive wave of her arm.

Adella grabbed the door handle, and as she turned it, she felt someone on the other side turn it at the same time. Expecting it to be her brother, she let go, stepped back and waited for him to enter.

But it wasn't her brother.

It was Joel.

He looked at her immediately and then at his wife. He paused and momentarily took in exactly what he saw, his mouth slightly open as though he was going to say something.

Their eyes met for one brief moment.

"Oh Joel!" Mrs Polwarth said, "My dear husband, where have you been? I have nearly bled to death."

He walked over to the bed and briefly glanced at Adella again, "What happened?"

Cynthia started to explain, and Adella saw her opportunity to leave. She stepped as quietly as she could through the open doorway and began walking down the steps.

She made her escape.

Almost.

"Miss Maxwell!"

She heard her name called from the top of stairs by an all too familiar voice.

She stopped halfway down, but did not look round.

"Miss Maxwell," she heard him call again, this time more insistently.

"What?" she said defiantly not looking round.

"Thank you for helping my wi-" he paused then continued, "thank you for helping Cynthia."

She turned round, her face like thunder, "If you wish to thank me then you can start by telling your wife that I am not the liar she thinks I am."

Comprehension spread on his features, his wife did know more than she let on.

"No?" she said with a wry smile, "I didn't think you would be man enough to tell her the truth. But what does it matter? Since the whole world makes me out to be a liar and fortune hunter, why not her as well?"

There was silence for a few moments as they stared at each other. Adella waited for a reply, and Joel unable to give one. It was broken only by Cynthia calling in the distance,

"Joel, Joel! Has that dreadful girl gone yet? Joel!"

Adella raised her eyebrows and said, "Best go and tell your wife I have gone," and she turned and ran down the few remaining steps.

But he ran after her and as she tried to open the door he kept his hand on it stopping her.

"You should not care what my wife thinks of you. She knows nothing about you except what she has made up in her mind."

"Let me out. I do not wish to speak to you." She spoke in a cool low tone, but she was secretly afraid. She could not let him know it.

"I just want to explain. I promised you I would and I will. Will you turn and look at me?"

"You are going to tell me now?"

"No – I cannot. But I will."

"So you keep saying. I really do not understand what all the secrecy is. You just wish to hurt me further."

"I do not. I do not wish to hurt you."

He was so close behind her she could almost feel his breath on her neck. "Listen to me. I have younger brothers. My father -"

"Your father would not have approved of me. I know that," she turned round and met his gaze. She continued, "'our father would not have approved of me. I am not stupid. He is right. I am no match for you and I never was. I never will be either. Even after she is dead."

"You do not understand; my father – he is – I cannot say what he is. But my brothers. They. . ."

"Yes?"

"They are younger than me and need – they need guidance."

"Guidance?"

"Yes, they would have had nobody to help them."

"What does that mean?"

"I cannot say anything more. I wish to tell you more, but not now. Now is not the time or place. I have said too much already."

He stepped away from her and she noticed the sudden distance between them.

"I do not understand why you persist in hounding me at every turn. I have told you that I have moved forward and that I do not wish to speak to you or have anything to do with you. Yet here I am. Stood in front of you. In your house."

"I am sorry. I will let you leave."

She turned to the door and let herself out.

It was blessed release for Adella to get out of that house.

She paused and swept a glance up and down the street for a sign of Leonard. She would wait outside for he could not be much longer.

She stood under a nearby tree, and tried to look as inconspicuous as possible as she fought to get her composure back. There were a few people about, a family getting into a carriage, a couple walking arm in arm along the street. She exhaled deeply and leant against the trunk of the tree, still shaking.

He had lied even to his wife. Of course he had. She would be the first person he would lie to! The woman was such a fool, so obviously devoted to him, singing his praises and good virtues when he was the biggest deceiver in all of England. They deserved each other. But what of her actually speaking to him? She was determined not to but when it came to it she could not help herself. What did she expect; an apology? For him to stop and beg for her forgiveness?

The cool wind blew on her face and it made her put her bonnet back on. As she was tying it, she noticed a little girl stood on the steps nearby with wide eyes staring at her. She was knee high, dressed in an expensive dark red coat. Her hair was shoulder length with soft dark curls.

"Hello. What's your name?" Adella asked smiling and glad to be distracted from the previous few minutes.

The girl said nothing, but ran over to a man a few feet away and hugged his leg. Adella looked up and her face fell. It was Frederick Garner.

They recognised each other instantly. Mr Garner picked up the girl and said, "Good afternoon Miss Maxwell."

Adella gave a sharp nod of acknowledgement to him. She was determined not to say anything further or be overly polite. He did not deserve it.

"This little girl is called Sarah." Frederick said pausing, then continued. "Sarah Polwarth."

It took a few moments for her to realise what he had said, and what this child represented.

It threatened to overwhelm her.

She walked backwards.

Turned suddenly.

Her eyes filled with un-shed tears and she ran down the street, not pausing to think that Leonard might need her. He would understand, he hated Joel as much as she did.

She ran and vaguely remembered that she should go back to the Alther's. But she did not care now. The look on Mr Garner's face was imprinted on her mind, a mixture of smugness and pride. She shut her eyes trying to eliminate it, but it was no use, it was still there.

He had a child.

She continued on relentlessly, breathless and hot. If she passed people, she did not see them. They were a blur.

It was only when she reached her front door that she stopped. The key would not fit in the lock, her fingers trembled too much. She threw it down in disgust and slumped on the step and sobbed uncontrollably.

**12**

———————

Joel slowly turned back and made his way to his wife's room. His legs dead-weights leading him unwillingly away from the path his heart was urging him to take. He knew when they arrived in Bath that things would get worse, but he had not anticipated his first meeting with Adella would awaken the fierce love that had lain dormant for so long. Each time he saw her his whole body cried out to tell her the truth. To speak tenderness and warmth. To run after her and hold her in his arms and never let her go.

But he had to wait.

As he paused in the doorway to Cynthia's room he quickly buried such overwhelming urges. Instead, he reminded himself of the vows he made to his wife on their wedding day, and reluctantly moved forward. He couldn't allow himself to be weak now. Not after all this time. There wasn't much longer left.

"Well? Has she gone?" Cynthia said when he finally walked in.

"Yes." He said in a low tone.

"Good. I can't stand her. Why did it have to be her who came to help me?"

Joel moved forward and sat on the bed. He looked directly at his wife, "You are too ungrateful. Miss Maxwell did not have to come and help you, and all you do is criticise her."

She turned her nose up indignantly. "My arm aches so much! Where is Doctor Preston? I need him." She looked at the bandage on her arm, "I am sure this is tied too tightly and the cut hurts terribly. I want my maid. Make yourself useful for once and ring for her."

Joel stood up quickly and sighed, "I am sure Dr Preston will be here soon. Try and be patient."

He walked down to his study, unable to spend a second longer with Cynthia. She was a witch today. He needed time alone to think over seeing Adella again. If Cynthia wasn't ill, he would have confronted her about how she knew about Adella. But he could not argue with her, sick, dying woman that she was. He had certainly not told her himself and the only other person who knew was Frederick.

Frederick wouldn't betray him.

But one other thought crossed his mind. It was possible she had seen his pictures of Adella, painted when they were in Sidmouth. Adella was not changed that much since then. Her eyes still the most beautiful dark brown eyes and her hair was still dark and full with the odd curl escaped in much the same way as he remembered. But there was an unmistakable sorrow in her eyes now. He saw it the first moment his glance fell on her beautiful face, and he knew he had caused that anguish.

A few minutes later the study door was flung open. In ran Sarah, with Frederick right behind her. Joel lifted her up into his arms.

"Hello my sweet girl," he said into her hair.

"Is Cynthia alright then?" Frederick asked.

"Yes. She is resting, though I do not think she will be happy until Doctor Preston arrives."

Frederick rolled his eyes. "She is never happy unless there is a doctor attending her."

"She is not always happy then."

Frederick gave a small laugh, "Indeed, Doctor Preston has the patience of a saint to put up with the likes of her. Do you think she is the most troublesome patient he has?"

"Maybe she is," Joel said smiling a little.

"Well I shall ask him when he arrives. . ."

"You will do no such thing!"

"Very well, but it will be on the tip of my tongue when I see him. I hope you realise how much restraint it will take." He suddenly became more serious. "Joel. I saw Adella a moment ago, what was she doing here?"

"She was helping Cynthia, bandaging her arm, why?"

Frederick glanced at Sarah.

"Oh," Joel said looking at his daughter.

"It was unavoidable I am afraid, we happened upon her outside the house, and she asked who Sarah was, I had to answer her."

Joel rubbed his brow with his hand, "How did she react?"

"How do you think?"

"I assume she did not know of Sarah before then?" Joel asked as he walked to the window.

"No, her reaction was. . .well, she was upset, I could see it in her eyes. She ran off quickly."

Joel stood silently. Looking out of the window yet he saw nothing of the street outside. Her eyes always did express what she was feeling.

He wanted to keep Sarah's existence a secret from her. Why, he did not know, but he knew she must feel the betrayal even further by Sarah's existence in the world. He wasn't ashamed of his daughter, well, not exactly. It was just that he always wished that her mother was Adella. He clenched his fist and felt the hardness of his nails digging into his palms. No pain he could feel could compare to hers right now. Finally, his reverie was broken by Frederick speaking.

"You should not feel too bad. It was inevitable that she would find out."

Joel turned his head slowly, but he could not meet Frederick's eye. "I suppose you are right. But I cannot help thinking how I would feel if our positions were reversed and I had found out that she was mother to another man's child."

"It may well happen yet unless you act quickly."

He lifted his head and this time held Frederick's gaze.

"No," he said. But there was self-doubt in his voice.

"You cannot fool yourself to believe that she will save herself for a man she thinks cares nothing for her, who treated her -"

"Enough!" Joel shouted, and the sudden outburst of anger made Sarah start to cry. Joel picked her up again and spoke soothing words, rocking her. "We must not argue in front of Sarah, I will not have her upset. She is too precious to me."

Frederick said nothing, but went to the desk and sat silently as Joel calmed and distracted Sarah. They were interrupted by a knock on the door. It was the nurse maid who took Sarah away.

After only a brief pause Frederick resumed his onslaught, "The only way to truly prevent Adella from marrying some unworthy fellow, is to marry her yourself as quickly as possible. Tell her now."

"No. It's not right. I may not love Cynthia, but I am not a fiend, or an adulterer."

"Really? Doesn't it say in the bible 'anyone who even looks at a woman with a sinful desire of wanting her has already sinned in his heart.'"

Joel said nothing.

Fredrick continued, "She would make an excellent mother to Sarah, and then there would be your own children too."

"Stop it!" Joel said firmly. "Just stop it Frederick!" His breath was heavy. "I know she would make an ideal mother to Sarah. You know how much I long to marry her. But you forget – I know her and I know she would never lower herself to become my mistress. When I am free from the shackles of my marriage I will tell her and not before."

"You are a fool." Frederick said with a cool note of disgust in his voice. "You need to give her time to adjust to the truth."

"So you keep telling me." Joel stared at Frederick for a few seconds and then left the study.

Some distance away, Adella still lay sobbing in a crumpled heap on her doorstep. Her mind awash with thoughts of the same little girl. That beautiful child, so innocent. She should have been their child. It was her eyes that haunted Adella, she had his eyes.

Of course she knew they were married, children were a natural consequence of it. But it still cut deep. Seeing their marriage announced in the paper five years ago was one thing, but seeing first hand their child was another. However much she tried to reason and excuse her deep emotions and rise above the mortification and betrayal, she could not. She tried not to blame the child, or hate her. That sweet innocent little girl who looked so like her father. Her tormented mind continued until she felt a hand on her shoulder.

"Adella?" a familiar concerned voice said.

She looked up, a little startled, then focused her eyes on the woman's face.

Flora.

"Adella. What is wrong? Why are you crying here?"

"I – oh Flora!" Adella said trying to stand up, but it was no good, she could not get up. Flora crouched down and put her arm around her.

Eventually as the sobbing started to subside, Flora lifted her up and, seeing the key on the ground, opened the door and led her inside.

Arm in arm, Flora took her to the kitchen, sat her down and put the kettle on the cooker. "What you need is a nice cup of tea. That will make you feel much better, and you can tell me everything."

Adella managed to smile a little and nodded.

It was nearly two hours later when Flora, still in the kitchen, heard the front door open. She knew it would be Leonard, and hurried herself out to the hallway to meet him.

"Flora! What a pleasant surprise."

Flora's heart leaped, and she lost concentration for moment as she tried to suppress a blush, "Good afternoon Doctor Preston. I, I have been helping Adella. . .she, oh dear, she was upset earlier. Something happened. . ."

A concerned expression spread over his face, "Where is she? Is she alright?"

"She is resting upstairs. I took her up there myself, but not before she told me some things –" she dropped her voice, "things about Mr Polwarth."

Leonard sighed.

"So it is all true?" Flora asked reading the expression on his face.

"Yes. It is true. But something must have happened earlier for her to be so upset. What Mr Polwarth did five years ago is old news."

Still with a serious countenance, Flora continued, "Adella tended to Mrs Polwarth's cut, and she was by all accounts rude to Adella. It appears she knows about her and Mr Polwarth, or rather that there was a history between them."

"But that would not upset her so much, Adella can stand up for herself. Did something else happen?"

"Yes. She was outside and saw their daughter, that is what has upset her the most. She said she was being silly, reacting the way she has, but she told me everything that happened in Sidmouth and I must say, she has been very brave over the whole thing. Far more than I could ever have been."

"I am sure that is not true!" Leonard exclaimed.

Flora smiled and lowered her head in embarrassment at Leonard's steady gaze.

Upstairs, Adella did not hear the conversation below. She could not sleep, though nervous exhaustion racked her body. How much more could she take? She wished Joel and his awful wife out of Bath. This was *her* home, he had invaded it by his presence. Had he chosen this town specifically? And why had he procured her brother to be his wife's doctor? He knew from five years ago what his name was, he must have done it on purpose.

Bitterness gripped her and every muscle in her body tensed as she held onto the feeling. All she wanted was release from the sadness that engulfed her. She thought she had managed to move on. She thought she would be able to cope with him being so close. But now she was not sure. She was happily settled in Bath and her life had purpose. Helping Leonard and the sick was dear to her heart. How could he come into her life now that she had forgotten him. Only occasionally did her thoughts stray to her 'unmention-able betrayal'.

She heard a knock at her bedroom door, and though she did not respond, Leonard and Flora came in.

They approached tentatively, Adella was lying facing away.

"Flora is about to leave," Leonard said.

"Oh," was the quiet response.

Flora took a step forward, "Adella, if you need me again, you only have to ask. I – I understand how difficult it is for you now and how much you need a friend. I have had a similar disappointment myself you know. When you are feeling better I will tell you all about it."

Leonard's eyebrows raised in surprise at Flora's words, but he said nothing.

Adella turned round briefly and took Flora's hand, "Thank you. You don't know what that means to me."

Flora took her leave. Leonard followed and showed her out, and returned to Adella a few minutes later.

"She told you what happened today then?" she said.

"Yes. We had a brief conversation downstairs. She has offered to run your errands for a short while, until the Polwarth's have left Bath. What do you think?"

Adella turned round, and sat up quickly, looking at her brother's face, she sighed, "I think that would be an excellent idea. She does not mind doing it then?"

"Not at all, she offered actually, and well, I said I would speak to you first. But it would be a temporary arrangement. Just until they are gone."

"How long will that be?"

Leonard sat on the edge of the bed, "It is difficult to say, Mrs Polwarth has not long left. I believe her mother and father are soon to arrive in Bath, though they have kept it from her that she is dying. She will think they are visiting for a short time."

"Kept it from her that she is dying? Surely not! How can they do such a thing?"

"In the brief times you saw her, you must be able to tell that she is not the sort of woman who would react well to such news."

"*He* decided to keep it from her didn't he?"

"Yes. But it is with the agreement of her parents. If she had a stronger resolve then they would tell her. But she is a delicate woman, always has been sickly from her previous doctor's report."

Adella looked down and sighed again. "She was not pleasant to me earlier. She knew who I was. I mean, she knew about me and Joel. But she obviously believed her husband's lies, because she called me a fortune hunter."

Leonard took hold of his sister's hand, and patted it gently, "You did well. I am proud of you. And you bandaged her arm most expertly."

The corners of Adella's mouth turned up in a scornful smile, "Does that mean that I can send him a large bill for my nursing services?"

"Do not worry, I will add it to the bill, and you will receive the money directly."

She frowned, "I will give the money to a poor family. I could not bear to have any money of his. But tell me, did you know about their daughter?"

Leonard nodded.

"Well, you are their doctor I suppose. But I think I would have preferred to hear it from you." She looked at her brother with mournful questioning eyes. "It was Mr Garner who told me about the girl, and he seemed smug about it too."

Leonard stood up and decided that the conversation was already in a dangerous place said, "Come down when you are ready."

She nodded, "I will come down in a short while. Dinner will not cook itself."

THE NEXT THREE weeks passed with no further incident. Adella did not see Joel or any of his friends or relations during that time. With Flora now running errands and helping Doctor Preston, Adella stayed at home and only ventured out when she needed to visit the grocer's. She was an excellent host to her small circle of friends and the Alther's, all of whom visited both separately and together during the week. Helen did not understand the new arrangements, especially why Flora was suddenly such a favourite with Dr Preston, and why Adella had become somewhat subdued and quiet.

"You must walk out with me to the park." Helen said to Adella one afternoon when she and Flora visited.

"Tomorrow," Adella said quietly.

Helen was unperturbed and the following day called and expected Adella to walk out after lunch.

"Flora is running errands for your brother again," Helen said. "She loves it. Rushes out of the office every time he enters the shop! She said to me she likes to have something to do. She said it as though I don't have a purpose! I do. Mine is to marry a rich man and I told her so as well. Do you know what she said? Nothing! She only scoffed! Well we will see. When I marry a Duke or an Earl or even a plain old Baronet would do, she'll be sorry. I will still look after her in her spinsterhood when I am a rich woman. Anyway, I would not want to do all that traipsing all over Bath with lotions and potions. Leave her to it, and you and I will have fun walking out."

Helen looked Adella up and down, "You look a little drab. You should dress more like me. If we are going walking, it is always best to stand out a little, so that the Gentlemen notice you." She swished her deep blue dress a little, as though flirting with a man.

"But I don't want gentlemen to notice me."

"More the fool you then," Helen said shaking her finger. "Still if you look drab, I'll stand out more."

"Helen, I really do not wish to go out, besides, I have a lot of work to do in the house. Mary is ill and I am left to do her work too. I am very tired," Adella said.

Helen waved her finger again, "I won't take no for an answer!" she hunted about and found Adella's coat and bonnet. Adella lacked the will to argue any more and was forced to go further afield for the first time in weeks.

They headed out arm in arm to Sydney Gardens. Helen explained, "I have been there before and I thought it exceedingly grand," she lowered her voice a little to a whisper, "and there were some handsome gentlemen walking about. It's quite the place to be seen in Bath you know."

"No I did not know. I have only been there once or twice myself."

Helen led Adella onwards, and they soon found their way around the people going about their business. Carriages, chaises, omnibuses all clattering on the road. Families, children and adults alike all busying themselves walking here and there. After five minutes, Adella was glad to be out. The sun shone brightly and it warmed her heart. She forgot the torment of the last few weeks. Maybe Helen wasn't so bad after all.

Helen chatted incessantly about the latest fashions and who she had been getting to know, though Adella did not hear much of what she said. It was only when they walked through the stone gate that led to Sydney Gardens that Helen paused speaking. They walked about the grass under the trees, Adella admired the gardens and Helen didn't notice them for fear of missing anyone important.

They turned a corner on the path and suddenly Adella stopped.

She did a double take.

There in front of her was Mr Garner. He was with another gentleman, considerably older than himself, but his tailored suit and pristine appearance gave the immediate impression to Adella that he was a vain man.

She had not seen them coming and quickly started to move away, but it was too late, Mr Garner saw her and making a bow to both ladies said, "Well well well. Miss Maxwell. How delightful to see you again. You look positively glowing. We have not seen you at South Parade for some weeks. I wonder why?" Then indicating to his companion said, "This is my friend, Mr Yates."

Helen fluttered her eye lashes at both men and after giving her best practiced curtsy said, "Oh Adella does not run errands for her brother any more. She is above all that now!"

"Is she?" Frederick said, not looking at Helen, but staring at Adella.

Adella frowned, "Come Helen, we must move on, I have to get back home, I have many things to do."

"You have?" Helen betrayed.

Frederick smirked.

"Yes!" Adella said through gritted teeth.

"I'm sure Miss Maxwell could spare a few minutes to walk through the gardens?" Mr Garner said and offered his arm. Mr Yates offered his to Helen, who eagerly took it with a pathetic giggle.

Adella resolutely refused Mr Garner's arm, but walked forwards. It was not long before her fast pace made them outstrip Helen and Mr Yates. She hoped that he wouldn't be able to keep with her, but alas, he did.

They walked on in silence. Adella most unwilling to speak one word to this man unless propriety demanded her response.

Mr Garner spoke, "It is a very fine day is it not? Not the sort to get stuck inside with household chores. I do hope I am not keeping you from any important work you have at home."

Adella glanced fleetingly at his face, "My work may appear to be insignificant and unimportant to someone like you, but I take pride in looking after my brother, he is very good to me."

Frederick said quietly, "So good that he keeps secrets from you?"

Adella stared at him, she knew he was baiting her further, but his words intrigued her.

"Of course he has secrets from me. He has many patients and can't go around telling me everything about them."

"Ah, but I am talking about a specific secret, and a specific patient we both know well."

"What do you mean?"

"Did you not wonder why he spent an evening with Mr Polwarth and I a few weeks ago?"

Adella paused, wondering what he might mean. "He is called to South Parade many times, Mrs Polwarth is his patient after all."

"I was not speaking about his visits to Mrs Polwarth. No, I was thinking of the time he came with the sole purpose to speak to Mr Polwarth."

"Who my brother chooses to spend his evening's with is no concern of mine." But there was already a feeling of dread arising in her.

"Indeed. But surely, if he chooses to spend an evening with your former fiancé; who tells him why he denied you in Sidmouth and all his sordid little secrets. Every last detail in fact. Surely he should not keep that a secret from you?"

Adella's mouth dropped open.

Frederick continued on, still with a curved smile, "Do tell me, what are you more amazed at, that I too know that you were blameless and that you were engaged to my friend, or that your brother knows the full truth and has said nothing to you?"

She blushed deeply and she managed to say, "You are lying. There is no way Leonard could know and not tell me. I only told him myself a few weeks ago."

"Indeed, but I am not lying. I was there when Joel told Leonard everything. It was one Saturday night a few weeks ago, and we all sat around the fire and smoked cigars as Joel told Leonard why he abandoned you."

Cigar smoke. It was that evening Leonard came back smelling of cigar smoke.

"I do not believe you, Leonard would have told me as soon as he knew. I know my brother and he simply could not keep something like that from me. You are an evil man to suggest it." She stopped walking and looking round saw that Helen and Mr Yates were no where to be seen.

"You doubt me, but I will not take it personally, however much I am wounded." There was a note of sarcasm in his voice. "If I were treated as you have been, I too would be cynical and twisted. But I tell you the truth. Ask your brother if he knows. You will be able to tell by his reaction when you do. After all, you know him so well and he is so good to you."

Adella could take no more and started to walk back towards the direction where Helen would be. Mr Garner walked leisurely behind her.

At last, she saw them in the distance. Running now, she approached them.

"Adella! We thought we had lost you! Come and walk with Mr Yates and I. He has been telling me all about his latest business ventures. It's very interesting, though I haven't the faintest idea what he is talking about." She gave a small giggle and fluttered her eyelashes at Mr Yates.

Adella flushed, her face contorted with anger. "It was a big mistake coming out today. You should not have made me! I am so annoyed at you Helen, you only think of yourself."

Helen laughed a little and glanced at Mr Yates, said, "Adella, what are you talking about?

"Just that you are the most selfish, self-centred girl I have ever met!"

Adella walked away, then after a few strides started running.

She ran all the way home. Her mind clouded with Mr Garners words. She knew that as soon as Leonard was home she had to confront him about Mr Garner's accusations. Which, of course, she knew were completely false.

**13**

---

Mr Alther stood behind the counter with an array of glass bottles and jars in front. Each with a liquid or powder in it; yellow, white, grey and clear. Each labelled with a name that meant nothing to Flora, but placed in front of them for a purpose. Flora was next to her uncle, patiently waiting for him to speak. She knew him well enough now not to disturb him as he concentrated on the task ahead.

He picked up a bottle that looked empty but as he swirled it round a little, a few drops of liquid could be seen at the bottom. Mr Alther gave a satisfied nod of his head, then leafed through the pages of a book, and ran his finger down the paper. He stopped and tapped a particular part of the page. He had found what he was looking for.

"Right. I am ready now Flora. This is what we need to make - " but just as he was about to continue the door to the shop opened and an elderly woman walked in. A gust of wind went through the shop until she closed the door, clearing the thick air a little. The woman was dressed in black and wore a large bonnet that covered her head. Her face was screwed up, and it matched her ragged clothes.

"Oh no. Here we go again," Mr Alther muttered to Flora. "It's Mrs Smith, or at least that is what she calls herself. Watch and learn with this one."

Flora looked at the woman expectantly, wondering what she wanted.

"Good afternoon. How can I help you?" Mr Alther asked.

The woman looked about the shop to see if there were any other customers. She took a few more steps forward.

"I want -" she paused, and looked about again.

"Yes?" Mr Alther said leaning forward slightly.

"I want -" she lowered her voice to a whisper, "Arsenic."

Mr Alther rolled his eyes.

"Oh yes, we have plenty of that!" Flora said brightly and turned to the shelf to her right.

The woman's eyes flashed victoriously, Mr Alther put his arm out to stop Flora as she reached up, "Sorry Flora. But we do not sell Arsenic to just anybody."

Flora stopped and a confused frown came over her face. Her uncle continued as he stood defiantly, "We need references before we can sell such a dangerous poison."

"Who from?" the woman asked.

"As I have told you before, from a magistrate, doctor or such. Somebody trustworthy who can vouch for it's use."

"I don't know anyone like that."

"Then I'm sorry, you can't have the Arsenic."

"But all I want to do is kill. . .rats. Thousands of them all in my house. Little vicious things scratching away all the time." She made pawing motions with her hands.

"Sorry. I can't help, not without the references." Mr Alther finished off his speech by waving her away with his arms.

"I'll go to Mr Greene's the other side of the city, he'll sell it to me."

"Try if you like. He won't sell it to you either. Thick as thieves are us chemists when it comes to selling poisons."

The woman sniffed. Then she turned and shuffled out leaving behind her another gust of wind as the door opened and closed. After she went, Mr Alther turned to Flora, "A strange one that woman. A bit peculiar in the head. That's the fourth time she's been in asking for Arsenic in as many weeks."

"You had better tell me what else you don't sell to just anybody, so that I don't make a mistake."

"Oh not much else. Mainly the poisons. Don't want to be responsible for a string of murders." Mr Alther laughed a little. "I don't like selling anything like that to strange people. We have a duty to protect the public from those that would poison others."

"Quite right," Flora said.

Mr Alther looked at his niece over his glasses, "use your intuition Flora, look at the person and what they are asking for. If you are in any doubt, just say."

"Now, back to making Tincture of -"

But before he could finish, the door to the shop opened again, and this time, it was Dr Preston who walked in.

"Afternoon everyone," he said and removed his hat. His eyes betrayed a quiet sadness, but he brightened a little when he saw Flora behind the counter.

"Good afternoon Leonard, er I mean Dr Preston." Flora said.

"I have that Opium you wanted Doctor," Mr Alther said.

"Excellent."

Mr Alther reached for a box under the counter and took out a small sealed brown paper bag. "Now pay attention

Flora. Some doctors like to use Opium for their patients pain relief, others prefer Morphine. Dr Preston, could you tell Flora why you prefer Opium?"

"Well, it is quicker really. The effects are more obvious and direct. If the patient is in a lot of pain it gives instant results. Now, if the patient has more of a dull ache, then Morphine is better."

Mr Alther went on, "And of course, they are both as highly addictive as each other, and they must be strictly regulated. Not all doctors tell their patients about the addictive qualities of them though."

Leonard nodded, "Indeed. That is true. I always tell my patients, and I try not to use either unless I have to. But this patient needs something strong."

"Hmm I suspected as much. Not long left to live then eh?"

Leonard shook his head, "Sadly no. Not long left."

Leonard was about to leave, having obtained his Opium, when the door was flung open yet again. It was Helen. She slammed the door shut and straightened her bonnet in an agitated manner.

"Well. I thought she was a nice girl, but I can see I was wrong! Saying such things! How dare she!"

"What ever is wrong, Helen?" Flora asked as Leonard quietly moved to the door for a quick escape. But large man as he was, he could not avoid Helen's notice in the small shop.

She turned to him giving him a shrewish look, "Not so fast Dr Preston!"

He instantly stopped, hand on the door handle. Helen continued, "It is your sister who said those things. I went to see her out of the goodness of my heart, and all I got was an earful of abuse."

"What? From Adella?" Flora said with a small laugh.

"Yes. From Adella. I took her for a walk in Sydney Gardens, and she – she told me I was selfish and that I was self-centred and oh, other things. What do you think of that?" She took out her handkerchief and dabbed her eyes delicately.

Leonard and Flora glanced at each other, but it was Mr Alther who spoke. "Sounds like she spoke the truth. You are selfish and self-centred."

Leonard tried not to laugh.

"Oh really! I thought at least with my own family I would get some sympathy!" Helen cried.

"But surely, if Adella had said these things, there must have been a reason?" Flora said.

Helen gave a dismissive wave of her hand. "Oh I don't know, she disappeared off with Mr Garner and I was with Mr Yates, and then suddenly she ran towards me and that is when she said those mean things. All I did was go walking with her."

At the mention of Mr Garner's name, Leonard started forward a little. Flora saw it, and they locked eyes again.

"When you called for Adella, was Mr Garner with you?" Flora asked.

"Of course not. We saw him in Sydney Gardens and he seemed eager to walk with Adella. Though I don't see why, she is not anyway near as pretty as me and she's ancient; an old maid I'd say! But I think Mr Garner was trying to vex me, he gave me knowing glances before he walked off with Adella, I'm sure of it. Anyway, Mr Yates, is as rich as Mr Garner and probably richer, he works in the Stock Market you know. I think I might prefer him."

"Did she say what Mr Garner said to her?" Leonard asked.

"No."

Leonard looked at Flora, "He must have mentioned or spoke of - " then glancing at Mr Alther and Helen who were listening carefully he stopped. Flora nodded.

Helen stamped her foot, "What, secrets? You two have a secret about Adella? Tell me what it is? I must know! How dare you have secrets without telling me."

"Sorry Helen, I don't know what you are talking about, Dr Preston and I have no secrets," Flora said flatly.

"Hmm," Helen looked back and forth at Leonard and Flora, but neither gave an indication of guilt.

"Well, the next time I see Adella, I will speak to her about it," Leonard said and he put his hat on.

"And get her to apologise!" Helen said.

"Yes, and get her to apologise." Leonard turned to the door, bid his farewell and left.

ADELLA WAS in full slumber when something woke her. The first rays of dawn were starting to seep through the curtains of her bedroom as she came into consciousness. She heard footsteps and knew it was Leonard. However quiet he tried to be, she would always hear him. She was sure he had been out all night with a patient and would be tired, but she must speak to him straight away.

Forcing herself up more quickly than usual, she hastily dressed, worried that Leonard was about to leave the house again. She wasn't about to let him get away. Her soft soled slippers made her steps almost silent as she went downstairs and stood in the kitchen doorway.

Leonard had his back to her, cutting bread and cheese.

"You were out all night then?" she said looking at his dishevelled clothes she remembered he wore the day before.

He turned round quickly. "You should not creep up on me like that. I think you have added a few more grey hairs to my head!"

He turned back, and continued cutting.

"There is ham in the pantry if you want it," she said.

"Thank you." But he did not move, and the quiet noise of his chopping of cheese and bread was all that could be heard.

"I spoke to Mr Garner yesterday. The first time I walk further than the grocer's in weeks, and suddenly there he is." She made an involuntary gesture with her hand.

Leonard turned around, "Yes, Helen mentioned it. What happened, did he upset you? She seemed to think you had spoken out of turn to her. Of course Flora and I didn't believe it. But that doesn't matter for now. What did Mr Garner say to you?"

"He made some wild accusations." She gave a nervous laugh. "He said that Joel told you the reason why he abandoned me."

Adella watched as he flushed, opened his mouth to speak, but said nothing. He looked away.

There was no surer sign of the truth. Her hand flew to her cheek in dismay. "He was not lying. How long have you known?" she whispered.

"A few weeks," he muttered looking at the floor.

"And you never thought to tell me?" Anger seared through her and she stepped forwards. 'You've known all this time and you never thought to tell me?"

"Look Adella, I can't tell you. He made me promise not to say anything."

"He made you promise! You should have made no promise of the kind."

"He told me as a patient tells his doctor, and I cannot betray that trust. And anyway, he only told me on the condition that I said nothing to you."

"Why? Am I your sister or not? Do you not know where your loyalties lie? What he did to me....you know what he did to me and now you know the reason and you will not tell me! These five years I have wanted answers. You have only known him for a few weeks and now he tells you!"

"I cannot. I cannot." He shook his head. "If I do tell you, you will go and see him. I know you will. Besides, he will tell you himself soon enough I assure you."

"But I will not speak to him if you tell me I will not tell another living soul. He would never know."

Leonard paused, then he shook his head once more. "No, even if I was unprofessional enough to tell you, if you knew the truth you would speak to him. You would not be able to stop yourself."

"Then I will tell him Mr Garner told me," she said.

"No. He would know it was me who told you."

Adella sighed deeply, more in the sadness from his betrayal than in anger. "I cannot believe you will not tell me. My own brother."

"I have not liked keeping this from you. Just know that, he is not the man you think he is."

"You are right. Not only has he wounded me five years ago, but he has turned my own brother against me. Is there no end to his evil? He is not the man I thought he was, he is a devil in disguise. Sent from the pit of hell to torment me."

"I – I cannot say anything further. But he is not a devil, he is an honourable man. If you knew the truth, but I cannot say. . ." His voice drifted off and he turned back to the sideboard, his head hung low. 'Damn him, why did Frederick tell her? He is the devil and I do not trust him," he whispered.

"I can see arguing with you is pointless. I know what to do next." She turned and left quickly as silently as she had arrived.

Leonard stood for a few minutes, lost in thought. It was only when he heard the front door that he realised she was no longer in the kitchen and wondered where she might be going at this early hour. He hoped it was to cool her anger, though suddenly he suspected she might be going to Joel. If she was..... he turned and walked to the front door to go after her. Then stopped himself. Perhaps it was a good thing she went to see him, if Joel would tell her himself then he would no longer have to keep the secret. He should have told her exactly where he had been all night, forewarned her, but he didn't have the strength. The death of a patient always left him feeling tired and numb for days afterwards.

## 14

Adella pulled hard at the door bell and stood back. It rang loudly and echoed in her ears. Her eyes scanned the front of the building. Then she checked the window.

Nothing.

She rang the bell again.

*What was taking so long?*

Eventually the door opened. A footman looked her up and down.

"I want to see Mr Polwarth."

"I'm afraid he is not accepting any visitors except on business," he answered in a cool tone.

"Business?" More anger seared through her. She didn't think she could get any more enraged than she already was. But now it reached new heights.

The footman spoke again, "If you would like to leave a card I will pass it onto Mr Polwarth."

"Card? I will not leave a card. I demand to see him!"

She pushed past him into the hall.

"Come back, you are not allowed in," he shouted.

"Where is he?" She reached for the nearest door and flung it open.

"Stop!" the footman said from behind her, but she ignored him and stepped in the room.

The footman grabbed her shoulder, "I'm sorry sir, I tried to stop her. Miss, please come with me. You can't go in there."

She shook herself free and was able to see Joel a short distance away inside the room. He was seated in an arm chair by the fireplace. His face wore a look of surprise. "Get off me!" Then she turned to Joel and shouted, "You are not going to push me aside. You will speak to me whether you like it or not."

Joel stood up and paused momentarily, "Matthew, let her in, and close the door behind you."

The footman did as he was asked, but with a look of disdain directed at Adella. Once it was shut, all she could hear was her own breathlessness.

Their eyes locked. He stood waiting for her to speak and she noticed he grasped the back of the chair.

"I want answers," she said.

He spoke in a quiet resigned tone, "Yes. Yes I know."

"You told my brother everything. Yet you would not tell me," she spat.

"No. But I will tell you now."

It threw her off guard.

"You will?" she said frowning.

"Yes. I will tell you everything. Ask any question. I will answer it."

He indicated to the armchair opposite him and she looked at it. After a moment's thought she sat down still in deep confusion. He sat down too; a safe distance away from her she noticed.

"Why did you tell Leonard your little secret and not me?"

"I didn't think he was so little to be trusted."

"It was not him! He won't breathe a word, it was your friend Mr Garner who told me of the cosy little night you spent together talking about me and how you abandoned me. Yet I am the one who knows nothing of it. Tell me, is this your way of punishing me further?" She shouted now, and her voice became more angry with each word. "If it is, I would very much like to know what I did to deserve all this. Because all I ever remember doing was loving you and giving my heart to you." The last words she spoke were full of anguish. Bitter tears rolled down her cheeks.

At those last words he stood up and came towards her. But before he reached her, something stopped him. She looked up into his face towering above her as he shut his eyes, and drew breath.

"Goodness Adella. You cannot know how it pains me to see you thus."

"I know nothing of your pain. Neither do I care."

"No. I'm sure you don't." He placed himself back on the chair. "Now the moment of truth has come; to tell you everything, I find myself faltering. I have waited so long."

She did not expect that for an answer.

He continued in a soft low tone, "I know I have hurt you. I know I have continued to hurt you. But you see, I had reasons. . ."

Adella stared at him. "Reasons? What possible reasons would make a man behave as you did?"

"Believe me, I do."

She folded her arms and with a defiant tilt of her chin said "Tell me."

He looked down and with a smile said, "I am fearful of your response."

"And you are smiling. This is no time for jest. It is as I thought; you are a miscreant and you take pleasure in my misery."

"No," He said with a firm shake of his head.

"Just stop making excuses and tell me what I want to know. I will be the one to decide if you are scoundrel or not. Tell me at once what I did."

"Good God, it wasn't what you did. I promise you that. It wasn't because I wanted to cause you pain. Nothing could be further from the truth in fact. I loved you. God alone knows how I loved you." He took a deep breath. "I left you. . .I abandoned you, because. . .because of my brothers."

His eyes searched her face. She noticed a vulnerability about them.

"Your brothers?"

"Yes. You see, my father – he was controlling. Before I met you, he tried to force me to marry Cynthia. I didn't want to, so he imprisoned me for two months. When I got out, it was on my 21$^{st}$ birthday and I ran away. First to Scotland with Frederick and then Sidmouth. Where I met you."

"You were imprisoned by your father?" She gave a hollow laugh. "Nobody would do such a thing."

"My father did, in his own house."

"What do your brothers have to do with it?"

"That day I left you, my father had found me. He threatened to lock up my brothers unless I married Cynthia. So I had to choose; you or them."

He paused, still staring at her and she at him. "I had to choose them, can't you see? They were children – Michael, the youngest, was only fourteen. I had to protect them."

In one swift movement he crouched down in front of

her. His nearness did not affect her. She was confused. So completely confused.

He grabbed both her arms with a firm grip. "I loved you. I did not lie to you in any way about my feelings. I wanted to marry you, but I had to give you up. I had no choice. I couldn't let them go through what I did."

"You loved me?" she whispered.

"Yes. I still love you. With all my heart. Adella, I have longed to tell you. But I thought – I thought it best you hated me. I hated myself. It was better you didn't know the despicable truth about my family."

He stared at her, waiting for a reaction.

"If this is true, why did you change your name and lie to me about who you were?"

"I was hiding from my father. I wanted to tell you so many times."

There was still a niggling doubt in her head.

"You are lying now. You only want to seduce me and finish the job you nearly did five years ago. What sort of man locks up his own son? You have made it up. It is a lie."

"No. No I am not. You have no reason to believe me. I have no way to make you realise I speak the truth now. But it is the truth."

She struggled free from his grasp, stood up and stepped back against the wall. Her hand touched the wall as though to ground herself.

"I love you still Adella. I have always loved you. Every day of the last five years, you are the one who owns my heart. It was you I dreamt of. Your face I saw as I shut my eyes at night."

He walked slowly towards her and stopped just a few inches away.

"No – this is no explanation. Why did you just not tell me. You are a liar."

"I am not. Not any more." He gave a small laugh, "You cannot realise how many times I wanted to tell you."

He came closer. His lips almost touching hers.

"I love you Adella."

She couldn't breathe. He was so close. She was trapped but powerless to move.

*What if it were true?*

He pulled her to him and kissed her softly on the lips. Tentatively at first, then with more force and passion as he seemed to gain confidence. She didn't move at first, then what seemed like both an age and an instant, she realised what he was doing. She tried to pull away, but he moved his arms around her waist and pulled her closer, encasing her in a strong grip.

She struggled again, and he released her from the kiss.

She whispered, "Please, let me go."

He let his arms drop but stayed close to her.

"It is your turn to torment me now." He said in a deep low tone. "You cannot realise what feelings you stir in me."

"Please - " she tried to continue, but he interrupted her.

"I love you and now that I am a free man, I must ask you. Marry me. This time, we can be wed in a mater of days – as soon as the death certificate is written."

She moved away from him, "A free man? Has Cynthia died?"

"Yes, a few hours ago."

"Your wife has been dead a few hours and you are proposing to me." She paused, then said in a low tone. "It is disgusting."

"But - "

"It revolts me."

"I never loved Cynthia. I was forced to marry her, against my will, against everything that I was. I loved you and now I am free, I have to take this chance, and take it quickly."

"Why? If you truly love me then you would court me properly and honourably."

He sighed, "I wish that I could. But my father is going to try and make me marry a wealthy widow. Michael is still not 21. He needs protection – as does my daughter. But this time I am not so young and easily coerced. Marry me Adella. I am going to stand up to my father and be rid of him forever. I have some money of my own, we won't be rich but you'll not want for anything. Certainly we'll have more than a tutor's salary." He gave a wry smile.

Confusion racked her mind. She wasn't sure what she felt. To finally know the truth after all this time. Then to suddenly be asked again to marry him. She rubbed her temples, but it was in vain.

"I need time to think." She said eventually. "I can't switch my feelings on and off. It's been five years. If what you say is true, do you expect me to fall at your feet? It has taken me too long to get over what you did. While you say you have loved me, I have hated you."

"You believe me then?"

"Yes," she said quietly. "Yes, I suppose I do. Though I am sure I will regret it."

"You will think about my proposal?"

"If you are determined to stand up to your father, marrying me will make no difference."

"It will to me."

She wanted the words to be true, but there was a nagging doubt. She needed space, and time to think. She needed to get away from him, but for a strange reason couldn't muster the strength to go.

"I need more time to think this through."

He nodded. 'I will visit you tomorrow and we can talk again."

"No, I do not want you to call. Not yet. Not until your wife is at least buried."

He sighed, "Then after the funeral I will see you again."

She nodded and moved towards the door.

"At least allow me to escort you home."

"No, I do not wish for it. I want to be alone."

"You always were too independent. I will not give you up again Adella," he said.

She did not reply, just slipped out of the door and to freedom.

**15**

———

Adella closed the front door and slumped against it. She was numb and as the seconds ticked by she knew she had to act. How did she get home? She didn't remember a single moment of the walk back. But yet, here she was.

She slowly made her way upstairs and went quietly past Leonard's room. The door was shut and she surmised that he was asleep after his long night. It was what she had hoped for. She could not face speaking to anyone.

She curled up on the bed, her mind a turmoil. She wasn't sure what affected her the most. The fact that he still loved her or that he had given her up.

Yet now he wanted to marry her again and she wasn't sure what she wanted.

Could she forgive him? After all this time to know why he abandoned her , denied her. It was an anti-climax. Damn the day she ever met him.

The worst of it was that he was going to try and hide his brother and daughter for her. She should feel flattered he loved her so much he was willing to go to such lengths. But she only felt guilt. Guilt because he was using her as an excuse.

All those wasted years. All those years of thinking she did something to make him leave and yet it was not her fault.

Sometime later she heard the afternoon post arrive. It was unusual for letters to arrive so late, but she made her way down in a haze. The writing on the envelope she immediately recognised; her fathers.

Quickly she opened the letter. Her mother was ill and could Leonard spare her for a few weeks while she recovered? Her fathers words did not alarm her as they normally would. She was strangely numb to her mother being ill. She would go of course. Family duty came above all else.

Family duty.

It was what drove Joel away from her, and it drove her away from him now.

She went back upstairs and to the washstand, poured out some water and washed her face. She wanted to remove any trace of Joel Polwarth that still lingered on her lips. She pressed the cloth hard on her mouth to wipe away the feeling left from his harsh stubble. Then she gathered a few clothes and other belongings together, and packed them in a large carpet bag.

Before she left, she sat at her desk and wrote three separate letters in a swift hand. Then, from the bottom drawer of her bedside table took out a small parcel wrapped in cloth. Pulling back the wrapping to reveal a small leather-bound volume, 'Alroy by Benjamin Disraeli' was the title on the spine. The book fell open to where a neatly folded handkerchief marked the page. The handkerchief was still white and clean considering the amount time it was hidden. It was more than five years since the night before Joel left Sidmouth with his father.

Adella recalled the night she had felt her arm being shaken gently, and someone quietly calling her name.

"Adella. Adella."

She opened her eyes slowly, "I'm sorry Joseph. Did I fall asleep?"

"Yes," he smiled, 'but it has been a long day. And you will insist on embroidering my initials on all of my handkerchiefs. Even though it is not necessary."

"I have not finished this one yet, look only the 'J' is done." She held up the cloth, "I will have to do the 'W' tomorrow."

He took hold of her hand, slid it into hers, and gently squeezed it. "Do you not find Alroy an interesting story?" he asked.

"Not really. You do?" She took the book out of his hands, neatly folded the handkerchief and placed it between its pages.

"Yes. I think it an underrated novel."

"Well, we cannot expect to like all the same things, and agree on everything. When we are married, I do not think we will be one of those couples that always argue. But at the same time, I think it would be very dull if we agreed on everything."

He smiled again and looked away, but not before Adella noticed a distant expression in his eyes, one that she was no stranger to now. Then, wishing him to turn back she said, 'I suppose I ought to go to bed. I have a busy day tomorrow. I am taking Mary out for a long walk. She seems to have a lot of excess energy these last few days. I think it is all the sugar her mother keeps feeding her."

He turned to face her, his brows furrowed, "You should

tell her to stop giving her sweets, it is not her who has to deal with the consequences. I hate to see you treated in such a way."

Adella smiled, "Your concern for me is very touching."

"Good, because I mean it all. Once we are married, you will not have to put up with it any longer. We will have our own children to look after, not other peoples."

"You will still have other peoples children to teach," Adella said.

"True."

Adella yawned, "I must go to bed now."

"Very well," he said, "but I will not let you go until you have kissed me to apologise for falling asleep while I was reading to you."

"I will have to fall asleep more often. . ." But any further words were stopped short by his kiss.

But that was over five years ago. Adella stroked the embroidered 'J' with her thumb. She never did add the 'W'.

With a deep sigh, she placed the handkerchief back inside the book and quickly covered it up again with the cloth. After placing it inside her bag she picked up the letters, took one final look around her room and closed the door behind her.

As she walked past Leonard's door again, she silently slid a letter underneath it then paused, arrested by a pang of guilt. But she managed to move, and walked downstairs. Any regrets were snuffed out by the memory of his refusal to tell her what she wanted to know. She went quickly and quietly from room to room in search of anything she needed to take with her, determined now that nothing would stop her leaving. Before a few minutes were up she was out of the house and on her way. She stopped briefly at the post office, then hurried on to the train station. She paced the platform, back and forth several times as it filled up with other passengers. Half of Bath were travelling to London it seemed.

She did not have to wait long for a train. There was one that left fifteen minutes after she bought her ticket, such luck she had not seen for so long. After she boarded the second class carriage the train stood annoyingly at the station for longer than she wished. There was a worry in the back of her mind that Leonard may have woken and come after her. She was determined to go even if he did turn up – indeed he could not argue with her, she was going to nurse their mother. Only when she heard the whistle and the train started to move away did she relax.

LEONARD RANG the door bell of South Parade and was directly shown up to the drawing room. He was breathless as he walked in. Joel and Frederick were seated in armchairs.

He was greeted warmly by both of them.

"Did Adella come and see you this morning?" Leonard asked.

Joel nodded.

"I knew it! What happened? Because she has left Bath! All I have is a short note telling me where she has gone."

"Gone?" Joel exclaimed. "But I never expected her to leave. She said she needed space. But are you sure she has left?"

"What did you say to her?"

"I told her everything. I asked her to marry me. She said she would think about it. Damn it. How can she run away?"

"She has only done what you did to her," Leonard said in a flat tone.

"Yes. You are right. But she's really gone?" Joel said, his expression stilled and grew serious. "Fled Bath because of me?"

"She has gone to Aylesbury to our mother and father."

Leonard handed him the note and Joel devoured its contents in one glance.

*L,*

*I have gone to Mother and Father. While you were asleep, a letter from father arrived asking me to nurse mother for a short while. Do not worry yourself, father says she is recovering but needs assistance. Besides, I need to get away from Bath and from Joel. I will write when I get there so you know I arrived safely.*

*A*

FREDERICK TOOK the letter from Joel and quickly read it saying in a sarcastic tone, "She doesn't give much away does she?"

Leonard snatched the letter back. "No. But she is angry with me and she would not have left Bath so quickly and without speaking to me. She knows you told me everything."

"Ahh yes, that would be my fault. It slipped out when I saw her yesterday," Frederick said.

Leonard was incredulous, "Slipped out! How can something like that just slip out! You told her deliberately didn't you? You could not tell her, so you told her I knew instead!" he shouted.

Frederick waved his arm dismissively. "What is done is done. Whether intentional or not."

Leonard struggled to find the words, "By my honour I didn't breathe a word, though I was a fool not to." He stood shaking his head for a moment or two, and gathered his tortured thoughts. "She has never hurt anyone in her life, the sweetest, loveliest girl, my own sister."

Frederick was now a little taken aback by Leonard's anger too, though it amused him somewhat before. Any mirth he felt quickly disappeared when Leonard turned to him. "And you, you are no help either. You told Adella I knew Joel's secret and whether intentional or not."

Both men stood watching Leonard's outburst.

Joel spoke quietly, "As soon as the funeral is over with we will leave Bath, so you need not worry on that account. I meant what I said before. I want her back, and I will not rest until I have her."

They were interrupted by a knock at the door. A servant entered, "The evening post sir," and he handed over a small parcel.

"Thank you," Joel said taking it and placed it on the side. He glanced at the package, then looked away, but he quickly snatched it up again.

Leonard saw it too. "That's Adella's handwriting."

They all watched as he opened it. He ripped the brown paper quickly, and revealed a book. Joel turned it over in his hand and pulled out a handkerchief held within its pages. There was a letter with it too. He opened the paper and read it eagerly.

Joel,

*I am returning these items to their rightful owner. I always wanted to return them to you and must do so in order to keep my conscience clear. When you read this, I will be far from Bath. I am returning to my mother and fathers house having neglected them long enough. My mother is ill and needs me.*

*The simple truth is that I will not be rushed into a marriage with someone I know so little. I knew you five years ago, but I have changed so remarkably since then. I think you must have too.*

*If you still love me as you say you do, then you will wait for me to come to terms with all I have learned today. I cannot say when that will be.*

*If you are determined not to marry the widow you must refuse because of your own wish to be free from your fathers influence and not entangle me in your escape. I want to remain free to decide my own destiny without being party to your reasons.*

*I do not know when we will meet again. I think it best at least that you do not attempt to see me until your mourning period is over. Six months is not such a long time.*

ADELLA MAXWELL

HE CLUTCHED the items close to his chest, closed his eyes and muttered inaudibly, "I will finish reading this to you, I promise."

"What are they?" Leonard asked.

Joel looked up, he held onto them possessively. "It is the book we were reading together the last night we were together in Sidmouth."

"And the handkerchief?"

"She was sewing my initials on it that same last night."

Leonard looked enquiringly at them, but Joel still would not give them up, even for the briefest examination.

There was a slight tremble in his voice, "I did not realise she still had these. She's kept them all this time."

"But why return them? What does she say in the letter?" Frederick asked peering over at the paper in Joel's hand.

Joel handed it to Frederick and then to Leonard.

"She is determined to keep you on tenterhooks," Frederick commented.

"Yes, but can you blame her?" Leonard asked.

"No, I can't blame her." Joel said. "She has every right to act in her own interest. However much I hate it."

Leonard left South Parade not long afterwards and instinctively walked towards the Alther's. Adella deserved better, from him at least. But it was not the fact that she left Bath, Flora was helping him now, and that gladdened him a little. No, he felt bitter regret he could not speak to her before she fled. He would go home, and once there write a long letter to her to try and persuade her to return to Bath as soon as their mother was better. Yes, a break was what she needed, and after a few weeks, Joel and Frederick would be gone, she could return and life could get back to normal.

When he got to the Alther's, he found the place closed as expected. The private bell was not answered either and he rang it several times. So he walked onwards towards his home, and though the light started to fade now, saw in the distance the figure of a woman he instantly recognised.

When they met he smiled, "Good evening Flora."

Simply seeing her face made everything better, no matter how bad things were.

Flora's face wore a stern frown. "Good evening Dr Preston. I have just been to call on you. My Uncle was with me, but has called on a friend momentarily." She indicated to the house behind them. She continued, "I received a letter from Adella in the evening post and it has troubled me greatly."

She took out a letter from her pocket and handed it to Leonard. He took it eagerly. It said very much the same as his own letter, except that she asked Flora to look after Leonard.

Leonard sighed, and handed back the letter. "She wrote to me as well, and told me she was going home," he said.

"But what else happened today that has made her leave in such haste? She said 'other reasons than my mothers illness drive me from Bath so quickly.'"

Leonard offered Flora his arm and she instinctively took it. "Come and walk with me a little until your Uncle has finished his visit and I will tell you."

It was a few minutes later that Mr Alther appeared and looked up and down the street saw his niece and Dr Preston. He approached them and they instantly stopped talking, though not before he heard Flora say "I am sure you did what was best."

"Keeping secrets again?" Mr Alther asked with a small laugh.

"No," Flora said, "We are sorting out what to do now that Adella has left Bath."

Mr Alther instantly frowned. "I was sad to hear she has left. I will miss her in the shop. But you must both try and persuade her to come back soon. Who will keep house for you now Dr Preston?"

Leonard and Flora looked at each other, and Flora tentatively spoke, "Well Uncle, in her letter, Adella has asked that I look after Leonard for her. Of course, I cannot keep house for him, it would not be proper, but do you think he could eat his supper with us, for Adella's peace of mind?"

Mr Alther glanced at them both, "Of course, not only for Adella's sake, but Mrs Alther would like the conversation too. She is always saying 'Dr Preston this' and 'Dr Preston that'. You are always welcome in our house."

Leonard gave a small laugh, "Thank you. But I insist on paying you for my food, I would not want you to be out of pocket due to an extra mouth to feed."

"Very well, but Flora, you will have to ask Dr Preston what his favourite dishes are so you can cook them for him."

"I wouldn't want to put you to any trouble Flora," Leonard said looking down at her.

Flora dropped her eyes from his gaze, "It is no trouble I assure you. It would be a pleasure."

They parted a few minutes later, and Leonard went home to write his letter to Adella. He posted it first thing the following morning, along with another letter to his mother, telling her to expect Adella. Though he knew she would most likely arrive before it.

Two days later he received the confirmation he hoped for, that she was home. Her letter was short and to the point like her last, it stated she arrived safely but nothing more.

So this was the news that reached Leonard the morning of Mrs Polwarth's funeral. He hoped the ceremony would be over with quickly. Through his work, he often attended funerals, each one a reminder that he wasn't always able to help the ravages of illness. Without Adella at home as support, attending a funeral was not a happy prospect. He thoughts immediately turned to another face, one that could lift his spirits. He would stop off at the Alther's on the way home, on some pretext.

As he approached the small chapel on Wells Road, he saw the mourners already gathered outside. They were all men, which was no surprise as female gentry rarely attended funerals. He recognised Joel and Frederick amongst the group and as he approached, Joel saw him and offered him his hand. Leonard instinctively shook it despite his former anger. He came out of duty to his deceased patient, and would play the part.

As Leonard looked at Joel's face, he noticed a deep tiredness wrought across it, despite this, he seemed on edge. "Thank you for coming today, Dr Preston. It means much to me that you would attend, you looked after Cynthia so carefully. I am much obliged to you."

Leonard nodded, and was about to walk into the church, when a gentleman next to Joel turned around.

Joel cleared his throat, stood aside a little and said, "Allow me to introduce my father; Mr Michael Polwarth," then, to his father he said, 'This is Doctor Preston, he looked after Cynthia here in Bath."

Leonard gaped and stared at the older man's hand held out to shake his. It was a well groomed wrinkled hand, and Leonard momentarily forgot himself, before he forced a mental shake and briefly shook it. After he did it, he wished he hadn't. This man, now stood in front of him, who looked like a harmless old gentleman was the cause of his sister's unhappiness for such a long time. Evil came in all guises, and this was the ultimate wolf in sheep's clothing.

Joel's father wore a questioning frown as he studied Leonard's face. Then his countenance changed, a smile of sorts played on his lips, until he spoke in a bright unassuming tone, "I would like to thank you from the bottom of my heart for looking after my dear departed daughter-in-law. I was exceedingly fond of her, and indeed always approved of my son's choice in marrying her. It is such a shame she has passed on, but at least Joel has a daughter to remember her by."

Leonard stood incredulous. Such lies, such insolence! But he could say nothing and simply met his piercing blue eyes with an equal steady gaze, challenging him. Mentally telling him with one look that he knew the truth. He hoped the old man could read it.

"It was my duty, and I am glad to have helped give her comfort in her last few weeks on this earth. I would do it for any of my patients."

They were interrupted from further conversation by Frederick, "Ah, Doctor Preston, I am glad you have arrived early. I was hoping to speak to you -"

Frederick pulled Leonard aside, his brief conversation with Joel's father over with. Leonard looked back at the elder Mr Polwarth again, as Frederick dropped his voice to a whisper. "What do you think of the man himself then? Surprised he is here eh?" He placed his hands in his waistcoat pockets. "I didn't think he'd come all this way, but he has surprised me again. Always out to shake people up that one. I'm sure he's up to no good here in Bath."

"But he has just come for the funeral has he not?" Leonard said.

"Hmph, probably, but he may well have come to keep an eye on Joel now he is single again."

They stood together silently for a moment, until Leonard tentatively spoke, "Do you think, he will make Joel marry again in six months time?"

"He can try, but Joel is finally going to stand up to his father. I know you were angry at him the other day, but Adella makes no difference."

"What do you mean?"

"It made Joel even more determined to get what he really wanted in life. And given a choice between his tyrant father and Adella, he's chosen Adella of course. Best not say anything to his father though. Else she'll be in danger."

At that, the carriage carrying the coffin pulled up and they were interrupted from further conversation as they quietly entered the chapel.

Leonard could not stop himself from glancing at the elder Mr Polwarth all the way through the service. More especially, when he saw the man nodded in agreement at various parts of the eulogy, given by Cynthia's brother where Cynthia was described as being loved by her husbands family, and having been lucky in her marriage.

He couldn't stomach the wake, and made his way, as he promised himself earlier, to see the only face that could lift his spirits.

## 16

________

The day after Cynthia's funeral saw Joel and Frederick still in South Parade. The house was morose and quiet, marking the period of mourning, and they found it increasingly difficult to speak alone. Not only were Cynthia's father and brothers there, but Joel's own father was also staying. Joel had previously tried to persuade him to stay in an hotel, but he would have none of it.

His father never got in the way, in fact he was the least troublesome guest anyone could wish for. But whenever he was in the same house, Joel got the strangest impression that he was listening to his conversation even when he wasn't in the room.

Joel was still set on hiding his youngest brother, and was not sure how long he would have before his father started to demand that he married again. He knew that he had at least six months, a suitable though not excessive mourning period. But there was the chance that his father would throw that aside for his own means. If mourning rules for men were the same as for women, then he would have two and a half years of no worry. But men were expected to get on with life immediately, to show they could handle such a loss quickly and to marry again especially if they were wealthy and needed a male heir.

And what of Cynthia's family? If he married within a year of her death, they would take great offence, but he was willing to throw away all convention, all propriety for the one thing he wanted more than anything else; Adella. His father he knew would have no scruple with the feelings of Cynthia's family. They served their purpose and he doubted whether, other than to see their granddaughter, they would be seen again by any of his family. It was a sad fact that though he never wanted to marry Cynthia, her legacy through Sarah was all that remained of the woman. He tried desperately to bury his indifferent feelings over her death; guilt that he did not really care that much about her, hated her at times and was glad to be free. It didn't help either, that when he thought about Adella, he smiled that he was free to marry her.

Joel and Frederick walked out alone every morning following the funeral and one such day as they went out, they planned to leave Bath that evening.

"We must pack and leave quickly if my father is not to know about it before we go. I can't stand to be around him any longer than I have to be. It will be difficult, and I wonder if any of the servants will need a bribe to keep quiet," Joel said.

Frederick studied Joel's face. It was set with a frown, "But surely he could have no qualm with you leaving Bath?"

"I do not presume to have any idea what he wants for me, and I am done with guessing. I cannot stay near him any longer. His presence overpowers me still."

"Then leave all the orders to the servants to me. You

need not worry, I will make sure he does not know. Though I cannot see any reason why he would do anything to try and stop you leaving Bath."

"Perhaps not. But I would rather not risk it. Who knows what he might have planned?"

Upon their return to the house, Joel felt more optimistic about leaving. His father was out and they quickly gave instructions for the packing. Sarah was to go with them, as well as her nurse.

At seven o'clock, Joel packed his own final items in his room, when there was a knock at the door. His heart thumped hard. It might be his father. With a croak in his voice he managed to say, "Come in."

The door took an age to open.

It was the footman.

Joel gave a small sigh of relief.

"Begging your pardon sir, but the carriage is waiting and Mr Garner is asking if you are ready."

"Tell him I will be a few minutes."

The footman left, and Joel slumped on the bed, his head in his hands. He had to master his anxiety. He was determined that nothing should stop him leaving Bath. Confrontation with his father or not, he was going. He stood up and went downstairs.

Cynthia's father and brothers were in the sitting room with Frederick.

"We are a little shocked at your sudden departure," his father-in-law said, "but I suppose you want to be alone to grieve. . ." The old man smiled sympathetically. He never disliked the man, except that he had been one of the many people who approved and pushed him into marriage with Cynthia.

"Thank you, yes, I would prefer to leave Bath immediately," Joel said.

"I hope you were not leaving without bidding your own father farewell?" said a cool voice from the doorway.

Joel's heart almost stopped as he instantly recognised who had spoken.

His father.

He turned around, flushed and tried to hide the surprise in his voice, "Of course not. Frederick and I are going away for a time," Joel said.

"So it seems." His father stood in the doorway with a hard piercing look in his eyes.

"Yes, well goodbye father. I thank you for attending Cynthia's funeral," Joel said as he stood up. But as he approached the doorway, his father made no move to get out of the way.

"Goodbye father," he said more loudly.

Their eyes met for a moment; Joel's in stern determination, as he desperately tried not to betray his growing fear, and his father's in cool detachment.

His father stepped out of the way. But as Joel went to pass by, his father grabbed his arm. It was a strong grip, and as he looked down at the hand he heard his whispering cold voice say, "You had better return home by the Midsummer Fair."

Joel nodded slowly, then finally after a few moments, his father loosened his grip and let go.

He was unable to think of much else than his father's last words as the carriage pulled away. He looked out of the window to watch the house disappear, and only sat back when he could no longer see it. Relief washed through him. He was away and free. For now. But before they headed for

Scotland there was one more call to make; Horse Shoe Walk.

He hoped that Dr Preston would be at home, though he had doubts that he might be, he was sure the doctor may be at an appointment. As the carriage stopped a few minutes later, Frederick leaned out of the window, and said, "It is the one on the left, the house with the dark green door."

"You are not coming in?" Joel asked.

"No. I think you best go alone," he replied,"But give Dr Preston my best regards."

Joel stepped out and looked up at the building, and rang the bell. Two stories high, with a slate roof, one of many terraces in the area built smaller for the middle classes. The door was soon answered by Dr Preston.

"May I come in?" he asked.

"Of course. What a surprise."

Joel stepped in as Leonard looked out and saw the carriage waiting outside.

"You are leaving Bath?" Leonard said after he closed the door.

"Yes, how did you know?"

"Your carriage is loaded with luggage."

"Ah!" Joel relaxed. For a moment he thought word about his departure reached Dr Preston.

"Please come through," Leonard led Joel through to the sitting room.

"I am sorry you find it somewhat untidy. Without Adella here to keep house for me, I am afraid I am liable to let it slip into disarray."

Joel replied in a serious tone, "I am leaving Bath and I have come to pay your bill."

Leonard raised his eye brows, "Yes, I suppose you have.

But I have not prepared it yet. So I should forward it onto you?"

"That will not be possible, I am going away for several months, and I cannot divulge where that will be. So I would be obliged if you would prepare the bill now. I can wait."

"Certainly," Leonard said. He stood up and opened the bureau.

He went through his papers, "Why are you going away? Are you hiding from your father?"

"In a sense yes. I still intend to hide my brother, and Frederick and I will be planning what to do," he said, 'so, I hope that in time. . ." his voice drifted off.

Leonard looked up, "You hope that in time you can marry Adella?"

"Yes."

Leonard sighed. "You better make sure she is not under any threat from your father. I will not have her in danger."

"I promise you, that will never happen."

Leonard's shoulders relaxed and he continued writing the bill. "I am sure you would not. . .intentionally. But I do rather wonder whether she would have you now at all, even though she knows the truth."

Joel stood up and chose not to hear Leonard's words. Such talk was not to be contemplated. Looking around the room, he tried to take in what he could of what Adella once called her home. It wasn't an unpleasant room, much plainer and smaller than what he was used to, he expected the furniture to be tatty and worn, but it wasn't too bad.

Leonard saw him looking round, "If you are wondering; Adella did not particularly like this room. She thought it a little poky."

"It is comfortable enough though," Joel said. "Much better than the rooms we had at Brayfern together."

"Indeed. It will never be grand, but it is sufficient."

"Have you heard from her?" Joel asked.

"No. Though our mother says she is well enough."

Joel said nothing, but went on walking slowly around the room, he picked up an object he found on the table and turned it over in his hand.

"Is this is one of Adella's hair combs?" he said and ran his fingers over the intricate flowers carved into the wood.

"Yes. She only took with her a few basic items. I haven't sent her other clothes and such because I'm hoping she'll come back to Bath now that you are leaving."

"Did she wear it much?"

"Sometimes. On more formal occasions I think."

A few minutes later, and Leonard completed the bill. He handed it to Joel, who, without questioning it, looked at the total and left a modest pile of bank notes on the table.

"I must thank you again for all your assistance with Cynthia,"

"I was just doing my job."

"But that does not lessen what you did," Joel said.

Joel left immediately afterwards and it wasn't until a few days later that Leonard noticed the hair comb had gone.

Adella sat herself in the window seat of the sitting room in her parents' house and looked out at the unceasing rain outside. It was now two weeks since she arrived back to her parents and long enough for her to grow weary of having little occupation. Her mother did not need much nursing now. The house, with three bedrooms, was modest and set amongst a row of town houses built for artisans and clerks, twenty years before. Adella grew up there, and little was changed in the street since the time she ran up and down playing with the other children.

She missed Bath and her brother, despite his sins, but she missed being useful the most; having a daily purpose. The daily chores of keeping house for her brother had been at times tiresome, but now, the lack of physical exercise made it harder for her to get to sleep at night. She did help with the daily tasks, but many of the chores were now done by the scullery maid, employed since her father's promotion a few years ago. Most of the time, there was something domestic to keep her occupied, but there was always several times during the day when she was left to dwell on her own thoughts.

Her mother entered the room and sat down in a nearby chair. "I am feeling much better today. I think getting up out of bed has done me a great deal of good."

"I'm glad."

"*You* might feel better if you went out and saw a few of your old friends," she said.

Adella turned and looked at her. "I saw Mary Matthews yesterday and all she did was talk about being married, and about the single men in town who might have me. She was so condescending. Made out that I would be lucky if any man would have me! All she did was talk about how wonderful being married was, then, a few minutes later all she did was complain about her husband. I do not think I could bear to sit through it all again. Why do married women look down on single women?"

Her mother smiled. "I am not willing to pursue *that* argument, dearest. You will get more angry if I tell you why. How about visiting Reverend Buyers and seeing what you can do to help the church?"

Adella sighed. "Perhaps."

"You must try and get out. Sitting about here brooding will not help in the long run. Idleness is not a worthy attribute."

"I know mother. I promise, I will try and make myself more useful."

Over the last few weeks, her thoughts had been full of Joel. She did not regret leaving Bath. She had questions though, questions about his family and his father. If it was true that he had been locked up as he said then it was truly terrible. What he must have suffered! She thought back to when they first met; when they were governess and tutor; his pensive nature. The distant look in his eyes. He had changed his name to hide from his father. What pains he must have suffered.

One thing was certain. They had both changed and five years apart could not be ignored. She thought she knew him then, but she knew nothing of his past. She knew nothing of his struggle with his father. For that alone she must be careful. She would not throw herself away in marriage even to the man she once loved without sober thought. Did she love him now? Could she love a man who chose his brothers over her however desperate the circumstances?

She stood up, suddenly frustrated at turmoil in her mind. A walk, rain or no, was what she needed.

The fresh air helped her clear her mind a little, though the rain was persistent, it was refreshing to be outside. She looked around at the houses and streets. She was haunted by the memory of the last time she returned home, five years before when she had been disgraced. Her parents hid the truth. They had told friends and neighbours that she returned from Sidmouth because the child had been sent to school. Adella was not sure if they all believed the story.

As she walked, she held her umbrella carelessly so that

the droplets fell on her face, but she did not notice. She walked on in any direction her whim took her; to several places through the town, past shops, to the church, until she returned home, emotionally and physically exhausted.

The next morning, as Adella readied herself to call on Reverend Buyers, a letter arrived from Flora. It was the third one she received in as many weeks, and she was both dreading and longing to read it.

Instead of sitting down and reading it there and then, she took it out with her to find a quiet spot. She found the perfect place as she approached the rectory. She passed through the church grounds and stopped on one of the wooden benches near the entrance. Looking around, the grass was greener from the previous day's rain, and with only a faint sound of birds and the occasional distant carriage, it was the perfect spot. There was no one else around, so she opened the letter, her eyes slowly taking in its contents.

*My dearest Adella,*

*I trust this letter finds you in good health. I was so very glad to receive your letter the other day and I was eager to reply, except that I have had so much to do lately I have little time to myself.*

*Not that I am unhappy. I know that I am fulfilling only one part of your duties, and that you would be able to complete them much better than me. I am only a small help compared to you, but I think Dr Preston is happy with my efforts.*

*He still misses you greatly. He is sanguine, I cannot deny it and I know he would rather have you here in Bath than miles away. But, oh dear, I have written too much, I do not wish to pressure you into feeling guilty, sometimes when I write I get carried away. Forgive me.*

*Be assured that I am still doing as you ask and am looking after your brother. He dines with us now every evening. Helen thinks it is because he loves her! I laugh, though I would not presume to know your brother's feelings, Helen still has enough conceitedness to believe that she can win any man she lays her cap at! I am not sure Dr Preston will bend to pick it up.*

*Besides that news, I am still having lessons with Uncle in the shop. Everyday I learn something new, though I know I still have much more knowledge to acquire, Uncle is patient with me. I must say, I do wish I visited them before, though I dare say mother could not have spared me. Helen was a bit of a handful as a child.*

*Now, I have been delaying, I know you asked in your last letter about my disappointment with a man a few years ago. I suppose I must tell all. For though you suffer now and have suffered for five years, I too have been greatly hurt in the past. Do you mind if I do not name him? I think it will help if I do not write his name. . .*

ADELLA GAVE A LONG SIGH, she took her gaze away from the paper, and for some minutes prepared herself to learn the details of something she feared would be similar to her own sorry tale. She continued reading.

WHEN I WAS TWENTY, *I received a proposal of marriage from a young man I had known pretty much all my life. We grew up near each other, and he was an apprentice Cooper. I accepted him straight away. There was no doubt in my mind that I loved him very much. But when I told my parents, they were unhappy and would not consent to the match. Though they knew him to be both respectable and trustworthy, they felt that we were both too young, and that he did not have sufficient money to support a family. So, they told me to call off the engagement and, if in a few years' time he was more prosperous, then they would agree. Of course, it was not long before I was 21 and I could choose my own road. But after careful consideration and despite my own disappointment, I agreed to my parents' wishes. I did not want us both to live in poverty and forever to be reliant on our parents.*

*He was disappointed, but accepted the decision after a short while. Shortly afterwards, he applied for and was taken on at an Engineering company in a nearby town and moved out of the village to be near his new employer. At first, I saw him often ; every two or three weeks on a Sunday afternoon. But gradually, his visits became less frequent and we lost contact for nearly two years.*

*I did not expect to see him again, and though I knew I still had deep love for him, I resigned myself that I must give him up in my mind. I thought I had.*

*However, after those two years, I happened upon him when I visited the town where he lived. We were cordial to each other and the chance meeting was not as embarrassing for us as I thought it might be. He inquired after my health and seemed genuinely concerned for me. I felt instantly that the flame of attraction was again ignited for both of us.*

*That following Sunday, he called on the family again and stayed a few hours. His visit was repeated the next Sunday, and for the first time I began to feel he wished to renew his addresses. He was certainly attentive. He was doing well in the engineering company and was certainly earning enough money to support a family. In short, he was prospering.*

*However, after about a month of his visits, they abruptly stopped. As the weeks carried on, there was no sign of him, so I wrote to him to inquire if he was well. In truth to try and see if he really did reciprocate the sentiments I still held onto and why he stopped visiting.*

*I received a reply a few days later. He told me that, though his sentiments were what they were all those years before, he regretted to inform me that he was now engaged and shortly to be married to a woman who was shortly to bear his child.*

ADELLA'S HAND flew to cover her mouth. She re-read the last paragraph several times, "so, I am not the only woman to have been put upon by a man!" she said out loud. "But poor Flora. What she has had to bear!" Adella read on.

YOU CAN IMAGINE *the anguish I felt. Not only to learn that my love was returned, but that we could never marry and he behaved in such a way to a woman out of wedlock. It pains me indeed now to think of it. I thought him not the kind of man to lose control of such base urges. But it was so and I have learned to accept it.*

*I did reply to him, to acknowledge that I received his letter and to wish him well. Though it pained me to be so distant and aloof in the letter, I could not speak of my sentiments. That would have been wrong, he was engaged.*

*I hear of him from time to time. He has several children now I believe, and is still employed by the same engineering company. He has been promoted several times. But I have not seen him since his last visit that time and it is just as well. I have long given up any feelings for him. I was consumed by shock and malice towards him for many years. I think it would have been better that he had not told me that he loved me. That way I could have borne the separation more.*

*So, that is my story. I hope you are not too depressed after reading it. I must assure you that though I still look upon what happened with a certain amount of acrimony, I have been looking forwards, not back. My life is so full now, and ever since I arrived in Bath I have not regretted that I am still a spinster (though Helen reminds me of it frequently!).*

*She still continues to pursue any man who is slightly rich, and I am a little afraid that she may be indiscreet with her affections in the hope that she will trap a man. But I can only hope that my Uncle and Aunt will make her see sense and get her to behave properly.*

*But for now, I must end my letter, as Helen has just come in to tell me that your brother has an errand for me.*

*I wish you well.*

*Yours*

*Flora Alther*


ADELLA PLACED the letter back in her pocket, though curiously she couldn't let go of the paper. She felt deeply for Flora, it was a sad tale indeed and her heart went out to her. If only she knew this when they were in Bath together! Both of them suffered and continued to suffer because of a man. Was there a man alive who was not a deceiver? Adella doubted it, until she was reminded of her own father and brother; they at least were honourable. But no, Leonard was not any more.

One thing was certain, Adella was determined to reply to Flora as quickly as possible, so she knew she had a friend who understood her suffering.

She stood up and continued her walk to see Reverend Buyers with hopes that a married clergyman of fifty could improve her opinion of the other sex.

When Adella arrived home, she let herself in and busied herself in the kitchen after checking on her mother. After tea she sat quietly reading and was roused from her book by the sound of a carriage pulling up outside the house. She peeked through the curtains and saw a fine set of livery. The carriage door opened and a gentleman stepped out. He looked up at the house, then at the door.

Adella's heart almost stopped.

It was Joel.

Hadn't she told him not to contact her until his mourning period was over?

She moved away from the window and in a moment of panic almost ran out of the back of the house. But no. She couldn't do that. His arrival was unexpected, but she had to face him.

*What would her parents say to him?*

Her mother was in bed resting, but her father was next door. How would they react to him after everything? Half of her wanted them to meet him, but the other half wanted to keep his visit a secret.

She was completely unprepared to see him. Her mind raced as to why he had come. Several possibilities presented themselves in her mind.

One thing was certain, she never thought he would see her childhood home, especially these last five years. She looked about the small sitting room, the walls and the furniture almost closing in on her. How strange it will be to have him inside; this was her sanctuary where she had wept in the arms of her mother when he abandoned her.

She waited in the doorway until she heard the knock at the door. Slowly she made her way, knowing she was lingering.

Calmly she opened it.

"Hello Adella," Joel said.

He looked anxious. Serious. Uneasy.

She felt herself flush. He was smartly dressed in a dark suit. Cleanly shaven and with a clear complexion, he was so different now to when she last saw him. Then he had been tired and worn. She wondered whether his new vibrancy was the result of his widower hood. He was still so very handsome.

He looked down momentarily then met her glance, "I had to see you. You left Bath so suddenly that I could not leave it six full months. Can I come in?"

She nodded, then turned slowly and let him follow her through to the sitting room closing the door behind him.

She stood in the centre of the room, he was still near the door, just a few steps away. Neither spoke for a few moments.

"I have left Bath for good," he said staring at her. He was still holding his hat, and in his nervousness, he brushed the rim.

"Have you?"

"Yes. I am going to Scotland with Frederick for a few weeks."

"You have not come to only tell me that?"

"No." He smiled and gave a nervous laugh. "I – I have come to – Adella, I was hoping you would come with us. We could be married in a few days."

She drew a deep breath. But before she could continue, he spoke again.

"Before you chastise me; I remember what you said to me the other week, but I have to ask again. I have this strange notion that you may have changed your mind. Besides, I wanted you to know that it was cruel of you to leave so suddenly. But I suppose after what I did to you, it would be a thoughtless thing to say."

The irony only struck when he pointed it out.

"My mother was ill. That is why I left so suddenly."

"Is she better?"

"Yes."

"Then will you come with me?"

His eyes were wide with expectation and hope.

"I can't," she whispered, her eyes fixed on his face. Though a part of her wanted to say yes. It was on the tip of her tongue. It would have been easy to speak the words in a confused rush.

He took a step closer to her, and again, until he was in front of her.

"Are you sure?" he asked taking her hand and keeping it in a tender grasp.

"I can't leave my mother. She is better than before but is still unwell, and my father is busy with work. There is no one else to nurse her or run the house." She glanced quickly into his eyes as she spoke.

"I see." He said, in a low deep tone. 'Is there anything I can say to persuade you to come?"

She shook her head. "I don't think so."

"You don't think so," he repeated with a quick smile. "Then there is the smallest chance. . ."

"No. I will not give you false promises. I am not unfeeling or indifferent to you, but I need more time."

His expression was pained. He dropped her hand, turned away and walked to the other side of the room. He silently looked out the window. She wanted to speak to him, reassure him. Why? When had she suddenly started to care how he felt or that she was causing him pain? Someone she hated for so long. It was difficult for her to remember that she didn't despise him any more. It was flattering indeed to be asked such a thing. But it was nonsense. To run away and marry him in such a hurry was not right.

After a few minutes he turned around and with a taut expression said, "I am going to confront my father soon, whether you come with me or not. But I would sooner you would. During those bleak years when I was first married to Cynthia, I dreamt I would be free again to marry you. Now I am here in front of you, you cannot blame me for asking again."

The lost look in his eyes almost undid her. She stepped forward, wanting to be closer to him.

"I too never thought for a moment that your reason for abandoning me would be so – understandable. But there are so many reasons to resist at the moment. I must stand by my decision. For both our sakes. You see that can't you?"

"I refuse to see it."

She continued unperturbed by his word. "If you are going to confront your father, what of your brother and daughter?"

"They will be safely hidden."

"You are not expecting your father to take to your disobedience?"

"No. He will cut me off and I am glad of it."

"How can you be? You have more money anyone could dream of, yet you wish to rid yourself of it."

"If you think wealth and happiness are the same, you are mistaken. Indeed, I am surprised at you. You never used to put monetary value above anything else." His words were harsh, but he spoke in a tender tone.

"You do not know me then. Have you forgotten the reason why I became a governess in the first place?"

"I remember and I do know you, but not as well as I would like."

There was a long silence between them. Neither seemed willing to break the reverie. Adella wondered whether she should sit down, or offer him a seat but it seemed so awkward and instead she clasped the top of the settee with her hands.

Eventually Joel spoke, "I was determined to take you with me, but now I am here, I cannot force you to do anything against your will. I will not treat you the same way I am treated by my father. I look forward to coming back when you will allow me to court you properly. Just as you wish and deserve."

"You must do as you will. But I cannot go." Then after a moment added, "However much my heart is telling me to."

He stared at her. "You would come if I could have longer to persuade you? Tell me, how many minutes or hours will it take to change your mind? Though I feel your mind has decided."

Adella was about to reply, but she was prevented from speaking by the door opening.

An awkward fear washed through her.

It was what she dreaded; it would most likely be her father.

How would he react?

Adella felt herself redden as the door widened further and her father came in the room. She took a guilty step away from Joel.

"There is a carriage outside, I wondered who might be -" he stopped and stared at Joel, then his daughter.

"Adella, won't you introduce us?"

Joel was by now stood straight and to attention.

"Father, this is –" she paused, then swallowed, and in a quick voice said, "This is Mr Joel Polwarth."

At the start of her words, her father had stretched out his hand for Joel to shake it. But as the name sank in, his arm faltered and he pulled it back to his side.

"Joel Polwarth?" he muttered.

Adella watched as her father's soft expression turned into a frown.

"If you are Joel Polwarth, then I should like you to leave," he said with a defiant tilt of his chin.

"No father," Adella said. "You must not force him to go. If I can forgive him, then so must you."

"You forgive me?" Joel's face softened.

"Yes. Of course." Adella said to him. Then she turned to her father. "Joel is here to – well to speak to me about some-thing, and it is difficult for you to allow him in our house. But please, do not force him to go. It is my decision is it not? You trust me don't you?"

He replied in a low tone, "Adella, after all he has done, how can you say such a thing? You need protection from him. I will not have him in my house."

"Father, please. I am old and wise enough to deal with him myself, indeed, our conversation was nearly over and he was about to go."

She looked to Joel, the surprise on his face told her he wasn't considering leaving yet.

Joel broke the tense silence, "Mr Maxwell, though I realise my presence here is not welcome by you, let me assure you that I am not here to cause mischief. I have acted badly in the past towards Adella, I know it and have felt it. But I have the highest regard for her, indeed I always have."

Her father stood staring at Joel for a moment. Adella put

her hand on his arm and said, "Please father, let us finish our conversation and then he will be gone."

He faltered for a moment, then with a resigned sigh said, "I do not like it, but I do trust you Adella. I will be next door if you need me."

She nodded and he left, leaving the door open a small crack.

Adella stood looking at the door for a moment. The embarrassment of the last few minutes washed over her and she forced calm on herself.

Only the sound of Joel's voice broke through her thoughts. "He is angry, and if it were my daughter I would feel exactly the same. But tell me, you really do not want to come with me?"

"I have given you my answer."

"Then I will return in due course."

She nodded and for a moment her mind wandered to what it would be like to be pursued in such a way.

"I really hoped I could persuade you to come with me. At least I can see you are well looked after and comfortable here." He looked about the room as though seeing it for the first time.

"I am, though I miss my friends in Bath."

"I saw your brother a few days ago and he is well. I think he would be glad to have you back. Though I mean to have you for myself so perhaps it is good practice for him. He should find himself a wife, then he will not need you."

A few minutes later she followed him out to the carriage, and though the sight of them together would give the neighbours gossip, she allowed him to kissed her hand before he stepped in.

Once the carriage was out of sight, her father wasted no time in joining her outside.

"What did he want?" he asked in a gruff tone.

"He wanted to marry me."

"What!"

"I told him no," she said and linked her arm through her fathers and led him inside.

"Good. I hope you told him never to come back."

"I told him I would not marry him at the moment, but he seems determined to win me. He has promised to return in a few months. Then I will see if he truly still wants me. Remember his reasons for abandoning me father? You must not forget what he was forced to do."

"Still, it is an affront to come here like that. You will take care?"

"I will father, I will."

It was a few weeks later, and Joel was being driven up to his family home in Frederick's carriage. The intervening time had been spent in a house rented by Frederick in Edinburgh. They used their days planning in detail how Michael and Sarah would be hidden. Joel's emotions quickly changed from fear and anguish, to a cool determination to never allow his father to control his life again.

Frederick, ever eager to help and listen was the best of friends during this time, helping plan where the best place to hide them was, and what to say to his father when he told him what he had done.

Michael visited Scotland too. Joel wrote to their father and requested Michael stay, and to his surprise, his father agreed to the trip. Whilst in Scotland, Joel and Frederick persuaded Michael to be hidden for the next year, until he reached twenty one. Though reluctant at first, especially to defy his father, he finally agreed. His concerns originated from the belief that nothing could be done to out-do their father, knowing how ruthless he was. But somehow, with Frederick's help, Joel had persuaded him.

Now, with Michael and Sarah safely on their way to their hiding place in France, Joel was returning to finally confront his father.

"Pre-emption," was the word Frederick kept repeating to him, as well as comments such as, "Never let the old man command you again," and "tell him that it all ends now." Joel smiled to himself at all the encouragement he had been given by Frederick over the last few months.

Frederick's words had helped, but were not needed now. Joel ceased to be ambivalent from the moment he saw Adella in Bath; his decision was finally made and he would not swerve from it. He wanted the thorn in his side removed once and for all.

"Nervous?" Frederick said as the carriage stopped outside the house.

"Yes," Joel said.

"I will not leave you," Frederick said earnestly.

Joel nodded and they stepped out of the carriage and entered the house. The weeks of planning and preparation were to finally come to a head within a few minutes.

But it was more than that. The years his father controlled him, kept him captive, controlled his every move. But no more. It was about to stop. It had to stop. There was no other option available. From this moment on, he was taking complete control of his own life; his father be damned!

**17**

———

"Is my father at home?" Joel asked the footman as he took his coat and hat.

"Yes sir, he is in the drawing room with your mother and two guests."

Joel and Frederick stopped and exchanged glances.

"Who are the visitors?"

"Mr Farrell and Rev Milne."

Two old family friends. Joel tried to hide the anxious expression on his face. He did not want to stall. Now was the time he had decided to confront his father, and it was late afternoon already. He started to walk towards the drawing room but Frederick grabbed at his sleeve, "A short while will make no difference. It will give you time to gather a few personal items."

Joel nodded and slowly walked up the grand staircase to his bed chamber. Before long, he found himself sitting on the bed. His hands gripped the side of the mattress. His mind wondered about the task ahead; did he really have the strength to do it? He managed to pull his thoughts together and to the task in hand. There was little he wanted to take, all of the furniture was his father's and he had most of his clothes already. But he did take a few items. A pocket watch given to him by his mother on his eighteenth birthday. He never used it. Several pairs of gold cuff links; they were not worth much, but they could be sold if he needed the money.

After one last look at his room, the room in which he had been held captive at the age of twenty, the room which still had bars outside the window, he went back down and found Frederick still waiting in the hallway. He was seated on one of the hall chairs, biting his nails. The hallway was cold, and there was a dull smell of damp about it. He would not be sorry to leave this place.

"Shall we go in?" Frederick asked as Joel reached the bottom of the stairs.

"Yes. I think our arrival may send the guests away."

"Maybe. We can but see."

Joel pushed open the heavy oak door and they entered. All the occupants within looked up. Joel's mother was nearest; stood next to a table with the tea things. His father was seated further inside the room, next to the guests. The room was not changed since the last time he had been there. Not surprising. The grand drawing room was always immaculately presented as the main entertaining room for guests who called. The public face of a family with secrets.

"Joel!" his mother said as he stepped in and kissed her. He noticed her eyes were deeply drawn and her skin paler than normal. "I have missed you so. You stayed away too long." She fussed over him, as though he was a child, but Joel enjoyed it. He knew it would probably be the last time he saw his mother. For a fleeting moment, he regretted his decision.

For only a moment.

"That is enough Clara. Joel is no longer a small boy," his

father said. He turned to the guests and continued. "Joel has been in Scotland, grieving for his late wife."

Mr Farrell, an elderly gentleman spoke with a bow of his head, "Yes, may I offer my sincere condolences for your great loss. Your daughter must miss her mother too."

"Yes, where is Sarah?" Mr Polwarth asked.

Joel glanced at his father, then at his mother who wore a look of expectation. For a moment Joel faltered, unsure what to say. But he quickly recovered, "I will tell you later."

His father raised his eyebrows, and smiled.

The conversation was unbearable at times. Joel could barely bring himself to take part in it and he noticed his mother spoke in the most part to Frederick; a few times he heard her asking after Sarah.

Finally, it was nearly an hour later when the visitors rose to leave. He watched his mother and father re-enter the room after seeing the guests out. They sat down on the sofa, and Joel felt a wash of vulnerability. He looked over to Frederick. He was stood by the window, and moments later moved next to Joel in a silent gesture of support.

It was now or never.

Joel took a deep breath.

He swallowed hard.

'Father, I have come home for one final time. I have come to tell you that I will no longer be a slave to your wishes. I will not marry Mrs Golding."

Joel watched as a cruel smirk spread over his father's face, "I know why you have come home Joel."

"You do?"

"Do you think I did not know of your plans to hide Michael and Sarah?"

Joel's eyes widened in disbelief, "What? How did - "

"Surprised?" his father said in a smooth tone. "Do you really think I wouldn't find out what you were up to?"

"I will not marry Mrs Golding." Joel repeated.

"Well, we'll see whether you do as I say. . ." His father stood up quickly and walked to the far drawing room door.

He opened it.

"Come through," his father said.

For a moment Joel could see nothing. Then he heard footsteps on the wooden floor.

Slowly, a familiar tall figure came into the room.

Michael.

Joel was paralysed for a moment until he finally was able to say, "Michael?"

He blinked hard. Michael stood next to their father; shoulder to shoulder.

"Did I convince you enough that I was on your side?" Michael said.

"I think you did judging from the look on Joel's face," their father said.

Michael laughed, "You really are a fool Joel. Father has changed his Will and I am to inherit the estate."

"Yes," their father continued. "Michael has shown me loyalty above anyone else. Much more than you ever have or ever will. What do you think of that?" There was a small smile playing on his lips.

"Michael. How could you?" Joel demanded.

"I do not see why you should get everything, just because you were born first." Michael sneered.

"After all I have done for you. . .all the times I have protected you from *him*."

Then suddenly his thoughts took another turn. He stepped forward, "Where is Sarah? What have you done with her?"

Joel put the question to Michael, but it was his father who answered, "She is safe. . .somewhere. Not France where you intended to hide her. If you wish to see her again, you will marry Mrs Golding."

"Never!" Joel shouted.

He heard his mother give a small whimper.

"You are despicable," Frederick said, "You have taken another man's child and hidden her?"

"Oh yes," Mr Polwarth said still with amusement in his voice, "Frederick, your loyalty to my son does you credit, but it is misguided. Such a waste."

Joel watched as the colour rose in Frederick's face. "You do not think you can get away with this? We will see what the Police have to say about kidnapping Sarah."

Mr Polwarth laughed, "I am not worried. I have a wonderful story to tell them. You sent away your own child Joel, and Michael has managed to make it back home to tell us that whilst on their way to France, she was kidnapped by gypsies. Isn't that right?"

Michael smirked, "Yes father, it was tragic; there was nothing I could do, there were too many of them. Goodness knows what has become of her. Sold into slavery probably. Or maybe if you are lucky they will keep her as a servant girl."

"So, Joel," Mr Polwarth said. 'If you wish to see your child again, you will do as I say."

"No! You will not hurt Sarah!"

But the words did not come from Joel or Frederick. It was his mother who spoke. She ran towards her husband and youngest son. "Please, you must not hurt her!"

"Shut up. Do not speak," Mr Polwarth shouted back at her.

She looked despairingly at her husband and cowered back.

Then, as though a hidden force pushed her forwards, she suddenly grabbed Michael's hand. "Michael, you must not listen to your father, tell me where Sarah is. She must not be harmed. She must not be locked away, not another one. . .please, Michael, you must not listen to him."

"Shut up!" His father grabbed her and pushed her away.

Joel took a step towards his father, fists clenched by his sides. "Leave her alone."

"She is my wife, and I can do as I wish with her."

"That is it isn't it? You have to have your own way. It's always been that. You have to be in control. Not this time. Not any more. I will go to the Police and we will see who they believe."

Joel turned and started to walk away, until his father's icy tones spoke again. "If you go to the Police, I will have her killed."

"No!" cried his mother again. "I will not let you hurt her!" She turned to Michael again, pleading. 'Michael, he cannot give you the estate, it is an entail. Joel will inherit, there is nothing you can do."

"An entail?" Joel said, with a gleam of triumph in his eyes.

"Silence!" Mr Polwarth roared. His face contorted for a moment then settled more into an inscrutable mask.

He turned to Michael with a nervous laugh and said, "Do not listen to her, she is unstable."

There was a deathly hush for a moment until Joel said, "An entail. The estate is an entail. I am the eldest son and I will get it whether you like it or not."

"Father, say it is not so?" Michael said, his eyes wide with shock.

Joel's mother spoke again, "It is an entail! You must not let him hurt Sarah." Tears formed in her eyes. "The lawyers know, he has paid them to keep quiet."

"It is NOT an entail," Mr Polwarth shouted, "What would you know? You stupid woman. SHUT UP!"

"Say it is not so father," Michael said, now with anguish in his voice. "Say it is not so!"

But Joel saw the moment's panic in his fathers face when his mother first spoke. Just one fleeting look of panic in his eyes that spoke the truth.

He stepped confidently forward. "So, all these years you have led me to believe that you could disinherit me any moment you chose to, when all along you have been using it as an excuse to control me!"

"Don't be a fool," his father said.

"I would only be a fool if I continued to believe the poison that comes out of your mouth. It should be simple enough to find out the truth about the estate, through official means."

Joel stared at his father. For the first time in his life, he felt power over him. It had been a long time coming. Joel watched as his father slowly turn red. He knew his anger was about to explode.

With one swift movement his father grabbed a display knife from the wall and unsheathed it. It was five inches long.

Joel clenched his fists, waiting for his father to come towards him.

But his father made a lunge towards his wife. It took them all by surprise, and Joel only just managed to grab his arm in time. The knife was just inches from his mother's neck.

His father's grip was strong.

"Mother, get out of here," he screamed.

But she didn't move.

They started to struggle. Joel tried to get control of the weapon. His father resisting with all his strength. Somehow he pushed his father back a few feet.

"Now we will see which of us is stronger," Joel said through clenched teeth.

Frederick was quick off the mark, and tried to help by grabbing Mr Polwarth from behind.

But he elbowed Frederick hard in the face. He fell backwards landing on the floor.

They were a tumble of bodies as they both fell on the floor and rolled over, each trying to overcome the other.

Joel heard Frederick shout, "Michael, help your brother for God sake!"

But no help came.

After a few moments, Joel pinned his father to the floor, still fiercely holding his wrist.

The knife pointing towards him.

They stared at each other. Neither spoke. Each silently tried to impose his will on the other.

Just as he thought he overcame his father, Joel felt a sharp kick on his shoulder which sent him reeling backwards.

Michael.

Before he could react, his father plunged the knife into his right shoulder. He stared down at it. It went in a few inches. Pain paralysed him and he screamed out.

He somehow managed to grab at the knife. He tried to pull it out. It wouldn't move. His father staggered to his feet. Then, without sparing Joel a glance, he brushed himself down and fixed his cool gaze on his petrified wife.

She shrieked, and started to edge away. But he lunged

forward again and grabbed her by the throat and pushed her upwards against the wall. Joel watched helpless. He tried to stand up, but he was losing blood and he crumpled to the floor, fighting to stay conscious and crippled by pain.

All he could hear was his mother struggling to breathe.

"Stop him Michael. For God's sake. Stop him!" Joel cried.

But still Michael did nothing. Joel searched for Frederick. He was kneeling across the room. He looked dazed. Joel watched as Frederick reached inside his jacket pocket and took out a pistol.

Frederick tried to aim at Mr Polwarth, but his hand shook.

"Give it to me," Joel shouted. "Quickly."

Joel looked over at his mother, his father still held a firm grip around her throat. She was gasping for air. Her eyes bulged with fear as she desperately tried to struggle free.

Within seconds, the gun slid across the wooden floor and into Joel's hand.

He lifted the gun, and cried out in pain. He looked down at the weapon still lodged in his shoulder. His shirt that was already soaked in blood. He was running out of time. Despite the searing pain, he made one last effort to lift the gun and took aim.

A shot rang out.

Then everything went black.

ADELLA HAD SPENT most of the day at the church hall helping prepare it for a fund raising dinner that evening for the deserving poor. It was to be a grand event with many of the local dignitaries attending, including the Mayor. The price of the dinner was an extravagance she could not afford, so, she contented herself with helping to decorate, prepare food, and generally make herself useful in any way. So she helped hang bunting and ribbons, and decorated the table so it befit the most important ladies and gentlemen.

By three o'clock, everything was done, and she and the other five volunteers gained the Rev and Mrs Buyers heartfelt thanks for their efforts. So, at half past three, she had hardly stepped through the front door at home, when her mother hurried along the hallway to greet her, one glance at her intense frown told Adella she was agitated.

"There is a young gentleman here to see you," she said breathlessly. "He has been here for an hour, and he will not tell me his name. He insisted on waiting and would not hear of coming back later when I told him you would be some time. He kept asking where you were, I did not tell him the truth; well, he would not tell me who he was!"

Adella's brow furrowed. She knew straight away that it must be Joel. It was just over a month since his last visit, and yet here he was again. She had at least expected him to stay away for two or three months.

"Is he in the sitting room?" she asked.

"Yes, I think he is rich. He is wearing very fine looking clothes and he arrived in an expensive looking carriage. He would hardly speak to me either. Most rude."

He was obviously trying to hide his identity from her mother because he feared her response.

"Very well mother, I shall go directly."

Adella almost ran to the sitting room. Her heart thumped as she tried to compose herself. He had said he would return to court her. Well here he was still too early.

She entered the sitting room and saw the gentleman stood at the far side of the room with his back to her. She knew instantly who it was. The tall figure, the dark, slightly curly hair.

She had not expected *him* of all people.

"You!" she said, rooted to the spot. He turned around and she found herself looking into the face of Frederick Garner.

He stepped forward eagerly and gave a small bow, "Miss Maxwell. You may wonder at my sudden appearance. But I am here on a profoundly important errand. A matter of life and death in fact." His voice was low and quick.

Adella said nothing, but waited for him to explain himself.

He continued, obviously encouraged by her silence, "It is Joel. He lies gravely ill, and I have come to take you to him."

Adella drew herself up. "Ill?"

Frederick stared at her. "Yes."

"What ails him?"

"He was stabbed by his father, he has a fever caused by the wound, and the doctor believes he has but a small chance of survival. Yet, in this fevered state he is calling for you, and the doctor thinks that if you were to go to him, then his chances may improve. . .that he may even recover."

"His father stabbed him?"

"Yes."

"Because he would not marry who his father wanted?" She looked into Frederick's face. "He confronted his father, and his father stabbed him?"

"Exactly."

"But what of his father now? Surely Joel is not safe from him?"

"His father is dead, and Joel was the one who killed him. Though it was in self defence of both him and his mother."

She barely noticed the words before, but now she sat

down, pale and trembling and Frederick followed suit in the chair opposite.

"Then you will come?" There was a note of hope in his voice.

"It is all my fault. I should have insisted he did as his father asked. If I had refused him and given him no hope. . ."

She watched as Frederick felt in his jacket pocket, and pulled out a wooden hair comb. "Is this yours?"

Adella leaned forward and took it, "Yes! How did you come to have it?"

"I found it in Joel's coat pocket, he was carrying it."

"I do not understand. . ." Adella said, "How did he come to have it?"

"I do not know, all I do know is that you must believe me when I tell you that you are his only hope." Frederick shook his head as though trying to shake the memory. "If you ever loved him then you will come with me and hope to God that he is still alive when we get there."

Suddenly she stood up, seized by blind panic. "We must leave at once. If what you say is true, there is no time to lose."

Frederick nodded. "Gather a few clothes. I have a carriage waiting at the Inn along the road, I can have it ready in half an hour."

Adella ran to her mother and explained quickly where she was going.

"You must go," her mother said. "Whatever your feelings have been, it is the Christian thing to do – to try and save him."

In an urgent yet sad tone she said, "I must go to him. He may be dead, he may die yet, but I must see him."

"You are not going alone with that man? Who is he?"

"He is a great friend of Joel's, and he will see me safely to Bedfordshire."

"But you cannot travel alone with him! It is not right."

Adella faltered for a moment. Her mother had a point. "It does not matter. Nothing will stop me from going. Nothing. Especially propriety."

With that, she ran upstairs and quickly gathered a few items.

Fifteen minutes later she saw from her bedroom window the carriage pull up and Frederick jump out.

She quickly bundled a few more items into her bag, and hurried downstairs. When she got outside, her mother and Frederick were deep in conversation. She did not hear what they said, though her mother looked a little more relaxed than earlier.

"Adella," her mother said, "I have told this gentleman that if he touches you, I will kill him myself."

Adella looked from her mother to Frederick, and blushed deeply.

Frederick gave a small bow and in a serious tone replied, "And I have told your mother, that I do not wish to tarnish what is so dear to my friend. I will protect her and cherish her as though she were my own sister."

At that, Frederick helped Adella into the carriage and they pulled away.

**18**

———

Flora hurried through to the living area at the back of her Uncle's shop, Dr Preston had arrived a few minutes before for his evening dinner, and she was cruelly detained from him by a dithering customer. All the time she could hear the sound of Helen's flirting and laughing in the distance as she and her aunt entertained him. Finally the customer left, and her uncle closed the shop and counted the days takings.

She approached the sitting room, but before she could enter, Helen came out to meet her.

"There you are! Where have you been?" She lowered her voice to a whisper, "I have had to keep Dr Preston company for what seems like an age, Aunt is busy in the kitchen."

"I thought she was with you."

"No, not any more. It is your turn to speak to him now. I am tired of it. I have other things to do before dinner."

"What things?"

"All sorts of things, I don't expect you to understand."

Flora watched as Helen rushed off upstairs. She went into the sitting room, not unhappy that Helen was out of the way. Dr Preston was sat on the settee reading a newspaper. He stood up as she entered, smiled broadly and folded away the paper.

"Please, do not let me interrupt you from your reading," Flora said.

"No, not at all. It is full of rubbish. Besides, I can read it when I get home."

She seated herself in the chair next to him, "It has been a busy day in the shop. I am glad to be of help to Uncle and Aunt at such times."

"You enjoy working here? You would not miss it at all?"

"Miss it? Well I do not think my mother and father will want me home as long as Uncle and Aunt can make use of me. Do you think I am of use to them?"

"Of course you are," he spoke gently, "you are a godsend to them. They frequently say to me how quick you learn and how helpful you are."

She relaxed, "I would hate it if they did not want me here, I like it so much. Though sometimes, it can be a little disconcerting. For example, there seems to be a lot of people with colds at the moment."

"Yes, I hope you will not catch one from them," he said with a concerned countenance.

She smiled, "I will try not to. Besides, Uncle deals with most of those customers. He is protective of me in that respect."

"Yes, he does look after you." Leonard suddenly leaned forward and in a low voice said, 'But not as well as a husband would look after you."

Flora was a little taken aback. She avoided his earnest gaze, and fixed her eyes on her hands folded in her lap, and murmured, "No, I suppose not. But Uncle often says he does not know how he managed without me before."

But instead of sitting back into the chair, as she expected him to, Leonard stayed where he was. He was still staring straight at her; she could tell. Their faces barely a foot apart. He moved his hand to cover hers. Finally, his patience paid off and she lifted her eyes to meet his. He was about to speak when they heard Mrs Alther in the hall, shouting that dinner was ready.

He quickly withdrew his hand, and then stood up, ran his hand through his hair and said, "Yes of course. You are needed here aren't you. The shop becomes busier and busier these days, and your Uncle and Aunt need all the help they can get. Especially from someone so competent as you. Forgive me I – I think we should go to dinner." Then before she knew what had happened, he whisked past her and left the room.

Flora stood for a few dazed moments on her own; what did that mean? And why did he leave so abruptly? For one fleeting moment it seemed as though he felt the same as she: admiration, esteem.

Love.

For love it now was.

On her part at least. But he obviously did not feel the same. It was clear he only had brotherly feelings towards her. She had after all taken the place of Adella. She stood up, and gained enough presence of mind to go to the dining room.

Neither spoke to each other throughout dinner. Flora sometimes looked at Dr Preston but he kept his eyes firmly on everyone else and never tried to include her in his conversation like he usually did. She picked at her food. Hunger deserted her at the thought that she had somehow offended him. She kept going over their conversation in her mind but could not think what had upset him. She decided to speak to him about it after dinner, but her anguish was further deepened when Dr Preston left as soon as he finished eating. Something that he never did unless he was called away by a patient.

"Oh, I suppose he gets bored with us," Mr Alther said after he left.

"It's Flora's fault, she scared him off with her silence!" Helen said.

"I did not!" Flora replied, but she doubted her own words. Was she too silent? She should have tried to make conversation with him over dinner, asked him a question or two so that he had to answer and speak to her. She couldn't think what to say when they were all sat around the table. Later, with her thoughts in turmoil, she went upstairs for some peace from Helen's unending twittering to try and figure out what to say to Dr Preston when she saw him next.

As the carriage pulled away, Adella waved to her mother through the window. When they turned the corner and her mother was out of sight, she closed the carriage window and sat back.

Frederick, seated opposite, watched as she settled into the seat. She looked at him, and for the first time noticed the pale tinge to his face, and the dark shadows under his eyes. For a long while, neither of them spoke; they both sat and stared out of the window at the passing landscape. The houses became sparser and the trees and fields more frequent as they drove away from Aylesbury.

Frederick was only roused from his own thoughts by Adella's soft entreaty, "What kind of man imprisons his own son?"

"The kind of man who stabs his own son in cold blood and tries to strangle his wife straight afterwards," he replied.

"When he came to Sidmouth, he did seem troubled. There was something. . .quietly suppressed in his demeanour. I remember it well. I believed him to be of a pensive nature. I did not think he was hiding such an awful secret. How naive I was. If I knew, I could have helped him. Just a little."

"You did help him, though you did not know his secret."

"How?"

"By loving him for himself, rather than who he was. Joel Michael Henry Polwarth, eldest son and heir of Michael Polwarth, who happens to own near enough half of East Bedfordshire."

Adella smiled. "I could not help but love him, everything about him made me love him, and it happened so quickly. But I do think, in fact I know, he would not have looked twice at me if he had not been masquerading as a tutor." She sighed deeply, "I have often thought of the time we spent together. Though it pained me to think I was deceived, we spent many happy hours together. It is not the sort of thing that is easily forgotten, however hard you try. He was so knowledgeable, and yet he was not arrogant. He never made me feel stupid. He was gentle and thoughtful too. . ."

Frederick smiled back at her tender words and voice. "I do not think many men and women spend so much time together as you both did. You had a great advantage to get to know each other on intimate terms."

"Indeed," she blushed a little. "We met outside several times too, it was most improper, and I have never behaved in such a way since."

Frederick tried to hide a smile. But he failed, and Adella's questioning look made him speak. "I am sorry. It's just I can imagine you scampering about through fields going to meet Joel, and him waiting for you."

She blushed again and looked down. Frederick said no more. And they descended into silence for nearly an hour. Their silence was only broken when the carriage stopped to have the horses changed. They both got out for a short time to stretch their legs, and a few minutes later, were on the road again. Frederick's instructions to the driver and groom to heavily tip the Inn staff ensured a speedy return to Bedfordshire.

Adella's thoughts returned to the subject of his family. "Was his father always cruel to him?" she asked.

"No. Not when he was very young, but as he grew older Joel learnt how to stop his father from getting angry. He bore the brunt of his brothers' disobedience as well as his own."

"He received punishment if they misbehaved?"

"Yes."

"It is too cruel," she shifted around in her seat, "How can a man sleep at night when he does such things?"

"Probably with a sleeping draught," Frederick replied in a dry tone.

Adella did not acknowledge the joke, but asked, "Tell me, did Joel, did he ever speak about me? I mean, before Cynthia died."

"Yes, though he tried to forget you. But when he came away from Sidmouth he told me all about you and what he did. Then, I remember most vividly when he was drunk a few years afterwards, he spoke for hours about you. He was married by then of course. So, yes he did speak about you, but only on the rarest occasions. I think it pained him too much."

Adella looked out of the carriage window once more but

did not notice the passing landscape. She yawned, suddenly tired, more from emotional tension than lack of sleep. Frederick took the hint and remained silent for sometime. But eventually he found himself saying, "Does it bother you that he chose his brothers over you?"

"Not now. I understand he had to guard them. He did the right thing by protecting those who could not protect themselves. It's the sort of thing he would do. It is honourable. I only wish he told me at the time." Adella sighed, "I was trying to think whether the last five years would have been easier or harder if I knew the truth."

"And what do you conclude?"

"I don't know."

Adella wanted to cry but the tears would not come. Would he be alive when they arrived? What would he say to her? Her thoughts settled on the recent events in Bath, she asked, "Why were you so cruel to me in Bath?"

He looked up surprised, "I was not cruel."

"I think you were." she said in low tone, "I think you took pleasure in seeing me suffer."

"I am sorry if I seemed unkind. I did not mean to be, but accept my sincerest apologies," he said gallantly.

She gave a small smile and they were silent for a time until she asked, "He has the best Physician?"

"Of course. I would not neglect him now, and in that respect. Doctor Chapman is the best in Bedfordshire."

"Do *you* think he will die?" she asked tentatively.

"I honestly do not know. But the doctor thought he could have a chance if only he would rest. As I said before, *you* are his best chance of that happening."

"Then I hope he does recognise me. But surely, does he not ask for his daughter?"

The mention of Sarah made Adella flush a little, and she dared not meet Frederick's eye.

He eyed her pensively, "No, he does not call for his daughter. He calls for you." Then after a pause, he continued, "You should know when Joel married Cynthia, he did not go near her. After nearly a year of marriage, Joel's father found out that Joel and Cynthia had not . ." Frederick pulled at his shirt collar.

"I understand," Adella said and at last met his eye.

"Well, sorry I'm not used to speaking of such matters with a lady."

She nodded and he continued, "You see, when Joel's father found out that he had not. . .visited Cynthia's room, he threatened to do so himself."

Her hand flew to her mouth.

"Joel had no choice in the end. Cynthia thought she had the most understanding and thoughtful husband because he made no demands of her. Though, in the end, *she* wanted to conceive. But only because all her acquaintances thought she was barren."

"But he is a good father? I always thought he would be."

"Yes. He may have been indifferent to the mother, but he loves Sarah. About six months after Sarah was born, Cynthia became ill. Though it was some time before we all realised it would result in her death. She was ill many times before you see. Always complaining about something or other. Joel was patient with her, far more than I could have been. Anyway, they ended up in Bath as you know."

They hardly spoke for the rest of journey, with only the odd passing comment for politeness sake. Though both were each deep in thought about the man who lay ill; each willed and prayed that he would live. They stopped once more to change the horses, and this was done with swift efficiency.

The carriage entered Biggleswade and finally pulled up at Polwarth House at eight thirty. Adella eagerly looked through the carriage window at the house. It was a newer looking building than she expected. Smaller too. There were only two main floors, not including the attic and basement. She counted eight huge windows at the front, and a large stone porch way in the middle of the house that lead inside. The gardens extended as far as she could see; trees, fields and ornamental gardens that looked lovingly cared for.

Frederick immediately alighted the carriage, and handed Adella down. There were several servants waiting, and Adella felt slightly embarrassed. Did they know why she was here?

She heard Frederick as he spoke to one of them and gave him an inquiring look. He answered it. "He is still alive. But we should go up immediately," he said.

Adella exhaled deeply in relief and before she knew it, Frederick indicated for her to follow him through the main door. No servants' entrance this time. Her heart still beat fiercely, and she dared not look too closely around the large house and exquisite staircase she ascended. Joel's family home was sumptuous indeed but she determined not to be over-awed. Occasionally her eyes would fall on a portrait, or ornament, but her mind did not take in the details.

They entered a labyrinth of hall ways, and passed door after door, until finally they reached the end of a long corridor.

"He is in here," Frederick said standing aside. The large oak door was already open, and Adella hesitated for a moment. Frederick glanced down at her anxious eyes.

"I am not afraid," she said, "Though I am a little nervous."

Frederick nodded, but he offered no more help, and Adella walked trance-like across the threshold of the room.

She stood still for a moment and took in what she saw. A middle-aged man stood by the large bed; she recognised a doctor at work when she saw one. Joel was in the bed thrashing about, but as soon as she walked into the large room he stopped.

He gazed at her, "Hush, she is here. At last she comes to me," he whispered.

Adella stood and stared back at him. That face she knew so well, hated for so long. But not now. Everything Frederick said was true. She was suddenly afraid. Her initial relief that he was alive had been washed away by fear at the sight before her. He looked deathly pale, there was a grey pallor to his skin. She had seen it before in those who were soon to pass on. Frederick prompted her forward, and with a few steps she found herself by the side of the bed. He still stared up at her, unable to speak. His eyes were bloodshot, but there was a clarity about them. His hair was damp on his forehead. He wore a large night shirt that reached his whole length, but it clinged to his skin, damp with sweat. The bedsheets were crumpled at the end of the bed.

"Hello Joel," she said in a soft voice.

His eyes never left her as he spoke. "My name is Joseph, my name is Joseph, Joseph, Joel. No, no, no, no, Joseph. Must not let her know. Joseph Joseph Joseph."

"Hello Joseph. Joseph West," she said.

His tense body relaxed a little.

The doctor came forward. "As you can see, he is still very delusional."

'Hush Joseph," Adella said instinctively and sat on the bed beside him. She took hold of his hand and kissed it.

"Must not tell her, must not! She must not know the truth," he continued on.

"Could you get him to sleep?" The doctor prompted.

She nodded, "Hush Joseph. You must rest. You must sleep. I will stay here with you. But you must sleep. Close your eyes."

She heard a sob behind her and looked round to see a middle-aged woman dressed in black, she presumed was his mother. Her eyes were just like Joel's.

"Sleep," he repeated.

"Yes," she was handed a cool damp cloth and pressed it on his brow. He relaxed and sank down the bed.

"And when you are awake after your sleep we will take the coastal walk to Branscombe once more."

"Branscombe," he said and smiled, as his eyes closed. Adella pulled the bed sheets over him and leaned forward and whispered into his ear, "But first you must rest."

He opened his eyes again, "You will stay with me?"

"Yes. Close your eyes, and when you awake I will still be here."

"Branscombe. My name is Joseph West," he mumbled.

"Yes, Joseph West. Sleep now." She stroked his damp hair until a few minutes later he was asleep.

The doctor looked relieved. "If he can sleep like this for a few days then I believe he will pull through. But we must keep his strength up. He must have food and water, but not until the morning."

"I understand," she said.

"My poor boy," the woman said coming over to the bed.

Adella looked up at her. But she kept her eyes on her son.

All the time Frederick had watched from the back of the room. When Mrs Polwarth started to fret over Joel, he stepped forward and drew her away saying, "Better leave Miss Maxwell to tend him. Sarah will be arriving home tomorrow and you'll need all your strength for her." She nodded and withdrew at Frederick's prompt, taking one long last look at her son.

The doctor tended to Joel for a short while, and then, satisfied with everything, he left saying he would be back in the morning.

Finally, Adella found herself alone with Joel.

She stood at the end of the bed and watched his face, then the rise and fall of his chest as he breathed. She could not help thinking of the time they were alone in Bath, when he kissed her. His touch was unwelcome then, but now......now she was transfixed. She wanted nothing more than to feel his lips against hers. She moved back to sit on the bed beside him and lowered her head over his. One soft gentle kiss to reignite the passion she felt for him years ago. He was a stranger, yet she knew him so well.

"I will not leave you Joseph West," she whispered into his ear.

It had been such a long day, and she was exhausted from the revelations. At least his sleep was deep and peaceful, and she wondered how she might wake him in the morning to give him food. She pulled a chair up to the bed, and took hold of his hand again, and held it against her cheek.

"We shall walk again to Branscombe, I promise," she whispered and let her mind drift back to that precious day when they first discovered their feelings for each other. Her heart was now fully opening up to allow her love to return completely.

It was some time before she noticed someone else in the

room. Frederick stood tentatively by the door. He turned to leave, but she looked up.

"Please, do not go," she said and stood up.

"We both want him to live," he said.

"Yes, but at least you seem to be able to hold yourself together."

"It may appear that way, but inside it is a different matter. Maybe after you have slept you will feel better?" he said.

"Yes. I will sleep in the chair."

"The chair! You cannot sleep there. There is a bedroom next door."

"I promised Joel I would not leave him," she said with entreating eyes, "I cannot break that promise. I know he is unlikely to wake, but if he does. . ."

Frederick ran his hand through his hair, "Then I do not know what to suggest."

"Perhaps, a chaise-longue and blankets?"

He nodded and within minutes the servants brought an exquisite French Mahogany chaise, decorated in the finest gold brocade. It was big enough to be more than comfortable, and together with the pillows and blankets, Adella was sure it would be sufficient.

Adella slept fitfully that night. She was not used to sleeping fully clothed, and her makeshift bed was a little hard. She could see Joel from where she lay, thankfully he did not stir much.

She was woken in the morning by the distant sound of voices coming from the hallway. She wasn't sure what time it was, though sunlight seeped out from behind the curtains. Scrambling up, she quickly checked on Joel; he was still sleeping, then made her way to the door. But before she could go outside, the door was flung open and a police constable walked in. He stopped after a few paces, his eyes met Adella's. She equalled his stare with fortitude. He was a large-framed man, young, and obviously was used to having his own way by using his weight and size.

Frederick was directly behind him. "Look," he said, "He is still too ill to go anywhere. I do not understand why you insist on checking he is still here."

The constable didn't seem to hear Frederick, took off his hat, and made a small bow to Adella, "Sorry to interrupt Miss, but I have my orders."

The constable moved to the side of the bed to check if Frederick spoke the truth. Adella gave Frederick a questioning look.

"I – I should have told you yesterday," he said to her, "There was an inquiry into his father's death, and they may. . .they may charge Joel with murder."

Adella grabbed at his arm, and looked across at Joel sleeping peacefully. "No! They cannot do that. He did it to save his mother! They cannot let him hang for saving his mother!"

**19**

---

Adella kept her eyes on the Police Constable as he stood over Joel. He was eyeing him suspiciously, but after a moment seemed satisfied. He turned back and approached Adella.

"Are you his nurse Miss?" he said as he looked her up and down.

Adella shifted uncomfortably under his gaze. "Yes."

"She's nothing to do with what happened, so leave her out of this," Frederick snapped.

The constable opened his mouth as though he was going to to protest, but relented, "Well, you look harmless enough." He went to the door, and paused on the threshold, "I'll be back tomorrow to check again."

"We are counting on it," Frederick said in a dry tone, and the constable was gone.

Adella collapsed on the chair. "They cannot hang him for saving his own mother's life! We must hide him, they must not be allowed to do this."

"Don't worry, if it comes to it, I will see he is taken out of the country. Don't trouble yourself, it probably won't come to that."

"Oh?" Adella said with hope in her voice.

Frederick seated himself in the chair opposite. "They have taken statements from all who were there; except Joel and Michael. Michael ran off a few hours after it all happened, but luckily before we found out where Sarah was first, he told us *that* at least. They need his statement, and I have men looking for him. When they find him, and he tells them the same as the rest of us - that Joel did it to save his mother from being murdered, then its a clear case of defence of another. It's unlikely they'll charge him with anything."

"Unlikely? What do you mean unlikely?" she asked.

Frederick shrugged, "If they did press charges, there would be no punishment. Besides, they saw the strangle marks around his mothers throat." He reached across and patted Adella's hand. "Do not worry yourself, I have the best lawyers, they will see that he is not charged."

Adella tried to smile, but she found it difficult. She looked across at Joel sleeping peacefully. "After all he has been through, now this! It would have been better that he let his mother be strangled." Her eyes glistened with the passion of her words.

Frederick looked a little shocked, then his face softened. "You do not mean that. If his father was still alive, Joel would be dead."

Adella sighed deeply, "You are right. I don't mean it."

"Concentrate on getting Joel better, and I will look after the law."

Adella nodded, "I will send for a bowl of broth. Joel must gain strength." She stood up and walked over to him, pulled up the blanket, and then wiped his head with a cool damp cloth.

"I'll send for it," Frederick said, "and have the servants send up breakfast for you."

The next day, Adella cared for Joel as well as she could, though she felt several times a little dizzy and weak, it had been cold travelling in the carriage and she wondered whether she might have caught a chill. Joel opened his eyes several times, and though his look was fixed on her, he never acknowledged or tried to speak to her.

Still Dr Chapman was not worried, and maintained that Joel was progressing well each time he visited.

"His fever has abated, he is gaining strength, I see no reason why he will not regain consciousness soon," he said that evening.

Adella's face lit up, "How soon?"

"In a few days. You must be patient, the human body can repair itself, but it needs time. His wound is clean and healing well too. But, Miss Maxwell, you look tired and drawn. I am more worried about you than Mr Polwarth at this present time."

He glanced at her over his glasses, and Adella turned away. "I am alright. I am worried about Joel, that is all."

"Then stop worrying, I am confident that he will fully recover in time."

Frederick arrived not long after, out of breath, and still in his riding boots.

"How is he?" he asked them both, though it was Dr Chapman who answered.

Adella waited patiently by the window as the doctor gave his prognosis on Joel, their voices a low murmur. She let her mind drift as she looked out of the window across the lawns. Their voices dropped to a whisper, and she was unaware of the frequent glances in her direction. A few minutes later, she was roused from her reverie by Frederick, who came over to see her. She noticed the doctor gone.

"So, Joel is much improved," he said with a smile.

"Yes," she said. "But what news of Michael?"

He paused, as though contemplating a white lie to alleviate her fretting, "none yet."

"Nothing at all? Surely the men searching must have an idea. He could not have gone far?"

"Not yet, but they have several lines of enquiry. We will find him. He has little money, so he'll show up soon enough," he said. "Have you eaten breakfast?"

"Yes."

He gave a quick nod of assent.

"You should take some fresh air? It will make you feel better, You've been shut up in this room for too long."

"I promised Joel I would not leave him."

"Yes I know, but he would not be happy that you are not looking after yourself properly."

"What makes you think I am neglecting myself?"

"You look tired and you are hardly eating."

Adella ignored his words and walked past him, she occupied herself by checking Joel. But he would not relent and followed her to the bedside.

"Take some fresh air, I insist. I will stay with him and call for you if he so much as stirs. All you need do is go out for a few minutes. Believe me, it will do *him* more good if you feel refreshed."

Adella looked down at Joel. "You promise to get me?"

"I swear it."

"Then you better send for a servant to show me the way out."

The warm sun on her face was reviving, but it was marred by threat of the law over Joel. This fact overtook any worries she had about his recovery. It was all such a tangled mess and she dared not think of anything further than one day to the next. If only Michael could be found. He was such a coward, and did not deserve a brother such as Joel.

She walked, but didn't stray far from the building, and wandered down the nearest gravel path, and admired the gardens. Though she noticed the beauty in front of her, her mind was too occupied to take in the smaller details of the gardens. She decided that she would write to her mother, and to Leonard. The latter was well overdue, she wanted to heal the rift between them.

Every step she took, she was acutely aware that she was treading on *his* ground, in *his* estate. He was heir to all this when she thought him a humble tutor. How he must have missed it when he was in Sidmouth. Such a beautiful place to grow up. But the thought was quickly quashed. His father had been a tyrant, and he turned his back on it all.

She walked for twenty minutes, then unable to stay away from Joel any longer, retraced her steps back into the house. She allowed herself more time to look at the interior decoration. It was all so finely furnished, she dared not surmise how much the house alone was worth. It made her own upbringing feel so humble.

After taking a few wrong turns, she finally found herself back in the room with Joel and Frederick.

"He has not stirred, he snored a bit, but that is all." Frederick said with a small smirk.

Adella could not help but smile in return.

"Do you feel refreshed?" he asked.

"A little, though I am glad to be back," she said as she gently stroked Joel's hair.

The next day passed in the same way as the day before, with Frederick still unable to alleviate Adella's fears over Joel's arrest. Michael, it seemed, had hidden himself well.

At night, Adella slept well, and without waking at all as she was used to doing. She only woke in the morning, much later than her usual hour by the maid. Her head pounded and she felt hot. But as soon as the blanket was removed she began to shiver. Then, trying to get up, she found her legs were unable to take her weight, and slumped back.

"I'll fetch the doctor," the maid said looking at her. Adella was in no state to argue. As soon as she was alone, she tried several more times to get up, but it was useless. She was too weak.

When Dr Chapman arrived, he examined her. And, just as he was about to give his diagnosis, Frederick arrived and heard the news.

"You have a high fever, and must be removed from Joel's presence immediately," he said sternly. "I am uncertain if it is a contagious fever, but we cannot risk Joel catching what you have."

She fought back the urge to cry, "I promised him I would not leave," she replied her voice distraught.

"If you stay and he catches what you have, it may kill him." Dr Chapman said.

"Then get me out of here. Quickly," she said trying to scramble up one last time.

The Doctor looked at Frederick. "Can I suggest she is removed to your house? It is an imposition, but I would like her as far away as possible to lessen the risk."

"It is not an imposition. We will leave immediately."

"Who will look after Joel?" Adella asked, as she was carried out of the room by the two of them.

"Myself and his mother, she has been wanting to attend to Joel," Frederick replied.

Adella did not answer. His own mother would have to suffice.

IN BATH, Leonard quietly ate his breakfast before his morning appointments when the post arrived. He recognised Adella's handwriting straight away, and tore the envelope open. He had a great amount of eager anticipation that it contained a reconciliation. He was not disappointed. As he read her forgiveness, then news of Joel and all that had happened in the last few weeks, Leonard was moved by their plight. He had been right to keep Joel's secret. Joel's father was a man of no morals. He was shocked at what happened and a little surprised that Adella clearly forgave her former love so quickly, especially after suffering for so many years. But when he thought about it, he understood why she forgave him. Upon reading her diagnosis of Joel's condition he knew that if he survived, he would have a long recovery. But, he knew Adella to be an excellent nurse.

As he sat and contemplated the letter, his mind inevitably turned to his own situation. He had been dithering for days. But now, as he saw what harm there was in the world, he decided once and for all. He must take action now. There was no time to lose.

He ran to the Alther's. On foot, it usually took ten minutes, yet this time seemed to take forever. It wasn't helped by a number of patients and acquaintances who delayed him by their polite enquiries after his health. Finally, he rang the private bell, he waited an impatient few moments until the door was opened by Mrs Alther.

"Dr Preston, I didn't expect to see you so early. Is there an emergency? You're very out of breath," she said.

"Yes, yes there is," he said through gasps.

"Come right in, I'll get Mr Alther to open the shop for you."

He followed her through to the back, "I do not need the shop, I must to speak to Flora."

"Flora? Very well, an unexpected errand no doubt. I'll run up and get her."

"Quick as you can," he said trying not to alarm her.

He waited in the sitting room and took a few moments to fully recover from his rushed arrival. It did not take him long to get back his breath and just in time for when Flora entered.

"Good morning Dr Preston," she said brightly, 'You have an urgent errand for me?"

He turned round, and could not help smiling. She stood inside the door and he took a moment to take in her full beauty. Neatly dressed as ever, today in a white patterned dress, her hair was loosely tied. Her face was clear and bright, eager to hear how she might be of use. He stepped forward, and for a moment faltered. He was desperately unsure of the reaction his words were about to create, but with fresh determination he started to speak. He had to act, and act now.

"Good morning Miss Alther." He gave a deep bow. She looked a little surprised at his formality. "I have come here because I have news of Adella."

"Oh how wonderful," Flora said and stepped forward, "How is she?"

"She is well, though at the present time, she is Bedfordshire."

He indicated they they should sit, and Leonard spent the

next few minutes telling Flora of Adella's news. She sat, her hands in her lap, saying nothing, and allowed Leonard to speak without interruption.

"I do hope that Mr Polwarth recovers. So, she has forgiven him. It is as I expected. And she has forgiven you?"

"Yes. She has and I am glad of it. " He shifted in his chair, "But it is a sad tale indeed, that two people in love should be separated for so many years," he leaned forward, "when they clearly should have been together."

Flora nodded, "Yes, I do hope there is a happy ending for them. They deserve it."

Leonard knew it was now or never. He knelt in front of Flora, and looked steadily into her bewildered eyes, "They are not the only man and woman who deserve a happy ending."

He took hold of her hand. "Flora, if I thought I could read your feelings I would have declared myself before now. I have been so unsure, but now, I care not if this changes our friendship forever. Flora, I think you the loveliest woman I have ever met, and I – " he shifted uncomfortably, and blushed at the words he was about to say, 'I love you. There – I said it. I love you." He let out a small laugh, unable to hold his emotions together any longer, then continued, 'Is there the smallest chance that you would make me the most fortunate man alive and have me as your husband? If you wish to remain working here with your Uncle and Aunt, I would not mind. Your happiness is all I care about. But I hope - I hope that you would be content with me."

Flora trembled a little. Then, gently and yet unconsciously squeezed his hand. "Oh Dr Preston, yes – oh yes. I have loved you for many months too. I have not – that is, I did not think you could love me in return," she said shaking her head.

"Not love you! What man could not love you? And I beg you, do not call me Dr Preston any longer; call me Leonard, dearest."

She gave a shy smile. "Leonard, I love you."

He seized her hand. "Flora, I cannot tell you how many times I have wished to tell you how much I love you, or how when we meet I have wanted to keep hold of your hand and do this."

He lifted her hand to his lips and kissed it softly. "And then take you in my arms and do this." With his eyes fixed on hers, he straightened up and pulled her gently to her feet. Holding her to him, he bent his head and their lips met; tentatively at first, then with all the fervour and passion that had been pent up for so long. The minutes passed by in a delicious haze until Leonard became aware of someone moving about in the next room.

Fearful of interruption by the Alther's or, worse, by Helen, he released Flora and said hurriedly, "I will speak to your Uncle, unless of course, you think I should travel to see your father?"

"No, speak to Uncle, I know my father will be happy with a letter," she gave a nervous laugh, "and he would not refuse any man who asked for me now, he has long given hope of my marrying. It will come as a great surprise."

Leonard stood up, but kept hold of Flora's hand. "Then I will go to your Uncle now, and write to your father straight afterwards. I do not want anything to delay. But the fact that you are not married only makes my happiness more complete. If the men of this world cannot see your true worth, it is their fault! They are all blind."

She smiled in return, and with a kiss as a parting gesture, Leonard left the room to find Mr Alther. He was in the dining room, and his reaction was as Leonard hoped.

Mr Alther seized Leonard's hand and shook it violently unable to speak, then said, "I congratulate you on your wise choice for a wife. I wish you every happiness. But I am sure you are well matched. Flora is a sensible girl. I'm not sure how we can cope in the shop without her now. She has made herself indispensable."

"Flora and I have already spoken of that and I have assured her that should she wish to continue to help here, she has my blessing."

"Hmph. We will see. I think married life will suit her, and she will soon lose interest in helping me. Especially when her own family comes along."

Leonard could not help but smile at such a thought, "Perhaps."

The letter to Flora's father had to wait several hours before Mr and Mrs Alther would let Dr Preston leave, such was the excitement in the household.

When Mrs Alther was told of the news, she proclaimed, "I am sure I guessed you loved each other," and clapped her hands together several times.

"Guessed?" Mr Alther said, "You never told me! I don't think you guessed at all."

"Oh hush, I do not tell you everything Mr Alther, that would make things far too dull. It is good that a husband and wife have a few secrets from each other. Remember that Flora."

"Oh no. You will not give Flora marital advice." Mr Alther said, "What other secrets do you have from me?" he said suspiciously.

Leonard and Flora watched in amusement together as Mr and Mrs Alther argued.

Finally, when Helen entered the room to see what the noise was about, they broke the news to her. She was all agog with amazement. "But why would you want to marry Flora? She is so old! Wouldn't a younger woman suit you more?" Helen said, "Not me of course but, oh I don't know, someone else. . .anyone else."

Leonard took hold of Flora's hand and kissed it, "I can assure you Helen, that no other woman will do for me."

He was smiling, but was secretly annoyed, but now was not the time for arguments with his future sister in law. Nothing could cloud Flora's happiness either, she was secure in the thought that soon enough, she would not have to put up with Helen's constant set downs.

Leonard left, only after he insisted that his patients could not be kept waiting any longer, and it was only after he was on his way home when he remembered that he did not give Mr and Mrs Alther the news of Adella. He smiled to himself, he was sure that his dearest Flora would tell them. In the meantime, he decided he must buy an engagement ring as soon as possible.

~

As soon as Leonard left, Mrs Alther turned to Flora, "I knew you would make a good match. You are a sensible, warm young woman. I knew it would not be wasted."

"Can you not stop smiling Flora," Helen said, "It is most irritating. He's only a Doctor. I have plans for a much better husband, though having a sister married must improve *my* chances."

"Make your own match where you choose, I am happy with mine." Flora replied.

"Well, I suppose you will be comfortable. But his house is so small. I do not think you will have room to breathe when Adella comes back." She gave a brittle laugh.

The sudden mention of Adella made Flora remember that other news. "But I do not think Adella will be coming back. In fact, I think she will soon be married herself."

The Alther's were all amazement when Flora told them all about Adella and Joel, and all that Adella endured the last few months she was in Bath. Helen of course, was jealous of the match. "I cannot understand how *all* the men in the world like choosing dull old women as wives!" she said.

"They are not engaged yet. When he recovers, Leonard thinks it is a foregone conclusion. But he is still very ill."

This seemed to console Helen. "It sounds as though he may die before they will have a chance to wed. Does he have a younger brother?"

ADELLA WAS WELL aware of the days as they passed. Frederick's house seemed more lavishly furnished than Joel's and her own sick bed was in the most sumptuous room she ever saw. The finest red brocade curtains, French chairs that she was sure were worth more money than her fathers house alone. Her four poster bed was made of the finest mahogany dressed with silk sheets.

She was dreadfully ill for several days, and as the fever took hold she was glad for her nurse maid, a young woman called Claire who had been in Frederick's service since childhood. She was attentive and patient, never questioned why Adella was there, and followed her orders to the letter.

Frederick visited once a day to report the news of Joel, though he stood by the door and would not enter the bedroom on the doctors orders. Joel was recovering well and on the second day came the news she so longed to hear. He was fully conscious.

"He was not awake for too long; he was tired," Frederick said with a note of relief in his voice. "He is asleep again now."

"Did he ask for me?" Adella asked.

Frederick looked confused for a moment, "Yes, well no, actually. He didn't, but he didn't say anything really, a few mumbled words, that was all."

Adella tried not to let her disappointment show. She should not expect him to ask for her, or remember that she had been there. He was well. That was all that mattered.

It took Adella over two weeks to recover fully from her illness. Joel gained in strength, and had been sitting up and eating, but still they remained separated. The doctor was too concerned over Joel's frailness to allow any risk of further illness, so Adella remained under Frederick's care.

Frederick still had not found Michael, there was a promising lead in Cambridge, and he was ever confident that Joel would not be sent to prison. The lawyers had been getting a convincing case together and even without Michael's statement, it was a clear case of defence of the mother.

Finally, Dr Chapman visited Adella and he pronounced her fit to visit Joel. She was fully recovered for a few days, and she paced her room in eager anticipation, agitated at the thought of finally being able to speak to Joel as she once did; five years earlier. But what would he say? How would he receive her? Her mind was unable to rest at the thought of seeing him. She was anxious. Anxious that he might have fallen out of love, that his feelings so strong had faded through his illness. Then there was the matter of how much she changed over the last five years. She was a woman now, not the girl he knew.

When Frederick arrived back that evening, he arranged to take her to him the next day by his own carriage. She hoped to go that evening, but the Doctor said that Joel needed more sleep, and was unable to do anything for more than a few minutes. Nothing amused her, or could take her mind off the following day. She planned in her head what she would say to Joel, yet everything sounded stupid. She slept fitfully, and awoke late, making her rush to get ready.

Adella stepped out of the carriage once again at Polwarth House, she could not help but think of the last time she arrived at the house nearly three weeks before. Frederick accompanied her to Joel's room, but this time, he left Adella outside in the hallway while he went in to see if Joel was ready.

Adella could hear mumbled voices from within, and shortly afterwards, Frederick came out.

"He will be ready for you shortly," he said.

The valet came out of the room afterwards, and disappeared down the hall. Frederick, not content with small talk turned to Adella. "I will go home I think. I will not be needed for now. Send word when you wish to return, if indeed you wish to return as my guest."

"I don't think Joel will want me to stay here. Will he?"

"I rather think he will not let you leave," He then made a small bow and walked away.

The valet returned a few minutes later carrying a shirt then disappeared back into the room.

Adella tried to occupy herself while she waited. But the hallway yielded no help, dull wallpaper and one portrait was all that was on offer to occupy her mind. Finally, after what seemed like an age, the door opened once more and the servant said, "You can come in now Miss, the master is ready to see you."

Her legs nearly gave way. Nerves finally got the better of her, but somehow she found herself walking slowly through the open door.

**20**

———

As soon as she was inside the room she looked straight to the bed.

It was empty.

She scanned the room, and there he was, directly to her left. He was seated on the same chaise longue she had used as a bed a few weeks before. There was a rug wrapped around his legs, and he wore the clean pressed shirt the valet carried a few minutes before. She dared to look at his face, and noticed that he was newly shaved, and his hair had been cut. He was still a little pale, and had lost weight; what he already had to lose. He was still very much the man she once knew.

She stood in the middle of the room, not knowing what to say. Finally, she met his gaze.

Joel watched her, then broke the awkward silence, "I would stand up and greet you properly, except that I am not sure whether I could do it. It took me nearly ten minutes to move from the bed to here."

Adella smiled, yet she could not move nor say anything, all she could think of was how his presence filled the room.

"Will you not sit down?" He indicated the chair opposite.

She moved silently in front of him and gently sat perched on the edge, her hands clasped on her lap.

There was another awkward silence. How different it was to the last time she had been in that room and she was in charge of Joel's care. She heard Joel's voice over the confused thoughts in her head. "They told me you came and nursed me for a while."

"Yes."

"When I was ill, I thought I dreamt an angel visited me. Now I know it was true. Will you forgive me that I do not remember you being here?" His voice was soft and gentle.

"Yes."

"Will you not come and sit closer? He held his arm out to her and she instinctively took it and let him draw her in. He moved a little to pull himself towards her.

He took hold of her hand, "Adella, I still love you," he said seriously. "You know you are the only woman I have loved don't you? I am telling the truth, though it pained me in my soul to part with you. I love you more, much more than I did five years ago. I broke a vow to you then, will you trust me this time, and marry me now? Let me fulfil the promise to wed you made so long ago."

"I do not want you to marry me out of duty!" she cried. "I could not bear it."

"Duty!! Duty!!" He said with a sigh. "I have come too far to do anything that I did not wish to do." He shook his head, "I am no one's slave now except yours."

"But what of the law? What if you go to prison? What if they try to hang you?"

"They will not. The lawyers visited yesterday, and have told me everything. The Police Constable has stopped coming each day. It is a formality, tomorrow, they will have a hearing now they have my statement and Frederick has found Michael, no charges will be made."

Adella relaxed. Her shoulders dropped and she let out a deep breath.

"Michael found? Frederick did not say anything. And he has given a statement too?"

"Yes. We found out this morning, though he is too proud to come home. But in time I hope he will return. I do not blame him for being deceived by our father. So you see," Joel said with renewed hope, "there is nothing to stop us marrying except your agreement."

"But when we met in Sidmouth, we were so young. I am different now -" she tried to continue, but was interrupted.

"You are different, but you are still the woman I fell in love with. The woman my heart longs to claim as my own."

Deep in her breast, her heart spoke the same, "I want you to claim me. But we were thrown together in an artificial way. When we fell in love we were barely adults. After everything we have been through, let us not ruin each other's life by marrying in haste. We should spend time reacquainting ourselves with each other, and only marry if we grow to love each other still; as the man and woman we are now. Not as some romantic idea of the past."

"The voice of reason again," Joel said with a note of bitterness. "You always were sensible. Whatever argument you come up with, I shall not relent. I mean to marry you Adella. I mean to win your heart again, and I will never give up trying." There was a deep passion in his voice that made her heart quicken. To be pursued in such a way would be irresistible, and they both knew then, that despite her protestations, their union was inevitable.

He grasped her hand harder and turned it over in his

own, lifted it to his mouth and gently kissed the palm, sealing the unspoken promise that they both shared.

"I insist that you stay here, and not with Frederick," Joel said after a while.

"I would like that very much. Though, do you think it appropriate? People will talk."

He grinned, "I hope they will, then you will have to marry me if your reputation is in tatters!" His face darkened. "But then, I suppose they will have enough to talk about already with everything that has happened recently. I would sooner you promise to marry me now. But as I said earlier, I am your slave, and I will do anything you ask of me."

Adella gave a playful smile. "Then my first command is that you kiss me, and remind me again of those days we were together in Sidmouth."

"You better come closer then," Joel said smiling.

She did as he asked and as their lips finally met in a soft passionate kiss, the past was blotted away in an instant.

After many minutes, Joel spoke. "I have dreamed of doing that for five long years." He gently kissed her cheeks, eyes, her mouth rhythmically. "And when you are my wife. . ."

But he did not have time to continue. There was a sudden knock at the door, it opened and Sarah ran in. She flew into Joel's now empty arms, and Adella stood up and smoothed down her dress. Joel's mother walked in a few moments later.

"Papa, can you come and play yet?" Sarah asked.

"Not outside, no. But I am glad you have come in, I want you to meet someone important. This is Adella," he said looking seriously into his daughter's face.

Sarah looked up at Adella, then stepped forward and

held out her hand for her to shake it. She was as pretty as Adella remembered.

"Frederick says that you are going to be my new Mama and that I must be nice to you, else Papa will be upset."

Adella shook Sarah's hand, "I am pleased to meet you Sarah."

"Now Sarah. Adella has not yet decided if she is going to live here forever. But she will be our guest for now, and Frederick is right, we must be nice to her, or I will be very unhappy. Do you understand? Will you make Adella feel at home?"

"Yes," she said nodding with great exaggeration.

"Good girl. Now run along, and I will see you later."

He kissed her forehead, and she ran out, closely followed by Joel's mother. When the door closed, Adella spoke first, "You should be proud of her. She is a lovely girl."

Joel sat back and smiled, "I am. She is the only good thing that came out of my marriage."

The reference to Cynthia made Joel hesitantly look at Adella to see how she reacted.

"It's alright," she said, reading Joel's expression. "I accepted a long time ago that you married. You need not shy away from mentioning it. We must be honest no; no secrets. Cynthia was, Sarah's mother after all. You must never let Sarah think badly of her."

"I won't."

"You look tired," Adella said and sat down beside him once more and brushed away a lock of hair from his brow.

"I am a little. I think I should rest for a while."

～

Dᴜʀɪɴɢ ᴛʜᴇ ɴᴇxᴛ ꜰᴇᴡ ᴍᴏɴᴛʜꜱ, Adella spent much of her time taking charge of nursing Joel back to health. He gradually regained his strength, and was able to walk about and become more active. It was a common sight around the Polwarth estate to see Adella and Joel walking about arm in arm. One sunny afternoon, they were out in the grounds with Frederick and Sarah in tow.

"I'll race you to the pond," Frederick said to Sarah.

Joel and Adella watched as they both ran off into the distance laughing. Fredrick allowed Sarah to win.

Joel watched Adella's face, a soft smile on her lips. Then she turned to Joel, "I think Sarah is the only woman who will ever have command of Frederick."

"Oh, I don't know. I think Frederick is ready to fall in love, if only he would meet with a woman who he likes." He guided her to a nearby bench.

"He will, I'm sure. It is possible he has already met her and does not yet realise she is the one."

"There are plenty of women in the area who would love to be Mrs Garner."

"I'm sure there are. I look forward to meeting a few of them in the future, and watch as they tussle for his attentions."

"So you are happy to stay here?"

"Yes, I am beginning to think of Bedfordshire as my home." She stretched her arms out. "I am content." But then her face clouded a little. "Joel, there is something I must tell you. I have to leave for a few weeks. Leonard's wedding date is set, and I wish to attend."

"Very well. We can travel whenever you like."

Adella grimaced, "I must go alone. You are not well enough to travel all that way."

"I am!"

"You are not, and besides, I would prefer to go alone."

"Why?"

Adella sighed, "because I think it would do us both good. To see how we bear the separation."

"I will not be able to bear the separation." He grabbed her hand, "Haven't I told you enough times that I love you?"

Adella put her hand on his cheek. "Yes, you have, more than enough times. I love you too,"

"I want to marry you."

"Yes, but..."

"But?"

"But, it is my brother's wedding, and I would hate to miss it. I have decided. It must be this way. Please don't make this any more difficult than it already is."

Joel felt helpless but deep down he knew further argument wouldn't help matters.

"You might stay in Bath, and I'll never see you again. You'll find another man and marry him instead. It would be what I deserve."

"I promise you now, that I will return."

"And you won't fall in love with, or marry another man?"

"I promise."

"Can I still not persuade you to marry me? I would be much happier if I knew we were engaged when you left."

But as soon as he said the words, he suddenly regretted them, "I'm sorry. That was thoughtless of me after what I did to you - breaking the engagement."

"It's alright, but when will you realise that I have forgiven you?"

Joel thought for a moment, and with a slow smile said, "When you agree to marry me of course."

Frederick returned with Sarah a few minutes later, and

this time she dragged Adella off, and left Frederick and Joel to walk back to the house behind.

"Why so glum?" Frederick asked, "You look like you have received bad news."

"Adella is leaving for three weeks. Her brother's wedding and she is to be bridesmaid."

"And?"

"She will not let me accompany her to Bath," Joel said.

"I think it is a good thing. Let her go," Frederick made a dismissive gesture with his arm, "the separation will do you both good."

Joel stared at Frederick in utter disbelief, "How can you say that?"

"Only, that the separation will make her realise how much she loves you, and there can be nothing better than her attending a wedding. It will make her wish to be a bride. I guarantee she will come back here eagerly expecting you to propose again. How many times have you asked he now?"

"I've lost count, but I think it must be at least once a day. You seem to think you know a woman's mind. Though I see your point. But what if she realises that she does not wish to marry me? What then? Have you thought of that?"

"Then I shall say only this: has she, over these last months shown anything other than the deepest affection for you? Do you not think that she would have left here already if she did not love you?" He crossed his arms in defiance and his mouth hinted at a smile.

"You had better be right," Joel said, "Otherwise, we will have a prolonged stay in Bath, while I try and persuade her to marry me. I won't let her slip away from me."

"Both of us stay in Bath?" Frederick said taken aback, "I have interfered enough in your affairs of the heart. Leave me out of it."

"Of course both of us. I thought you liked Bath. Besides, you are the one who told me to let her go away. I hope you realise how miserable I will be, and how you will have to cheer me up when she's gone."

THREE WEEKS later and Joel stood by the drawing room window, his hand on the frame tapping his fingers impatiently. His mother and Sarah played quietly nearby. Despite Sarah's earlier entreaty to play too, Joel could not face it. He looked out again at the single track road that led up to the house.

"I'm sure she'll be here soon," his mother said.

"It's nearly six o'clock. She ought to be here by now. I should have travelled to Bath to collect her myself, despite her insistence I stay here."

"She did not want you to have a set back in your health."

"I know."

Finally, Joel saw the carriage appear at the bottom of the lane. He straightened his jacket. "Come mother, Sarah. She is here."

He led them outside and they all waited for the carriage to stop. Joel grabbed the door and yanked it open.

He peered in and his eyes instantly locked onto Adella's. She grinned at him, and he offered her his hand.

"I thought you would never get here," he said and kissed her hand.

"Neither did I! But I am here now." She looked at him, "Your health has improved I think? You have much more colour in your face and you don't look so tired."

"I am nearly fully recovered."

"I'm glad of it."

"Aren't you going to help me out as well?" Frederick's head popped out of the carriage door.

"I'm sure you are quite capable of doing it yourself."

Frederick alighted the carriage. "You could at least thank me for accompanying Adella back."

"Of course, another debt I owe you," Joel said.

They all entered the house, and refreshments were sent for.

"Tell me, how was the wedding?" Joel ventured after a short while.

"It was lovely," Adella said. "Simply lovely. Flora looked like a princess, and Leonard; well he was the happiest I have ever seen him. He did not stop smiling all day. I am glad he has found such a lovely girl. I don't have to worry about him any more."

"When exactly was it?" Mrs Polwarth asked.

"Three days ago," Adella answered.

"And was it well attended?"

"Oh yes, the families being there of course, and all the doctors and chemists in Bath attended too. Also - "

But Adella was interrupted by the arrival of the refreshments, and she used the opportunity to pull Joel away and speak to him on her own at the other side of the room.

"It was a lovely wedding, but there is something I have not told you," she said in a whisper.

"Oh?" Joel moved closer.

"I was miserable without you. All I did was think about you alone in this house, and how I wished you were with me."

Joel breathed a sigh of relief. "Then we will never be apart again?"

"Never again," she replied shaking her head.

He seized her hands, "Then let us set a date, my love, before you change your mind."

"I will not change my mind, and let the date be as soon as the banns can be read. I cannot wait any longer."

"I will send for the Rector immediately," he replied and he drew her into a tender kiss to seal the promise.

# EPILOGUE

Frederick poured himself a Brandy, lit his cigar and seated himself in the large chair by the fire. "How was the honeymoon?" he asked Joel, with a mischievous smile full of deeper meaning.

"It was everything I dreamed it would be," Joel said raising his eyebrows. "You really should think of getting married yourself."

"Hmm, and how was Sidmouth?"

"Just as I remembered. Our former employers, were a little taken aback when we both turned up on their doorstep, but they were gracious and acquitted Adella after I explained everything. In fact, they were reproving of me, not that I didn't deserve it."

"And did you take the coastal walk to Branscombe?" Frederick asked.

"Yes. It too was as I remembered," he said. "Though I do not recall much of the scenery now I think of it." He said with a distinct sparkle in his eyes.

"I thought as much," Frederick said with a small laugh.

They both looked round as the door opened and Adella came into the room.

"Ahh and here she is," Frederick said standing up. "Mrs Polwarth, how are you? You look radiant though, so you need not answer. I trust married life suits you?"

"Frederick, how wonderful to see you. But call me Adella," she said and offered her hand.

"I will not call you anything other than Mrs Polwarth, for though it be formal, I wish to remind myself all the time that finally Joel is married to the woman he loves."

Adella laughed, "I am sure you will tire of the formality eventually. But Joel, what do you say to this?"

"Leave me out of it. Though I shall not stop Frederick calling you by your legal name, however formal it is. I like to hear it too."

"Very well," Adella reluctantly said, "but I shall return the formality, until you realise how ridiculous it sounds, Mr Garner!"

"A battle of wills. I shall enjoy it Mrs Polwarth. But I must leave, I only dropped by because it has been exceedingly dull here without you both, and I was terribly bored. But I will leave you to yourselves now. If I were the bridegroom, I would want my bride all to myself the night before the rest of the family descend. They all arrive tomorrow?"

"Yes, and I shall not stop you from leaving," Joel said, "I do want my bride to myself. Be off, and return tomorrow when Mrs Polwarth and I shall be glad to see you." He exchanged a tender glance with Adella, and added, "Not too early though."

THE END

Dear reader, if you enjoyed this novel, I would really appreciate it if you would leave a review. It really helps other people find my books.

Read the second book in this duet series Hidden Hearts:

*Louise's Secret, A Historical Victorian Clean Romance:*

*In the heart of Victorian England, 1855, 'Pride and Prejudice' meets Gaskell's 'North and South' in the captivating tale of Louise Thomas — a daring heiress with a passion for engineering wonders, and a heart seeking a love that respects her boundless thirst for knowledge. Owning a sprawling estate in Devon, Louise is no ordinary aristocrat; she's a woman on a mission to find a love that can keep pace with her interest for scientific and engineering marvels.*

*Enter Charles Lucas, a preeminent engineer whose world revolves around intricate blueprints and grandiose bridges, with little time for romantic entanglements. But Louise's intellect and mystique capture him in a way no other woman has. As their paths entwine, Charles uncovers troubling rumours about Louise's past. Torn between their shared love for innovation and the shadows lurking in society's cogs, will their budding romance endure, or will hidden truths tear them apart?*

www.ingramcontent.com/pod-product-compliance
Lightning Source LLC
Chambersburg PA
CBHW061522210726
48287CB00006B/1789